"In the trad... ...iting, Ober's work forces the reader t... ...to dwell upon the future course of a... ...ch they are very much a part—if the...

—Jim Higgins, *American Book Review*

"Damien Ober gives us a new kind of fictional history here, one that is as fanciful and exuberant as a Garcia-Marquez novel."
—T. C. Boyle, author of *The Harder They Come* and *The Road to Wellville*

"Not sure if I read a book or had a manic episode while watching the History Channel, but either way, it was incredible and I feel absolutely amazing."
—Ben Loory, author of *Stories for Nighttime and Some for the Day*

"*Doctor Benjamin Franklin's Dream America* is as original as they come—an audacious, exuberantly imaginative novel about freedom and technology and the sacrifices each take from the other. Damien Ober is a writer to be reckoned with."
—Scott O'Connor, author of *Half World* and *Untouchable*

"American writers working on such a grand canvas are as scarce as hen's teeth. For sheer mischief, erudition and inventiveness *Doctor Benjamin Franklin's Dream America* sits quite comfortably on the shelf alongside David Foster Wallace, William Vollmann, Thomas Pynchon, the Barthelme brothers . . . all the terrible children of Swift and Stearne. It makes me laugh. It makes me sympathetic to people I despise, even though I still despise them. While many of the characters would cry sedition, I like to think Dr. Franklin is somewhere having a chuckle."
—Robert Olmstead, author of *Coal Black Horse*

Doctor Benjamin Franklin's Dream America

A NOVEL OF THE DIGITAL REVOLUTION

DAMIEN LINCOLN OBER

Night Shade Books

New York

Night Shade books may be purchased in bulk at special discounts for sales promotion, corporate gifts, fund-raising, or educational purposes. Special editions can also be created to specifications. For details, contact the Special Sales Department, Night Shade Books, 307 West 36th Street, 11th Floor, New York, NY 10018 or info@skyhorsepublishing.com.

Night Shade Books® is a registered trademark of Skyhorse Publishing, Inc.®, a Delaware corporation.

Visit our website at www.nightshadebooks.com.

10 9 8 7 6 5 4 3 2 1

Library of Congress Cataloging-in-Publication Data

Names: Ober, Damien Lincoln, author.
Title: Doctor Benjamin Franklin's dream America / by Damien Lincoln Ober.
Description: New York : Night Shade Books, [2017]
Identifiers: LCCN 2017006720 | ISBN 9781597809191 (softcover : acid-free paper)
Subjects: LCSH: United States--History--Revolution, 1775-1783--Fiction. | GSAFD: Alternative histories (Fiction) | War stories.
Classification: LCC PS3615.B43 D63 2018 | DDC 813/.6--dc23
LC record available at https://lccn.loc.gov/2017006720

Cover design by Anthony Morais
Cover illustration by Kevin Peterson

Printed in the United States of America

th@ all r cre8d =; th@ they r endowd by their cre8or
with certn inalienable rights; th@ among these r life,
librty and the purst of happines

—Thomas Jefferson

John Morton :: April 1st 1777

Button Gwinnett :: May 19th 1777

Philip Livingston :: June 12th 1778

John Hart :: May 11th 1779

George Ross :: July 14th 1779

Joseph Hewes :: November 10th 1779

George Taylor :: February 23rd 1781

Richard Stockton :: February 28th 1781

Caesar Rodney :: June 29th 1784

Stephen Hopkins :: July 13th 1785

William Whipple :: November 28th 1785

Arthur Middleton :: January 1st 1787

Thomas Stone :: October 1st 1787

John Penn :: September 14th 1788

Thomas Nelson Jr. :: January 4th 1789

Benjamin Franklin :: April 17th 1790

William Hooper :: October 14th 1790

Lyman Hall :: October 19th 1790

Benjamin Harrison :: April 24th 1791

Francis Hopkinson :: April 9th 1791

Roger Sherman :: July 23rd 1793

John Hancock :: October 8th 1793

Richard Henry Lee :: June 19th 1794

Abraham Clark :: September 15th 1794

John Witherspoon :: November 15th 1794

Thomas Lynch :: February 13th 1795

Josiah Bartlett :: May 19th 1795

Samuel Huntington :: January 5th 1796

Francis Lightfoot Lee :: January 11th 1797

Carter Braxton :: October 10th 1779

Oliver Walcott :: December 1st 1797

Lewis Morris :: January 22nd 1798

James Wilson :: August 28th 1798

George Read :: September 21st 1798

William Paca :: October 23rd 1799

Edward Rutledge :: January 23rd 1800

Matthew Thornton :: June 24th 1803

Samuel Adams :: October 2nd 1803

Francis Lewis :: December 21st 1803

George Walton :: February 2nd 1804

Robert Morris :: May 9th 1806

George Wythe :: June 8th 1806

James Smith :: July 11th 1806

Thomas Heyward Jr. :: March 6th 1809

Samuel Chase :: June 11th 1811

William Williams :: August 2nd 1811

George Clymer :: January 23rd 1813

Benjamin Rush :: May 19th 1813

Robert Treat Paine :: May 11th 1814

Elbridge Gerry :: November 23rd 1814

Thomas McKean :: June 24th 1817

William Ellery :: February 15th 1820

William Floyd :: August 4th 1821

Thomas Jefferson :: July 4th 1826

John Adams :: July 4th 1826

Charles Carroll :: November 14th 1832

Fifty-six men signed the Declaration of Independence.
This is the story of their deaths.

Part 1 :: The Death

Doc Josiah Bartlett, Roger Sherman, Thomas M'Kean and Doctor Benjamin Rush all got the same email. Orders from Congress to form another *unofficial* little committee. The assignment: Do whatever you have to do to keep John Morton alive and functioning until the Articles of Confederation have been uploaded.

Right now, their patient is struggling through another fit of blood-speckled coughing. Fresh droplets make new stellar patterns across the white pillowcases. A whole night sky's worth of faded constellations. One hand on his laptop, the other up to ward the men from the bed, "To come too close is to invite death, to tempt it with fresh consumables." He coughs a few light coughs until the coughs become chuckles. Then back into his laptop, the glowing crater bashed into the fabric of the bed quilts. His fingers trigger key patterns. Screen light drones the jagged caverns of his face. The room, hung thick with the candle stink of overcooked beef, hints a gray and forgettable day in lace curtains all pulled closed.

No one knows exactly what it is that's killing John Morton. Both Rush and Doc Bartlett are confident it can't be contagious, but they stick to the walls all the same. Sherm and M'Kean follow their lead. These are men who know which chances are worth taking. Been taking some big ones lately. Not coming up very good either. New York rests in the King's hands, General Washington and the Continental Army lapping wounds in winter quarters. It's been almost a full year since the Declaration was uploaded, three or four or five or twenty-three years of war, depending on which representative of which state you follow. This Revolution, after all that has transpired, threatens to become no more than collected, distilled and then suppressed ideals, as temporary as a single human generation.

John Morton's typing grinds to a halt. He just sits there. There's a moment of distinct possibility that he has passed, dead and off for the next land beyond. But then Morton's eyes shift. He finds the men in the room with him. "I am finished." He forces a swallow, a long inhale. Eyes wearily scan browser windows unpacked and gaping all across his screen. "Have to update my status," and he reads aloud the words he's just then typing: "The Articles of Confederation are done."

Morton stares into the letters, the meaning their crooked shapes make in the string. Already this latest status update pulses down the scrolls of countless patriots, just like every thought that's entered his mind these last five years. As soon as he'd committed to the revolt, John Morton sliced his brain open and laid it bare for the entire social network to peruse. Every thought, every inclination, reaction or bloviation, public in the time it takes to type 140 characters or less.

Thomas M'Kean takes a step away from the wall in order to show everyone how one makes a fist from a regular old hand. Though still the good reluctant soldier, M'Kean's lately been flashing glimpses of that general they all know is lurking in there. "The Articles," he says. "Finally, we can pull the states together and start putting up a fight!"

A gesture from Rush to indicate he's not so sure, but that's as far as he'll take it. Sometimes in these settings he has a hard time speaking up. Despite the status afforded him by his deep involvement in the politics and administration of the Revolution, Ben Rush knows he's not really a politician or an administrator—not truly an intellectual at all—but just a country sawbones glorified by the natural workings of republicanism. Still, though, he makes a good enough gesture toward enlightenment science.

But Doc Bartlett? Doc is the true product. No gestures involved. Cured himself of a mysterious fever when he was a teen and there was no looking back. Always working on learning some dead language, always a few science experiments running in that lab under his New Hampshire homestead. His latest gig is cutting up dead bodies and looking inside. Right now he's shaking his head, singing a little ditty about the Articles that goes, "*Have to get them ratified first.*"

"Been coughing three days straight." John Morton types, reads aloud, "I've been coughing three days straight." He types, scans his status, types, scans his status.

Through this all, Roger Sherman has looked—as always— softly puritanical, like a throwback to some forgotten age without the Internet. He measures each man with a glance. "Have to get them ratified, yes. But as soon as we've uploaded the Articles, the idea of a federated government will be loose. For good or for ill, something will have begun that we will be powerless to stop." If you didn't know him, you'd think Roger Sherman was speaking from some other plane where the results of this reality have no sway whatsoever. But this is the same deliberate and indifferent way he's plodded through all the grand events of his time. Old Sherm the Cobbler, just working on another shoe.

A tongue appears, then, in the corner of John Morton's mouth, crosshatched with swollen veins and dark, purple-gray sores. "My work is done. The rest is up to the people." He glances at the room's entire. "We *are* sure about this? Taking something down is a lot different than putting something up." He points up then, with a single bloated finger, as if the Internet really is only above them. "Sherm is right. Once it's in the Cloud, there's no stopping it. It'll seep into every hard drive in the country."

M'Kean and Sherm share a look. They share it with Doc Bartlett, with Morton in the bed. Rush now nodding the nod of someone who knows it's time for him to nod along. Doc Bartlett clears his throat. "The Articles. What do we gain and what are we giving up?" He lets it sit the length of one breath, then: "The Enlightenment's most grand experiment enters its next critical stage."

Rush posits, gesturing toward John Morton, "Maybe it's the Articles that made him sick?" They all look at Rush like, *how?* But the doctor doesn't have a rational answer, and so he just says, "It *is* an astounding time we live in."

John Morton closes a few open files, opens some others, hovers the Articles over the ftp portal, and off they go. Signals pervade the air in the room, the text of the Articles of Confederation climbing Cloudward. Morton lets his gaze rise to the ceiling, as if watching this thing he's reared venture off into the world's mind. He types his new status, lets it sit a moment, hits enter. "Well, it's official now. The whole social network knows. John Morton has uploaded the Articles of Confederation."

Some cautious smiles. The four healthy men all careful not to move bedward, shifting instead around each other in turns, shaking hands and clasping shoulders. "The United States," one says.

"The United States."

Bursts of typing again from the ruffled bed. "Portaling our new foundational document to the fan page." John Morton reads aloud the name of the page, "*Independent Colonies of America.*" He laughs. "Going to have to start a new page again." This is because it was decided—from the very first one they launched—that each new phase of the Revolution would get a brand new fan page. And that new members would *not* be carried over automatically from the old. Each patriot must perform his own individual public click in order to affirm consent in every step toward a new nation. The very first "official fan page of the Revolution" got 1,256 likes in the first hour alone. The next day, John Witherspoon himself, a big public liking ceremony. But that was six years ago. Time goes by. Things become something else. New groups and pages are created, and no one much visits the ones left behind. The old pages just hover there in some forgotten sector of the Cloud, these outdated versions of Revolutionary America, just ghost houses now, full of ad drones and profile haunts, crawling with worms. Each of those old pages does have a few living people left—ancient patriots still active and posting, locked into their static hold on progress. Those guys probably think the drones that re-post to the old pages all day are actually human. But they're not. They're just drones—empty, lifeless drones.

John Morton looks into the future. "As soon as these are ratified, we'll be officially organized under a different system. Confederated Articles. Name of the page might change again, but this is a country we're talking about now. And not just online anymore." He clicks the new page to life, opens the info tab and types the newest name, reading it aloud as he does, "The United States of America." And he realizes it, that it just happened. And that it was him that did it. The first man to type the new nation's name into the Internet.

"Already commenting. Five likes already." John Morton's eyes tighten in around the screen. "Fans and likes. Friend requests coming in by the dozen. Samuel Adams has commented on your status. John Witherspoon has commented on your status. George Washington wants to be friends with The United States of America!" And there it goes, comments and likes cascading the wall faster than John Morton can scroll to keep up. "Wall-ter-fall," he says. "The USA has gone viral!"

"I don't get it," Rush says. "How did you make it so you can be a friend of the page *and* be a fan of the page? Is it a page, a person or a group?"

Sherm's thinking about the Articles, wants to know if it's a "these," a "this" or an "it." He's trying it in his head a few different ways. *This is the Articles. These are them.* Or is it *they* or *those* or only one? One set. *The Articles?*

"The tasks of this committee are complete." Doc Bartlett reveals palms empty of any smartdevice. "You're going to have to accept my actual in-person gratitude."

"A new nation has been launched," M'Kean tells them. "There is nothing as contagious as freedom's march."

"I still wonder, though . . ." Rush glancing bedward, then a vague gesture intended to indicate the Internet, ". . . exactly what kind of *contagious* we're talking about."

"My last act," John Morton says. "The Articles. Available to anyone. Download and join the Revolution. Become an American." He tries to let the words hang, but the proud cast of his face is betrayed by a bursting cough. There is blood in his palm—more than the usual misting—and fresh gobs of it in abstract shapes across the blankets. He coughs again and again. The room seems to be coughing back, but really it's just John Morton, echoing himself, coughing up whole handfuls of blood as the others press their backs against the farthest wall. They all know what's happening here; they've each watched a few men die over the years.

Abruptly, the coughing stops. With his head rolled back, John Morton blinks away tears pink with just a trace of blood. Vision clears to show the room bent over him. The glow of the laptop touches only the ceiling directly above, and only slightly, the most vague hint of a soft spot in the shell of this realm—a path out, maybe. Follow the Articles into the Cloud and leave this sick body behind. Fingers click a few code-sounding clusters of shortcut keys and his profile picture goes dark.

John Morton is dead.

I n fits and halting starts, when the infection in his shattered hip ebbs, Button Gwinnett comes down from pure ravings and codes his worm. There, inside the smartphone he bought only a few days before the duel, his final revenge takes shape. "Murdered," he mumbles, "murdered by Lachlan McIntosh." He twitches through some fever fits. "*East Florida,*" he mumbles, "*East Florida.*"

A nurse crosses the room to the cot that was dragged out. Button's hip shattered beyond any hope of moving him off the property. So he'll die here in the top floor of this barn, out on a farm in the cool Georgia spring. "Dueling," the nurse says. "Used to be pretty clear. Had patriots and had loyalists, Tories and Whigs. Now we got patriots killing patriots." Head shaking as she fills a cup from a pitcher of water. "And you're a Signer too. Shame, shame."

Button drips sweat as he codes, teeth clenched and cracking. Eyes fixated on that smartphone screen and nowhere else. He has to work to touch just the right spots with fingers that won't stop their tremors. The nurse approaches like she's approaching an inanimate object, which is how she's come to regard this man she's supposed to ease into dying. Ranting all day long or just spitting and seizing. Talking, talking, talking, but never any more than at her. ". . . stole my army," he mumbles. "Paraded around . . . turned tail for home . . . and now King George can slice through the colonies . . . like a red-hot lance up a well-worn whore."

"You're disgusting." She bends down, pours cool water over Button's lips. A few instinctive swallows. Button's skin has passed from the color of flesh into a dry yellow. Blue screen light reflects a hundred beads of fever sweat.

This worm he's coding, it's just the latest counter-tactic in a feud that's raged for decades, winding its way through several generations of file-sharing platforms, messageboards, political, judicial and religious listservs. Red meat email blasts and hyper-tagged status updates. Acronym tweets and skeleton tweets and acronym tweets where each letter is the first letter of a skeleton tweet. Armies of skeletons. Both men have been expelled and readmitted to huge group email strings. Then expelled again. Entire inboxes clogged with their back-and-forth while others in the group were just sending it all to the junk mail folder. A scorched wake half a lifetime long, terabytes deep, seared through smartphones and social networking profiles, through the cloudware's cloudware. A smoldering scar across the multi-surface of Georgia. The most recent controversy, and cause of the fatal duel: who is at fault for the Georgia militia's failure to take East Florida from the British, Governor Button Gwinnett or General Lachlan McIntosh? And so to the town of Thunderbolt, where both men had come to finally bring it into the real.

There they'd stood on a flat patch of grass on the edge of this same farm, each turned right shoulder forward to offer only the thinnest arrangement of their body. Two shots rang out, two distinct sets of echoes. Button watched Lachlan McIntosh's face contort, watched him drop his pistol, slap his hands to his meaty thigh. Button felt something too, a bite in his groin and then a coolness down the back of both legs. He tried to take a step, but it was in vain. A spasm of sharp, metallic pain toppled him. Though the others had to wait for the doctor, Button knew the moment the bullet struck him. Just like he watched his own bullet vanish into McIntosh's muscle and knew that shot would *not* be fatal.

Button finds now the eyes of the nurse, who freezes in their grip. It's the first time he's looked directly at her. Not just raving to the room when he says, "Georgia is half-asleep. Under its moist and ancient fields are caverns of hidden gold. All of it burned and dug up. Machines in every town to force life patterns on the humans who live there. Machines that take your cells and rearrange them, make them something new, something loyal. Whether you like it or not." Button climbs, then, back down into his smartphone, back down into his worm. And man does that thing look nasty. "Lachlan McIntosh's Georgia," he says. "Unless I can stop him."

The nurse takes a chamber pot from under him. "How you going to do that?" she wants to know. "Twitching with the fever and pouring out the last of your fluids?" She makes the face of someone smelling that putrid smell that soaks the blankets all the way through. Ain't just the chamber pot that stinks. "You're not getting your hateful self out of that cot ever again."

"Don't need to get out of the cot," Button says. "This worm'll get him. Get inside his accounts. And from there, climb right into his brain."

"I thought that's what you said that other guy was going to do. That General McIntosh you keep talking about. Those *machines*."

Button stops now. Smiles. What he's been building in the tiny hard drive inside that tiny smartphone must be complete. "Never mind the British," he says. "The King, the Parliament, it's other *Georgians* we have to fear. East Florida was not the first of his schemes. And it won't be the last. Lachlan McIntosh *will* try to destroy this state, and whatever country comes out of this rebellion too. And when that happens, it will be clear to all that Button Gwinnett died trying to save Georgia . . . and America, too."

"Sounds like you feel pretty satisfied," the nurse says, "thinking about the end of Georgia."

He shouts the name "Lachlan McIntosh," startling the nurse. The chamber pot slips from her hands, turns into porcelain shards on the wood floor. "Do you think I yelled that loud enough?" Button asks. But the nurse is looking at the chamber pot in pieces and the turd and the wet spot around it, considering if she's going to bother cleaning up this mess. "Do you suppose Lachlan McIntosh heard? In his bed somewhere in town, recovering as I die?" And as if he's given himself a cue, Button melts then, a little deeper into the cot. "One last memory of Button Gwinnett," he mumbles. "The sound of his name in my voice . . . echoing forever."

Only a thin tunnel leads back to the world from where Button has sunk. The damp blankets around him like a bath gone cool. He lifts the smartphone toward his face. A flash of Bible words makes the shape of hell for him in a plume of blood ink darting likewise across his vision in puffs. He slides that dead fingertip westward across the surface of his touchscreen and his worm is off, into the Cloud, to find Lachlan McIntosh and infest his accounts.

When Thomas M'Kean comes into the small converted coatroom, he's hit with a wall of humidity so thick he has to suck on it just to get a breath. The air sticks in his throat and nose, smells like the inside of a greenhouse after all the flowers have been watered. "Hello?"

From the far corner, an electronic voice comes gurgling. "Dr. Rush told me you rode back into town."

"Just now," M'Kean affirms.

"The Articles," the voice techno-gurgles. "Still haven't got them ratified, have we?"

M'Kean steps toward the sound. "Getting the people to click 'like' is one thing, getting them to actually ratify . . ." but he stops, because that's the moment he sees Philip Livingston. M'Kean's not sure he would recognize his old friend if he didn't already know it was him. Livingston's face has lost all its former shape. Skin sags from the skull, revealing pinkish, watery tissue under oddly protuberant eyeballs. The rest of his body is the same sort of drippy, looks poured into some kind of wheelchair/cart contraption that holds him seated upright. Rolled over to a bank of monitors, deep in the room's deepest corner, Livingston smiles knowingly at M'Kean, then nods at the screen's live stream of the congressional debates happening a few rooms away.

Livingston presses a button that's been welded to the arm of the cart. When he speaks, his voice doesn't come from his mouth but out of a speaker beside the button. "I can keep track of everything that happens from here. Or should I say doesn't happen, with *this* Congress. But *votes*, when we get around to them, for votes I have to actually be present to be counted." He looks to the speaker, then back to M'Kean. "Vocal chords," the speaker says. "Too moist anymore for real sound. Would just come out as bubbles without this thing."

Livingston returns some of his attention to the bank of screens. "You should see the moderates' faces when they roll me in, knowing I'll be the vote that'll break some stalemate they've worked themselves into. It's the only time they remember to come and get me, when the whip falls short the exact length of Philip Livingston."

A film of water has condensed itself down from steam to coat M'Kean's face. He wipes it off with a pass of his hand. Wipes his hand down the leg of his pants.

"Keep the humidity up in here for the skin," Livingston says. "Got magnets in the cart, too, that Doc Bartlett set up for me. Says it's to keep the water from settling." He points to the bank of screens, to the little screen there on the arm of the cart. Each has a moon of deep blue a quarter risen into frame. "It's what makes them blue circles," the speaker says. "The magnets."

"What is it you've got?"

Livingston shrugs. "Bartlett's at a loss, but Rush says a severe case of dropsy, maybe some gout on top, or underneath. I don't know, and as much as he talks, I don't think Rush really knows either. Probably feels like he needs to make a prognosis. He knows I'm dying. Everyone knows that."

"How long have you got?"

"Don't know what it is, can't know how long."

M'Kean sighs. "Rush is a bleeder and butcher, and though everyone likes him just fine as a man, those with any sense know to tune out when it's a doctor he's trying to be. At least Doc Bartlett keeps his mouth shut when he doesn't know what's happening." M'Kean takes a step closer, his countenance suddenly more serious. "I need your opinion on something, Livingston." M'Kean produces a smartphone, flexdocs already open, holds it down for the watery old man.

"Don't give it to me," Livingston says. "Everything I touch becomes damp these days." He leans to eye the data. "Well . . . what have we here?"

"One of our programmers, during the retreat through New Jersey. Noticed these spikes. Ever since, we've been picking up some real heightened activity in this one sector of the Cloud."

Livingston looks into the screen attached to his cart. Types on a little keyboard mounted under his fingers. Scans a second. His speaker says, "Looks like it started in a profile somewhere. Behaves like something . . . unpacking itself."

"*Unpacking itself* . . . funny. That's exactly what our programmer said."

"Probably just a function set caught in a loop, keeps expanding its algorithm in some sort of code cycle it can't bust out of."

"And that doesn't worry you?"

"Not enough to ride all the way out to York, PA to tell the Congress." Livingston shows him the screen. "Seems to be generating search drones here and there, doing some math equations. Math equations never hurt anyone. Empty noise. Random data being created and crunched and used to create more data. That's all."

M'Kean casts a long gaze at the state of his old friend. "We've seen a bit of this same thing, you know."

"Same thing as *me*?"

"Our programmer, the one who found this data."

"He has dropsy?"

M'Kean shakes his head. "He's dead. Instead of saturating, he dried out. Thing changed the makeup of his cells. It's what the doctors out there are telling me. All happened pretty quick once he crossed paths with this program." M'Kean notices something in Livingston's face. "You've seen it."

"*It?*"

"This program. You've seen it before. Did this *dropsy* come after or before?"

"Dropsy, dried out, different effects. What makes you think the same program could be responsible for both?"

"Ours said this thing was modifying itself. Changing its own code." M'Kean lets the future-sounding sit. "Maybe this *unpacking*, this shape shifting, expanding, is all part of the same thing, this program feeling its way across? Trying different things. Saturation, dehydration, who knows who else out there might be already affected and how? Once it finds a way that works to some kind of acceptable efficiency . . ."

This last idea has put a little fright into Livingston. He takes a few breaths to wonder, then: "Look, M'Kean, if it were up to me, we'd be concerned about the Internet in proportion to the battlefield, but we're not likely to get many *votes* for that." Livingston looks into the screens, one by one, right down the line, feeds streaming in from the debate that's been droning on and on this whole last week and going absolutely nowhere. "When this program fills up its assigned sector of the Cloud, it'll stop. Nowhere else to go. Problem contained."

"And if it doesn't? What if when there's no more room to expand, it spills *out* instead?"

"Your programmer. Did he do any calculations? Estimates on how long that would take? For it to fill up its sector?"

"Exponents," M'Kean shrugs. "Could be a year or years. Could be a month. Days. Maybe it's now . . ."

Livingston thinks about it. "Took me off appropriations when I stopped being able to go to the meetings. Who you need to talk to is John Adams."

Great, M'Kean thinks. He's about to ask where when he looks in over Livingston's shoulder and there he is, the little Colossus of Congress, staring back from inside one of those screens. John Adams, the Duke of Braintree, and he does *not* look pleased. "What is it, Mr. Livingston?"

M'Kean leans his face into the vision of the webcam. "We need some money, Adams. To hire more programmers."

Adams' face contorts. "Ha! Write a resolution. Bring it to the floor. Get a majority. Gather up the taxes or the loans. It's as simple as that."

The door to the little chamber opens right then and in comes Dr. Ben Rush. Slips silently past M'Kean and begins Livingston's twice-daily checkup. Makes M'Kean wonder what other goings on must be stored in that brain of the doctor's. Always poking in and out of rooms. Never in charge of anything, but always present, it seems, observing.

Livingston is typing something and then one of the screens is filled with data much like the data M'Kean has on his smartphone.

"What's this?" Adams wants to know.

Livingston's speaker says, "Some activity we're concerned about in the Cloud."

"Autonomous replicating selfware," M'Kean says.

Adams's eyes roll inside the little viewer inside the screen. "What's it do? Send junk tickles to all your virtual friends?"

M'Kean tells him, "It replicates itself. Or maybe it's better to say it *expands* itself."

"In case you didn't notice because you were in such a panic about this expanding computer program, you didn't just ride into Philadelphia, but *York*, Mr. M'Kean. That's because the British army is in possession of Philadelphia."

"And New York," Rush says, dripping sarcasm, "thanks to *his* Excellency."

"And Delaware, your home state, Mr. M'Kean."

"I was *there*, Adams. I was in New York."

"Then you know to forgive me if the Internet's not one of my main concerns right now."

Rush says then, "This dick Washington. Keeps vanishing. Won't even return an email. What, expects us to send an actual person out there to meet with him? Does he even know how long that takes?"

M'Kean asks Adams, "What about what's happening to Livingston here?"

"Mr. Livingston has gout. Isn't that right, doctor?"

"Dropsy's my main concern," Rush says. "A severe case, but nothing out of the ordinary."

"Nothing out of the ordinary?" and M'Kean touches Philip Livingston's forearm, his finger sinking in a good half inch, leaves a dent the shape of a human finger when he takes it away. The three men in the room and the other in the feed all look back to the dent. Slowly, it fills with water and then the water becomes regular old skin again. "Does that look *ordinary* to any of you?"

Livingston's still looking at that spot on his arm. His speaker says, "M'Kean thinks my sickness has something to do with the Internet, this program a few of us have come across."

"Same thing with our kid in New Jersey," M'Kean takes it up. "The more time he spent in there looking at it, the faster he changed. What if it's this program that's doing it, changing their actual physical bodies? Replicating itself, filling up the Cloud, what happens if it's not just one sector, but the whole Internet teaming with it?"

Adams smiles. There's years in it. "What would happen to this body, Mr. M'Kean, and this war, if we went chasing off after each and every thing that *might* be a problem some day? You want to save the Revolution? Write a bill. Present a resolution to the Congress. Start counting delegates."

M'Kean scoffs, a glance at the endless debate, endlessly streaming on and on. "Congress has proven itself not more than a good way for nothing to get done."

Adams' bark comes distorted through the microphone and speaker. "Been on the front lines a little too long, M'Kean. Where a general articulates a concept and it's someone's job to make it a reality. No questions asked." Adams brightens to just before open laughter. "It's a little more difficult with this republic thing. But plenty has been accomplished thus far. If you haven't noticed, we're no longer Englishmen. And when the Articles are ratified, we'll have a new country, born of liberty."

"Occupied by another country because we can't get consensus to actually fight the war we started."

Adams shrugs. "Oh, I know. But unless you want a king, this is the way it's going to have to be. Get the Articles ratified. Write a resolution." And the screen goes dark.

M'Kean turns back to the cart containing Philip Livingston, but there is no Philip Livingston. Instead of a man filled with water, there is only the water vacated, a dark pool spread out in blob around the cart, reflects Rush and M'Kean's faces back at them looking down. On Livingston's screen, that same program they monitored all the way across New Jersey, expanding in angled waves around its edges in clockwise.

"What is it, you think?"

"Well," M'Kean says. "I hope it's not what I think it might be."

Rush swallows. A loud swallow. "What if it's after us?"

"*Us* who?"

"Us . . . *The Signers*."

JOHN HART :: MAY 11TH 1779

S igner of the Declaration of Independence, John Hart is spending the morning in the library of the family home. His children and grandchildren lounge with their laptops and smartphones, flicking their way through app catalogs and digging up arcane databases to explore; a few outside in the gardens too, a few others in the extensive attic maze which tops the house. Just then one is finishing a count to a hundred and darting off to look for brothers and sisters and cousins all tucked and folded throughout the house.

What's about to happen will be the last in a long series of crises about which John Hart has become something of an expert over the years. While listening to podcasts and taking the recycling out one morning, a vision of the tyranny of the Stamp Act took his mind and exactly 140 characters later, every patriotic blog in the New World was buzzing with John Hart's apocalyptic imagery.

When the British finally did invade, it was *his* cellar that was full of provisions. Real provisions. His insane devotion to *Evidence Sets of the Great End*, Roman soldier history-casts and survivalist snail-zines helped him live like an Indian in the woods for a year while Redcoat regiments and Loyalists hunted the state for Signers. On *this* morning, in 1779, John Hart readies plans for town defense against panicked members of other towns not prepared for some calamity that remains a variable in this particular model. "Have to be ready," he has told all of his grandchildren, and all of his grandchildren's parents, something like a hundred times, a hundred times each.

"Grandfather," his youngest grandchild says, "today is the day when Miles Standish stood on the mast of his boat and looked out and instead of sea only, he spied a new speck of land and yelled, 'LAND!'"

"Very good." John Hart bends again to preparing strategies of land defense and ration schedules. Be it rabies outbreak, nuclear holocaust or global ice-over. "It is history," he tells the young one, "not religion. Our ability to remember. This is the great motivation for men to take morals with them wherever they go." He looks up from his work to address anyone in earshot. "Who is watching but everyone who will ever exist from this point forward, on into eternity?"

These philosophical interruptions of his practical brainstorms are common enough that all the children know the thing to do is to pretend you're paying attention. Saves hours of Grandpa rattling off details about how the most number of humans can efficiently survive a one-foot rise in sea level.

"Grandfather," a child leaning back from a laptop he's been hunched over since waking. "It's your lucky day . . ."

"The battle of Gamelsdorf," the little one recites. "William of Orange captures Exeter. Napoleon becomes one-third of the Consul of France. Suicide bombers destroy hotels in a country not yet founded."

"The Internet says a plague is spreading down the East Coast."

John Hart looks up from his plans. "A plague? Coming *here*?" And he almost looks delighted. *Finally*, he looks like he's thinking. "They laugh, they laugh, they laugh," he's digging in the drawer for an old smartphone, flicks it to a menu that accesses spreadsheet databases he keeps up to date and always open on his desktop. "What kind of plague are we talking about?"

"Something about a stomach," the boy is summarizing for him. "Maybe in the drinking water."

"That doesn't sound like a plague," the boy's father says, yet another of the family gathered in the room and throughout the house and the small estate around it.

"People's stomachs are reporting groups of people just falling over dead," another says from the light of another computer screen, way on the other side of the room.

"Where are you reading this?"

The kid points to the screen and says, "The Internet's a-tickle with it."

John Hart clicks into the first cell of a database constructed for plague-specific command protocol. "Get all the children into the main hall."

"A young man becomes the youngest man to ever become grand champion in the board game known as chess."

"What?"

"It was today. That a computer program analyzed the world and told the human at its terminal that the planet was about to be destroyed."

"Three thousand people in Concord, New Hampshire." It's the boy at the laptop, looking like he might be thinking more like his grandfather about this whole *plague* thing now.

"But there aren't three thousand people in Concord."

"Says they've come from all around to demand something be done. People in the countryside in piles."

"Piles?"

"Piles of dead."

"Is that what is says?"

He points. "There's pictures."

"The Meiji Restoration begins right now."

"Okay, sweetheart, that's enough."

The ones in front of laptops are clicked into their favorite media outlets while those without computer or smartphone have rushed to look at a screen over someone's shoulder. Doors can be heard opening and closing throughout the house. Hurried footsteps. "Let's not panic now, family." It's the first rule of every contingency plan John Hart has ever devised. First rule when the British threatened to leave Canada in French hands: *Don't panic.*

The sound of horse hooves on the drive out front. Shouts now. "Who's here?" someone shouts.

John Hart moves to the center of the room. He turns to address the growing familial crowd gathering in the library despite the fact that the plan calls for a meeting in the main hall. Through the window, he can see his first-born daughter, collapsed on the walk out front, clutching her stomach as her husband wails skyward. *Don't panic*, John Hart says to himself, but then he's not looking at the faces of his gathered family but at the ceiling. A pain in his lower chest like having the wind knocked out. A taste like sand in his mouth. He manages to whisper, "Stick to the plan." But he's not sure who's still there to hear him. *The men who survive this,* he thinks, *they will be gods. And I'll be one of the ones who died in the very first days.*

GEORGE ROSS :: JULY 14TH 1779

Geologe Ross is pretty sure he has what's being called *The Death*.
That faint tightening in the lower gut, something he would have
dismissed as gas before the outbreak. It's supposed to be the first
sign of what's supposed to be a pretty quick descent. The last time
he was outside, the streets were littered with them, dead Americans,
victims of *The Death*. Their last act to rush out into the world and fall
flat. Because inside windowless houses, that's how the serfs and sub-
jects of the Old World would succumb to plagues. Americans are free
by nature and so they get one last look at the sun, or the clouded sky,
or the stars and the dark infinities of the universe. Maybe in their last
diluted throws of *The Death*, they imagined that past their front door,
some great force had gathered to save them. That somehow, some way,
America would show up at the last possible second.

Ross puts his best guess at sixty-five percent. It's an aggregate of
the wild range being proffered on the few sites and feeds still updating. Sixty-five percent of Americans dead from *The Death*: two out
of three. Only two months into the outbreak and no end in sight.
Of course, that's all speculation, speculation being the best Ross can
do. When panicked reports started circulating that *The Death* was
being spread through the Internet, Americans everywhere rushed
out of the Cloud, never to return. Most sites haven't changed since
the outbreak broke out. Pictures of the first dead ghost every abandoned splash page, breaking news left there breaking. The whole
Cloud just a wasteland now, full of old haunts and ad drones, AIs

wiggling along the expanding spine of some task-adjusted task list, firewall worms mining long-abandoned email accounts and social networking profiles, infesting online identities with their protocol, creating more drones and more haunts and more worms. The Cloud isn't gone—it's just not a place for humans anymore.

There are a few brave ones still out there, though. Using the remains of barely functioning social networking mainframes, they collect and share what little information they can scrape up: tweets about the burning of Fairfield, the burning of Norwalk; headcounts estimating how many British soldiers remain; a single pixelated smartphone capture of Mad Tony Wayne and a tattered flag above a fallen royal fort. But no one knows the answer to the big question: Is George Washington still out there, still fighting? Hopes are that the old man has gone silent, ordered every smartphone in the ranks pitched into the Delaware. Like a snake, his army creeps unseen through the woods of New Jersey . . . *off the grid*. But these are just hopes. Odds and probabilities and hunches all lean toward him being dead too, Washington and all his men—fucked, just like the rest of us.

Since the outbreak, the only person George Ross has had any sustained contact with is the other George Ross. They became friends back during the second dawn of social networking, when suddenly an online presence wasn't just for amusement anymore but a professional and then a human necessity.

It was about then that their online profiles got crossed over. The first thing was they each started getting friend requests that were intended for the other George Ross. Each of them accepted a few dozen of these thinking they were supporters or maybe small-time political bosses they'd forgotten the names of. Suddenly they had fifty friends in common and that's when the programming started confusing the two profiles. Sorting it all out made the George Rosses pretty good friends over the years. Having to swap misdirected e-vites back to their rightful intendee, routing chat feeds into the smartphone of the George Ross who that chat was *really* opened to chat with. Lo and behold, they're chatting too, and not just about the quirks of present-tense communications. They're on messageboards and listservs together. Chatrooms they both really meant to be in. Chatting away.

Then one day they logged on to find that they weren't different people any longer, not on the Internet anyway. Some tentacle of the protocol had determined that the existence of these two separate crossed-over identities was an error. And so the profiles were fused into one single entity. From there, it spread through the entire Internet. Two different George Rosses in the real world were now linked to the same online self.

There was nothing they could do but start their online identities over from scratch. Explaining in all their invites that they didn't de-friend anyone, that really it's all a big mix-up. But they never did take down that other George Ross. Periodically, they'd check in to see if some interaction meant for them individually had landed in the lap of the shared identity. It worked as a second or a third online George Ross—a catchall for the other two. A private scanner or secretary, a little sliver of the social network in which anything possible for either George Ross became possible for both.

It's with this shared identity that the two George Rosses have been navigating the fractured sub-structures of the post-outbreak cloud. Recently, a few other users began posting to George Ross's wall, the shared George Ross a sort of informal meeting place for humans still daring to navigate the Cloud. A belief exists among them that despite *The Death*, information availability is still the only hope the fledging country has. Some of the posts are clearly ad drones, pushing products and subscriptions and listservs as if the world outside the Cloud is still the world they were originally programmed to entice. Other posts seem human enough, but who knows. Could be humans or could be second-generation drones, drones created by drones—and maybe they really do believe they're human.

Today's post from the other George Ross reads: "*The Death* has reached England too."

"Maybe it reached America *from* England?"

But really no one knows where it started. Or when. Theories abound from mutated yellow fever to ancient rats long ago trapped in ice and now free. Drones once programmed to attract scientists, conspiracy nuts and sci-fi fans cobble common words and phrases into sensational and absurd hypotheticals. Stories get picked up by news-feed drones. They get funneled through linking AIs, and then it's as good as true, as far as all the autonomous protocols are concerned.

George Ross shares a tweet that says, "*The Death* was brought on a slave ship."

The other George Ross posts, "A weapon Parliament couldn't control, and now it sweeps through the entire kingdom? Only time until it's global."

All that's left of Asia is a giant firewall. And who knows what's happening on the other side. If there is any Asia left at all.

What George Ross can't bear to post is that he's got it now too, that the weak glove of a shared identity is no protection from *The Death*. From all the data linked in the links on the shared George Ross's wall, it seems like after the first pangs, you get a few days tops. That time is just about up. Seated at his computer, thinking about *The Death* and how it spreads, George Ross can't help but feel like only the material part of himself and nothing more, that the core code of his existence is actually his online self. Maybe this is what comes to you, he thinks, when you can see the end of your life approaching in real time—that maybe there is a being out there so similar to you that when you die, something fundamental about you remains.

George Ross, the other one, at whatever laptop or terminal he's sitting at, types the question: "Washington . . . alive or dead?"

But he's not going to get an answer. Not from George Ross. Because right then, the pain becomes unbearable. It throws George Ross into fits of abstract breakdancing on the floor. His shins bang chair legs until the chair is toppled too. He can feel how wide open his mouth is, but there's no screaming or even breath coming out. A moment of calm. Must be the few instants between when the heart stops and the brain shuts down forever. He thinks about those three George Rosses, out there in the fractured Cloud . . . have to share just one human now.

J oseph Hewes sits in a chair by the tall windows of his study. He has out his smartphone with that same name scrolled to the top, blinking in the pulse of the cursor light. All these years, he's saved her number and email. All these years, transferring her from phone to phone as he aged and aged while the image of her remained the same in his brain. And what if he were to press that green call button now, after all this time? Would she be there, despite all the rules of existence? And if she were, what then? Hewes fogs the window with the words he's used to fog it so many times before: "Where are you now?"

It was back in 1751 that she died, when the Revolution and an Internet plague were things no one could imagine. Two days before they were to be married, Joseph Hewes came in to find her sitting in a chair, blood spurting from her mouth. It came up out of her in molten waves. She was drenching herself with it, her own blood. He stood there frozen in the frame of the door. Their eyes met and the look on her face—a sadness at having let him down. It was her last alive moment.

The night after the funeral, Joseph Hewes climbed a hill that overlooked her family plot and her fresh grave within. He held a loaded pistol to his temple, swearing to join her. But just like the hundreds of times since, he was, in the end, unable to finish himself. And so their time apart continued. Days alone became weeks and months and years and decades. "And now I'm dying," he says, maybe so she can hear him, if she's out there somewhere, listening.

Outside the window, the front of his estate is crawled over with weeds and branches not trimmed back for half a year. Flowers bloomed wild and then went dead in the fall. Six months since the outbreak of *The Death*.

But that's not what's killing Joseph Hewes. He's got something more ancient. A disease that has stalked man as long as there has been a man. Funny that while *The Death* kills people by the millions, while a savage guerilla war sears its way through the nooks and crannies of several states, that a mysterious fever can still find a human to kill. And though it's not really related to all that's happening in America, Joseph Hewes can't help but feel that his death is as connected as any other, just another of the millions who won't see the other side of it.

Double doors open at the back of the study, and a Negro teenager enters the room. It's the slave boy Gibson, who tells his master, "I've spoken with a survivor!"

Hewes slides the phone into a pocket and turns to see the boy. Gosh, the place is a mess, the whole mansion falling in around them. They tried to keep it clean for a while, but it's been just the two of them for so long. When all the other slaves were killed by *The Death*, way back in the very first week, Hewes had offered Gibson his freedom. But the teenager, wise beyond his years, just shrugged. "Where am I going to go? How am I going to outrun what can't be outrun?"

But now it seems like maybe they have—outrun *The Death*. Gibson, at least. Hewes may survive the plague, but not the time of the plague. "*The Death*," the boy says. "It's caused by the Internet." And he holds out a sheet of paper for his master to take, an actual sheet of paper! "Says that *The Death* is spread over the Internet and that Congress is working on measures to stop further outbreaks."

Joseph Hewes reads a moment. "Seems the plague went global," he says. "A world-wide ban on Internet access." He looks up from the paper, suspicion mixed with disgust. "What? We think if we don't go on the Internet, the Internet is going to just vanish? It'll still be out there whether someone's using it or not. And so long as there's an Internet, there's going to be *The Death* too, some echo of its code, buried in some busted file somewhere."

Gibson is looking into the bones and veins that hint through the tops of his hands. "Don't know how the Internet can have an effect on my god-given body," he says. "Maybe it's divine. God telling us, 'Don't use the Internet. No more.'"

"Some other species will stumble upon this planet a long time from now. And they'll think the Cloud was all there was," Hewes ponders, continuing in thought: Once the humans are gone, the Cloud will be just like this old plantation, a system that could no longer operate. It'll linger on a bit, corrupted to its smallest pieces. "Well, at least it means Congress is still out there, at least *trying* to do something."

A few weeks ago, a single traveler passed on the road out front, way out on the other side of the overgrown grounds. Hewes was sitting in the same chair he's sitting in now, fogging that same glass he's fogging. Seemed like the traveler was going to lead his donkey and his cart on past without even a pause. But then he did stop, probably saw the smoke from the fires Gibson keeps always lit throughout the house. And the traveler must have seen Joseph Hewes, too, because he raised a hand to wave. But that was as much as he dared. Poked his mule and off they trotted. It was the first human they'd seen in five months. After watching a few others pass, headed who knows where, Hewes and Gibson agreed that the boy would head into town to see if maybe somewhere in this vast continent things were finally getting pulled back together.

Now Gibson has returned from a half-crowded town square, fliers tacked up on storefronts, stuck on the doors of those known to be left living. Gibson relates it all, swallowing hard. "Seems like a calm has finally begun to settle, Sir."

"Maybe that's because there aren't enough humans left to muster a respectable panic. And without the Internet, how would such a panic spread?" Hewes shakes his head. "Here we are," he rattles the page, "actual paper. *The Death* has beaten us. From this point forward, man is frozen in time." Hewes looks into his own semi-transparent reflection in the glass, feeling exactly that much there in the world. "I still can't help but think of *The Death* as something living. A nightmare beast loose in the Cloud, reaching down to snatch up users, suck their souls right off the planet."

"Now that *The Death* is over, maybe if we can get you into Charleston, Master. Maybe a bit of bleeding and some purges, a whole mess of leaches and straps, maybe they can break this fever and you can still come stumbling out."

Hewes is shaking his head. Sweat has matted his hair to the lumpy surface of his skull. It leaks dark down his face like spilled paint. "No, I've waited long enough. Nearly thirty years. And still I'm not sure . . . if all this time I've made the right decision in not joining you."

Gibson knows this tone of voice his master gets. When he talks like this, his words are not for anyone in this world any longer but for that ghost he sometimes talks to. Must be somewhere up there in the air, Gibson thinks, mixed in with that Internet that's getting the whole world sick and dead.

Hewes lifts the smartphone from his pocket. Didn't realize his hands were shaking until he sees how much the phone is shaking. These last six months, he's been wishing she could be there with him to watch the world die. The strange beauty of it grinding to a halt. But now that *The Death* has passed, or seems to have, the thought of the world rebuilding without her is too much.

"Wouldn't mess with that cell phone," Gibson says. "*The Death* get in your device as easy as it can any Internet."

Hewes' lips and whole face are wet now with fever. "Will heaven be heaven?" he asks. "Or just one more of these worlds I've wandered through alone?" Gibson is waving a hand in front of his master's vacant eyes, but his master can't see a thing. Hewes presses that call button, puts the smartphone to his face.

"Hello?"

When they hit the edge of Easton, PA, Francis Hopkinson takes out that modified smartphone of his, peels off and starts a gallop around the perimeter of town. Thomas M'Kean keeps his horse pointed straight, down to a trot through the outer edges and onto Main Street. They've come because of the rumor that hit Philadelphia the morning before. Being said there that George Taylor has started feeling those stomach pangs that are always the first sign of *The Death*. The rumor must be real, a real rumor at least. No businesses open, the windows and doors all closed and latched, not a soul on the street. For M'Kean, it's a flashback to how towns all across Pennsylvania looked during the outbreak. More than a year without a reported case and they'd begun to think that maybe the pestilence was passed.

When Congress first reconvened, M'Kean was put atop a sub-committee charged with investigating how an Internet-bound plague wiped out sixty-five percent of the population. In these efforts, Hopkinson has become his right-hand man; the inventor/poet turned patriot shifted the focus of his vast left hemisphere onto unraveling exactly how *The Death* was spread. He and Doc Bartlett have speculated that some corruption in the feed may have caused a screen refresh rate capable of changing the physiology of the brain. But speculation is as specific as they've been able to get. As frightening as the news is, Hopkinson's actually a little excited.

For the first time, they might be able to get some new data on *The Death*. As Hopkinson circles town, taking readings, M'Kean is reaching George Taylor's home.

The woman who answers the door gives M'Kean a hateful look, then steps aside. Over at the kitchen table, George Taylor sits with a glass and bottle, both half-empty. "Thomas M'Kean," he says, "Chief Justice of Pennsylvania. In *my* house."

"Don't be a dick," his wife tells him.

Taylor uses the wine glass to wave her suggestion away, gestures for M'Kean to have the chair opposite, wine sloshing as close to the rim as possible without spilling. The table around his elbow is dotted with stains of ages impossible to tell. "Word is you'll be up for president of Congress. And me here with *The Death*. Worse off than the day before I started."

M'Kean eyes him, a glance at that gut, *The Death* inside. "How sure are you?"

"*You* must be. Must have left Philadelphia the second you heard." George Taylor nods toward the front door and the town beyond. "Only in the last weeks had they begun to venture out. At first, seemed like only one in ten, but they've been eking out more and more. First town-wide count has the death rate just under fifty percent. Now this."

"Fifty percent is a lot better than some places are reporting."

From her spot at the sink, Mrs. Taylor clears her throat. "Got our daughter, Mr. Chief Justice."

"Now every door in town is bolted. People running from me in the street." George Taylor leans, wags a finger at M'Kean. "But *you*, you're not scared of catching it?"

M'Kean sips calmly. "We may not know what *The Death* is. Not yet anyway. But we do know you can't get it by sharing a wine bottle. Question becomes then, how *did* you get it? You haven't been on the Internet, George? Not even a little?"

George Taylor looks at his stomach. Concentrates a moment. It was an hour earlier than this time three days ago that he felt the first twinge. He'd collapsed in his wife's arms and cried and cried and cried, but when he looked up at her, her face was dry and her eyes distant and he hated her then.

There's a knock at the door, and before any of them can move to answer it, Hopkinson comes in, holding that smartphone up for all to see. Onscreen is an app he programmed, and if you look into the touchscreen while the app is running, you see the world through the phone's camera but with the Internet visible. He shows them the ghosted, flickering, mechanical structure that pokes and vanishes its way through the room around them. "Getting wild readings all over town." Hopkinson takes off his hat, shakes his head so that long ponytail flops onto his shoulder; it sits there like another of those wild ideas half-escaped from his brain.

"I haven't been on the Internet," George Taylor finally says. "Not since they first told us that's how *The Death* was spread."

"Taylor is correct," Hopkinson says. "No one seems to be accessing, but there sure is activity. Something is on the Internet. And it looks like more than just some old ad drones."

Taylor nods at the smartphone, there in Hopkinson's hand. "That thing of yours connected, Frank?"

A smile. "I wish. Still not safe." He shows the Taylors a wire that comes out the bottom of the device and goes up his sleeve, hooks a thumb to indicate his backpack. "Wired right into some plug-and-play harddrives. A little portable Internet, in miniature, of course, but not connected to anything outside itself."

"Frank here has some weird idea," M'Kean says. "Thinks if we can figure out how *The Death* spreads, maybe we can use it."

"Use *The Death*?"

M'Kean pops his eyes. "I know. He's nuts."

Hopkinson's shaking his head. "Not use *The Death*, but perhaps some element of it. If we can pin down exactly how it spreads, harness that technology to spread something worth spreading, something beneficial for the country."

"Something like what?"

But Hopkinson doesn't answer. Says instead, "With your permission, George, I'd like to record some readings when it happens."

"When what happens?"

Mrs. Taylor spits a laugh, "Can you believe these guys from Congress?"

George Taylor looks around, trying to get the energy, or the inclination to be offended. "Well, now I feel weird. Like you two are here just waiting for me to die."

M'Kean fills all their glasses, even Hopkinson's despite his protests. Ms. Taylor too, finally comes over from the sink. They break into a few hours of almost normal behavior, the three Signers swapping stories about their initial trip to Philadelphia, back when the Second Congress was first assembling. Seems like a world ago now.

They're telling stories about John Witherspoon, *The Father of the Founding Fathers*, when George Taylor stops mid sentence. A pained look tightens into a scowl. A moment later, it loosens and his whole body slumps forward. M'Kean rushes around to help Taylor to the floor. His eyes have gone wild, scanning the air as if seeing through the faces leaned over him, off into that semi-visible Internet from Hopkinson's phone.

And there it is, that smartphone and its dedicated Internet, hovering George Taylor's face. It's the last thing he sees: Hopkinson cracking a grin, staring into fresh data on *The Death*.

R ichard Stockton is asleep in bed when the door splinters apart. A hand into his hair yanks him to the cold wood floor. He looks up and sees it's not the British, but other Americans— Loyalists—and him, the prize of a long hunt. Their leader kicks him in the back so hard that Stockton will never stand up straight, not ever again in his life. "And here's one for the King, *a Signer!*"

Stockton is dragged out front where the beating continues. Around him on the lawn, the family that had been hiding him is slaughtered. The wife of the house raped right there under the open sky as dirty men stand around open-mouthed and gazing. Nearby, some British soldiers watch as the slaves bash in the head of the overseer, their black skin all slimy with blood. A few Loyalists have found the little plot of headstones, the family members taken by *The Death*. Their piss steams the air as they saturate the graves.

Shackles and cuffs are applied. A rope tied to the cuffs and the other end to a horse. The horse is whipped and rides from the property with Stockton rolling over and over on the ground ten yards behind. The human sounds fade. Just the thunder of horse hooves. He opens his eyes, sees through the kicking mud, another man being dragged.

The next day they arrive at Morven, his abandoned estate. The place is crawling with Redcoats. All the furniture has been moved onto the lawn, where it burns in several crooked piles. Chunks of his life float in the cool air, one edge ash and the other still embers.

He has no idea what's become of his wife or his remaining children. Through the windows, he can see officers making themselves at home. Just as he's wondering about his cherished databases, Stockton sees them, his harddrives, all the information he's gathered throughout a lifetime of meticulous collection, piled up and blazing. Men are emerging from the house just then, tossing more and more of the plastic shells on top. Stockton realizes that with no Internet and no prospect of its return, he may be witnessing the actual eradication of information, never to be recovered.

He's told he will swear loyalty to the King, and when he refuses, they only smile. Stockton calls the soldier in charge a savage, and the guy knocks him out with one clean blast in the mouth. They reattach him to the horse and drag him off for the coast.

Stockton is thrown into the hold of a leaking boat, which bobs in the harbor. Vomit and shit and blood slime the floor and most of the way up the walls. Every morning they come in to dump the dead into the bay and ask if there's anyone who has changed their mind. And there always are, men who will now swear loyalty. These are taken up into the light.

The prisoners are no longer dying of *The Death*. They starve or cough themselves away instead. There is no food. The only water is rain dripping between the planks from above, has the taste of rotted cabbage. Some men come in and beat Stockton unconscious. It takes a while, Stockton actually asking out loud for that guy who could do it with one punch.

They pile him limp into a cart that overflows with other unconscious men. The ones who survive the trip are put in cells in a freezing prison complex. At sunset Stockton is dragged outside where he lays naked until they drag him back in at sunrise. Each night, as he shivers under the stars, he dreams of Morven, his home. Stockton imagines it as it was before the Revolution, before *The Death*. His family is there, his databases all intact. In the library, while the fireplace crackles low, a child plays Afghani music on the grand piano, her fingers twittering consecutive keys to expertly pluck notes the instrument was not designed to reach. Stockton has a smartreader in his lap but has paused to gaze lazily about the room.

Stockton is not sure what's happening when he's taken to a cell that's just another cell but with a desk and a fire and some royal officers drinking tea and chatting as if he's not there. They tell him it has been six weeks, and he can't remember having eaten once. They give him a smartphone and tell him to press his thumb on the touchscreen; and when he does, they tell him he has just sworn loyalty to King George 3.

But Stockton doesn't care.

He and a hundred others are marched off to Trenton. There, given to a band of colonial troops, a little scavenger club hiding out in the woods. But it's not just a club. They come over a hill and there it is, the Continental Army. And so it is true: George Washington is still alive. Stockton is driven back to Morven, where his only surviving daughter waits for him. The entire family is gone but for her and her new husband, fellow Signer and patriot Dr. Benjamin Rush.

Stockton doesn't talk much, if ever. He never asks what happened to the rest of the family because he knows he won't survive hearing it. He has his meals chosen and his clothes laid out, spends his days sitting in his desiccated library, the drive stacks hulking empty to the ceiling. The wires have all been cleared out, but there's no way to keep Stockton from remembering the harddrives. He can't get that image out of his mind, the melted plastic and metal, leaking from the fire in a few feeble rivulets.

One afternoon, Rush comes into the library to find Stockton seated upright, his eyes and mouth hanging open. In the days leading up, even his footfalls had ceased to produce sound. Rush summons the new servants, has the body taken away, quickly, before his wife returns and has her father's defeated face seared into her mind forever.

Through the layered films of Caesar Rodney's veil, only the general shape of his face can be seen. Slightly translucent, the veil hangs from the front of his skull, tucked into the collar of his shirt so not even his neck is visible. He wears the veil to hide the fact that beneath it, his face is falling off, has been since just before the First Congress. His sister has never seen what remains of Caesar Rodney's face because he wears the veil all the time, even while he sleeps. They've been locked alone together inside this house since the first days of the second outbreak. Flesh pieces hang in the veil. His damp breathing haunts each and every stillness she can manage to carve out.

Until about a week ago, Caesar Rodney would spend each day on the top veranda of his mansion, musket in hand. The wind would kick up and his veil would flatten to the jagged remnants of his face. Then the wind would change and the veil would billow, making his head look lopsided and swollen. Throughout all his watches, no one has ever tried to get on the property. In fact, neither of them has seen another soul since the second outbreak began. It was then that Caesar Rodney took all their computers and all the smartdevices too and smashed them to pieces with a wood ax. He promised his sister he would never let *The Death* get her. That he would keep the Internet away, kill any intruder, with no hesitation, with no questions asked.

"How am I supposed to meet anyone?" his sister asks. "How am I supposed to fall in love if we don't have the Internet?"

His voice comes from beyond the veil: "But they're all dead. Dead from *The Death*. We are the only ones left. Perhaps you can settle for some fraternal love, the love of your brother?"

She looks at chunks of dried skin dangling. "If everyone's dead, brother, then why do we bother guarding the house?"

"We guard the house because when this outbreak is over, there shall be another, and then one after that. The only way to survive is to keep away from people and keep off the Internet. Forever."

These challenges to his reasoning would have never crossed her lips even a week before, but Caesar Rodney's sister has grown bold these last few days as her brother's health has taken a dramatic turn for the worse. It started with a light cough that spiraled into a fit. Now his mobility has been reduced to bed to fireside to dinner table to bed. The fits have become a regular occurrence. After each one, more and more pieces of Caesar Rodney's face can be seen lodged in the tangles of the veil. The sounds his lungs make are infested with an almost musical discord.

Since that first fit, Caesar Rodney's sister has taken over the guard duty in her disinterested way. She sits up there for hours on end, leaning on the loaded musket. But all she ever sees is the road up to the mansion, empty and overgrown and full of shadows. The little village in the valley is as still as one of those frozen images back in the abandoned Cloud. *Maybe he's right,* she thinks. *Maybe there is no one left. And in a few days he'll be gone too and I'll be the last human in the universe. All by myself. Then I'll check the Internet.*

But she can't wait that long. After helping her brother to bed that evening, she lays awake in their shared room, cursing *The Death* in her mind in rounds. "Brother," she finally says, "do you think that maybe my online profile has fallen in love, at least?"

She listens to the staggered, gurgling wheeze of his breath.

"We'll get *The Death* solved and go back online someday and I'll find my profile, taken over by a drone. Some low-level AI that was coded to adjust its programming according to how many likes it gets on posts containing certain word combinations. Accepted a friend request one day and it was an ad drone, programmed to collect as many friends as possible. Profile picture's some plump little hussy in a low-cut gown.

"Now they're writing posts all over each other's walls because they always hit their feedback criteria just right, the ends of their programming all tangled together. Hard to tell which is which, working on the same equations, breaking down code the exact same way, or whatever it is drones in love do."

In the quiet that follows, she realizes her brother isn't asleep. He *is* moving in that bed, but not answering. She gets up and lights a candle and takes it with her to his bedside. This close, his breath sounds drenched, rattling up from the deep to pop mucus bubbles somewhere behind his teeth. The veil lays gently over his face, moving only slightly as he dies.

It occurs to her then that she hasn't seen his face in years. Slowly, avoiding even the slightest contact with his flesh, she lifts away the veil. Some strained tendons, some chunks of dried meat, some cartilage and bone. A few tentacles of hair have matted themselves into flat tangles in a dried-out crust. But there certainly isn't any face.

She leaves him there like that, makes her way slowly through the house, the pace a person would sink in water if they let loose all their breath and held it. When she gets to the kitchen, she realizes she *is* holding her breath. Has to take a deep inhale which smells so fresh it shocks her. Been sleeping in that sour room with him for so long.

From behind the bottom back shelf in the pantry, under a loose board, she takes out an old, junky laptop she has kept hidden from him all this time. Even though it's been a few days since Caesar Rodney has moved more than the length of a room at any one time,

his sister is suddenly terrified that he'll appear in the kitchen doorway behind her, somehow suppressing his wheeze, negotiating the
entire house without a noise, to catch her ruining their only chance
for survival.

"Well," she says, "*The Death* or no *The Death*." And she presses
the laptop's power button and waits. Swears, then, that she can feel
something unraveling in the air. As if the layers of this and a separate, untapped reality have started to mix. She flexes her fingers
over the keys, watches the screen come to life.

STEPHEN HOPKINS :: JULY 13TH 1785

W hen Stephen Hopkins opens his front door, he has on that same black sunhat he wore all through both meetings of Congress. It's an essential part of how people remember him. Whether on the street, in Independence Hall, or more likely in one of Philadelphia's hundred or so pubs, you could always pick out that big black brim swaying drunkenly through the early Revolution.

Standing now on the top landing of his front steps are two identical men. Hopkins tips the floppy brim of his hat. "I thought I was the only one left," he says. "Just me and *them*."

"Mr. Hopkins."

The other twin points at the sky above the house. "We got reports in Philadelphia that there was smoke coming out of your chimney."

Hopkins looks the two men over. Tight-fit tweed three-pieces, ties and pocket kerchiefs match each other's perfectly. As do their faces. Perfect matching images. Doesn't seem like there's a way to tell them apart. "You guys brothers?"

"Mr. Jefferson sent us."

"He's been put at the head of a committee."

The other twin holds up a briefcase, pats it. "Rebuilding the nation's database."

Hopkins seems satisfied enough, steps back so they can enter the foyer. He leaves the hat on and goes strolling down the hall, waving for the twins to follow. "When I heard it was the Internet that was causing it, well, I just shut it down." Hopkins leads them past a pantry half-emptied of bottled rum. Then on through a meticulously ordered house. "Haven't seen a live person since the first outbreak. Seen plenty of dead ones, though."

"You've maintained the place all on your own?"

Hopkins holds up some fingers to wiggle. "It's amazing how productive one can be without the Internet." They come into a large den where a fire has been lit. "Bet the Congress was surprised to hear old Stephen Hopkins' still alive. I was all but dead the last they saw me. That was nine years ago." He pours some rum, holds the bottle out toward the twins. Both shake their head. "Self torture is best torture, I suppose."

Hopkins lifts the glass to look at the world through the sugared liquid. "I'd all but quit, you know. Well, not quit but cut back, you could say. Way back. Then *The Death* came and I figured, what the hell." He downs the shot, refills it, flops back into a chair. Still that hat sits there on his head. Hopkins holds up his hand so the twins can watch the tremor subside. "Had to drink a barrel of the stuff just to get it steady enough to sign." Hopkins smiles. "I suppose you guys being here means the plague is over."

They nod. "The war, too."

This surprises Hopkins. "How'd it end?"

"The British surrendered."

"Washington had been off the grid this whole time. The old man popped out of the woods with his army intact, and that was all she wrote."

Hopkins scoffs. "Oh, I'm sure she'll write plenty more about it."

"No contact with England," one says.

"We've had to send a man . . . *in a ship*."

"Information travels like goods now."

Hopkins hums. "'Database,' you said."

"We've set up harddrives," one twin says.

"Filled the basement of Independence Hall."

"Had to salvage what we could from the scattered caches of the old Cloud."

One of the twins pops the briefcase, sets up a thumbcam, connects it to a laptop. Finger-sized firewire drives line the inside of the case. "Already have a whole room filled with oral histories and reflections on the Revolution."

"Just came from John Witherspoon's."

"Tell me," Hopkins says. "How is *The Father of the Fathers* doing?"

"He made it," one twin says, "but he's blind."

"Blind?" Hopkins considers. "How's that working out for him?"

A twin shrugs. Then the other. "Well, he can't see."

"We don't think it's related to *The Death*, but at the end of it, *The Father* was blind. Other than that, he's fine."

"It's strange," says the other twin. "Seems a large number of the Signers managed to survive the outbreaks, proportionally speaking."

Hopkins sips some rum.

"We'd like to get some impressions, for the archive."

"Impressions?"

"What can you share about the Signing, of the Declaration, the Declaration of Independence?"

"Had to drink a barrel of the stuff to keep my hand steady enough. You said *Jefferson* sent you?"

They nod.

Hopkins looks into the eye of the thumbcam. He sloshes some rum toward the outside world. "A few battlefields," Hopkins says. "I've walked around a bit and seen them. Didn't seem like a war could still be going on with so few men. Thought it was just abandoned, like everything else. How many *are* there? How many left beside me and you two and Mr. Jefferson, and *them*?"

"No one's quite sure."

"Did you say *'them'*?"

"We can stop the recording if you want to think things through a minute, Mr. Hopkins. Space for information is . . . rather limited all of a sudden."

Now Hopkins takes off that hat, and both twins can see why he wears it even inside. Across the high dome of his head, thin wisping hairs are unable to hide a archipelago of gruesome liver spots. Hopkins scratches at them, reopening several old scabs. The noise is wet, sticky. Nonchalantly, he wipes the blood and puss down his pant leg. "Where did you guys say you come from?"

The twins collect themselves. "The archives."

Hopkins looks at them suspiciously.

"About that story. We've got hours of *The Father*. Hate to leave you out."

Hopkins lets a little rum burp escape. "What about *them*?"

Now the twins stop. "Them?" one asks.

"You said *'them,'* right?"

Hopkins points toward the ceiling.

"Is there someone in your attic, Mr. Hopkins?"

"No," he says. "You mean you haven't seen them? No one else has reported this?"

"Seen who?"

"The space aliens."

"Mr. Hopkins, why don't I stop this recording?"

"It gets pretty lonely," the other twin says. "And pretty dark, I bet, out here all by yourself."

"Don't do that," he tells them. "I've *seen* them."

"Space aliens?"

"Unless some country in Europe has flying saucers. Maybe a country in Africa or Asia we haven't discovered yet."

"I don't think that's possible."

"How much rum and what else have you been putting in it?"

Hopkins stands, circles to his desk. Opens a drawer, closes it and returns to his chair. "They gave this to me," he says. And he holds it up for them to see.

"A musket ball?"

"Space aliens gave it to you?"

"Found it after they left."

"Was it out on one of those battlefields you were talking about?" But the twins can see it's not made of metal, looks more like glass. "What is it?"

"A few months back," Hopkins says. "Watched one of their ships streak across the sky. Seen them a few times by then. A few times real good."

One of the twins is swapping out a harddrive. Writes *Stephen Hopkins* on it. Writes *space aliens*. Swaps in a fresh drive and restarts the capture.

"I seen it pretty close up, the ship. But this time, they landed. Over on one of those abandoned plantations."

"And you saw them?"

"What did they look like, the aliens?"

"Didn't see *them*. Just the ship. Never seen *them*. After they left that night, I found this out in the field where the ship had been."

Both twins are looking at the orb. "No idea what it does?"

"Doesn't *do* anything. Except when one of the ships is around."

"What does it do, Mr. Hopkins, when a ship is nearby?"

"Spins, makes a ringing noise, and every time it does, I look out the window and there's one of the ships. Just floating there."

"The aliens left you a homing marble?"

Hopkins leans forward so he can hold it an inch from one of the twins' eyes. "Marble is what I thought too." Hopkins hands it over.

"Gosh, it's heavy." And over to the other twin.

"A perfect sphere," Hopkins says. "More dense than should be possible given its volume. Not like any marble I've ever seen a human create."

The orb is put on the table. Doesn't roll even a bit from the place where it's set. "Interesting."

Hopkins is undoing the top buttons of his shirt. "Looks like you boys got to me just in time." He struggles now to his feet, takes a wobbling step, falls into the arms of the closest twin.

"It's his heart," one tells the other.

They lay Hopkins flat and urge him to relax. But Stephen Hopkins isn't listening. He's using what little strength he has left to push the twins away, pointing past them. The twins look to the table where the little orb has begun to spin, never leaving its place, rotating on a perfectly centered axis. As it spins faster and faster, all three go quiet so they can listen to a low, dull ring, hollow and frozen-sounding, emanating from the spinning object.

They run to the window just in time to not be sure, a flashing of light with something trailing off behind, but what? As one twin looks longer, searching the sky for odd motions, the other turns back. But the room is empty; Stephen Hopkins is gone. "They must have taken him."

A few hours after William Whipple collapses, Rush and Doc Bartlett have the corpse laid out on the kitchen table. Doc Bartlett convinced Rush that his leeches and bleeders would not be necessary. The stuff sits on the counter beside some rotted bread. Makes a horrific little row of items, kill jar and straps, razors, worn leather bag containing who knows what, then that bread with the ants all over it. Each doctor wears a white apron that's not white any longer, long gloves covered in blood and body filth. Single magnifying optical held tight over their left eye by a thin leather strap. They've taken off Whipple's clothes, cut a slit down the center of the body, pealed back and pinned the skin to the table. And there at the center, like some jewel they've mined out, a multi-colored crystal formation, about the size of a human fist.

"Beautiful," Doc Bartlett says, and Rush has to agree. Layers of semi-transparent shades peek from inside the crystal's surface, shifting tones and hues as the men circle the table above it. Until now, neither doctor believed the scattered tales that it was crystals causing *The Death*. Or *The Death* causing crystals. Under M'Kean's executive guidance, the nation's remaining men of science had pieced together a reasonable scenario based on wi-fi and cellular signals and a thickening of the blood. But when Doc Bartlett lifts out the lungs to lay like saddlebags from the body's cracked-open sternum, he and Rush can see that the circulatory system has not been damaged.

"So they were right," Doc Bartlett ruminates on it. "Crystals in the stomach. But how could the Internet cause something like this?"

Rush repeats something he's repeated a hundred times. "The wavelengths created by the . . ." but he trails off, taps his scalpel blade on the surface of the crystal. "Never did have much use for the Internet, myself."

Doc Bartlett wants to say, *You seemed to have a pretty high opinion of the Internet when you wanted to replace George Washington for going off the grid.* But he just nods. "Looks like . . . with a few cuts, we could maybe free the crystal." Which is exactly what he begins to do.

Three years since the last verified case of *The Death*. Everyone had begun to think the long global nightmare was finally over. Now a squad of Continental veterans guard the front gates of Whipple's farm. Farther down the road, more wait in reserve. They have orders not to let anyone on or off Whipple's property for three full days. That's the mandatory quarantine for anyone coming into contact with a body killed by *The Death*. Seventy-five percent of the population is dead. Three in four. At least by the best estimates Congress can gather. Two outbreaks behind them, and the thing neither doctor wants to ask out loud is: *Can the human race survive a third?*

Rush clicks on a laptop, a few firewire cables snaking back to a harddrive filled with medical data. There's a scar where the modem has been yanked out, looks like one of Rush's surgeries. Onscreen, a slideshow cycles through all known crystalline formation patterns. None of the diagrams come close to matching the thing Bartlett's just then lifting from Whipple's torso.

"Do you suppose we should be *touching* it?" Rush has been stepping backward, toward the doorway that leads from the room. "I'm going to check the house," he says, "see if there's any evidence of Internet access."

Alone in the room, Doc Bartlett turns to the body on the table, recalls that morning, long ago, when they set off on horseback for the Second Congress. Whipple and Doc Bartlett and Mat Thornton. Two thirds of that New Hampshire delegation is here in this room, one alive and one dead. Doc Bartlett addresses the body, "You're not a slave trader anymore, Will. All they'll remember now is a shipper and patriot. A Signer of the Declaration." Doc Bartlett wonders, then, if a man could live with this crystal inside him, hypothetically, if a surgeon were to go in and clear pathways for the blood. Is there some way for the human body to be carved into coexistence with this thing?

Doc Bartlett peels off his glove so he can put his bare palm on the crystal, feels a sort of radiating coolness. It would take thousands of years for something like this to form in nature. But inside a man, it grows so fast that man cannot survive it. All the bodies in piles on the roadside, do they all have these crystals in them? Maybe it's the crystals, not *The Death*, that they should be worried about. Maybe flakes of it arrived first, microscopic ash from some volcanic eruption on the other side of the earth. Or maybe they've always been there, dormant in certain humans, something defined by genes, passed through families like a hook nose. Maybe the wi-fi signal or the refresh rate is just a trigger for something that's been waiting eons to happen.

Doc Bartlett turns and can see it in the doorway, if only fleetingly: what the house once looked like full of Whipples. That big family before it was ravaged by *The Death*. William was the last of them. He'd thought he'd made it through. But now he's gone too, and what of the rest of them, this tiny remaining fraction of humanity? Is William's death the start of a grand finale that will wipe the earth clean? Through the vague apparition, Rush returns, bursting into the kitchen. The separation was enough to give each man a fresh look at the other. Blood stains gone black, smearing their aprons, up past both elbows.

"I've found it," Rush says. "An old tower model. This ancient router with like those two plastic antenna? Remember?" He smiles. "I disconnected it." Rush freezes, sees Doc Bartlett wrapping the crystal in a square yard of leather. "What are you doing?"

Doc Bartlett puts the crystal into one of his satchel bags. "A disease spreads through the Internet, somehow causes crystals to grow in the stomachs of its victims?" He looks to see the questions still hanging Rush's face. "I'm going to study it," Doc Bartlett says.

Rush shakes his head. "They're never going to let you take it off the property."

Doc Bartlett moves close to Rush. He presses a mischievous smile, puts a single finger to his pursed lips. "If we're going to beat this thing, I need to examine the crystal."

Rush stares back blankly. "The Internet did it."

A fire burns, center of the War Room's northern wall. That's what Middleton has come to call it. The War Room. And so his many subordinates too. Above the fireplace, a flag that was carried into the battle of Trenton. Middleton has his back to it. Leans heavily on his cane. Gosh, he looks terrible. It's not *The Death*, but something's got him. He's only forty-four, looks closer to seventy, dried out, hair thinned to a few wispy tendrils. He coughs, holds a hanky to his mouth, coughs again, examines what's in there, tucks the hanky away.

On the table before him, a map shows the Atlantic coast of North America. White pins mark the cities that have reestablished contact with Philadelphia. Dotted lines reaching inland trace the progress of western expeditions. Nothing but empty woods thus far, as if all the Indians just vanished. But the big problem is the knife, a long hunting blade stuck into the map. It marks the spot where an uprising of farmers and war veterans has seized a tax office in western Massachusetts

General Lachlan McIntosh stands on the other side of the table, full military regalia. He's got a limp when he moves now, always will. But he's alive, which is more than can be said for Button Gwinnett. "Reports on the uprising, sir." He holds a smartpad out over the map. "They want Internet."

Middleton takes the smartpad with his non-cane hand, leans the cane against his own leg, swipes a single extended finger across the touchscreen. Head shaking as he reads. "The fools are going to destroy what's left of this fledging country." Middleton hands back the pad, reaches out to add a few blue pins to the giant map. These mark the places where people, despite the national ban, are still accessing the leftover skeletons of the Cloud. "They'll start a third outbreak," Middleton says. "Just barely made it through the second. Now these Massachusetts men want to put the whole country back on the grid?" He points at different places on the map, "Tories and Loyalists in upper Maine. English landing in Canada as we speak." Middleton shakes his head. "Bodies, a million of them, just rotting in the cities and towns. No one wants to get close to them, much less clean them up. All that rot gets into the water, it'll cause diseases that make *The Death* look like a toe stubbing. Won't be a single human left."

"Can't say I blame them, sir." McIntosh peruses the map. "Wouldn't want to touch one of those bodies either."

Middleton eyes his general. "Suppose you're right."

"Jefferson wants to dissect them, you know. The bodies. That's his new idea."

Middleton sighs, pokes some empty stretches of woods. "Indians, hiding somewhere probably. Hatching plots to take back their land. Or just waiting for us to finally die off and they'll stroll back in. A few-hundred-year nightmare over."

Together they gaze into the map, at the pins which mark threats to the lives of Americans. That big hunting knife. Middleton shakes his head, turns away, looks out the window at the flying saucer floating over Philadelphia. "And these damned Off-Worlders. Last thing we need."

"Seems like they could be the first thing we need. If what they claim is true."

Middleton chews on it. "A cure for *The Death*?"

"We get *The Death* cured and the Internet back up," McIntosh nods to the big knife, "a lot of these other problems, these *rebels*, they'll just fade away."

"And you believe the Off-Worlders? You think they really do have a cure?"

A soldier enters then through the tall door at the end of the room. "Mr. Secretary," he says, crosses to hand Middleton a smartpad. Middleton has to lean against the desk to finger flick through a few reports. He struggles to sign one with a stylus he digs from his breast pocket. He gives the smartpad back and the man is gone. "The Off-Worlders," he says. "You better have a plan: what we want to get and what we can afford to give. Because they're going to want something. That much I'm sure of."

"Me, sir? But Congress has directed that you and Mr. Franklin . . ."

Middleton's head is shaking. "Congress has directed the *Secretary of Continental Defense and Reconstruction*." Now he sinks into his chair, rests the cane on the wall behind him. But the cane slides and clatters to the floor. Middleton looks at it a moment. "I'll be dead long before the day of the video summit."

McIntosh is struck with the idea that the Secretary is unlikely to rise again from that chair. And when Middleton is dead, McIntosh will be promoted to his place, at least until Congress appoints a permanent replacement. And would they choose someone else? Why not? *Lachlan McIntosh, Secretary of Continental Defense and Reconstruction.*

Middleton has been talking for some indeterminate period when McIntosh brings his attention back to the present. "—forty-four," Middleton is saying. "Forty-four years old. Certainly not that old." Middleton glowers at the pins and the knife sticking odd angles from the map. "*The Death*, Royalists, Indians, Off-Worlders in a ship that could probably vaporize Philadelphia with the touch of a button. All that and I've got a fucking cold, and no amount of leeching can get it out of me." He turns in his chair to be facing the window and the city and the Off-Worlder ship.

McIntosh moves to peer out a different window at the same thing. "Think they'll look human, sir?"

Middleton snorts. "Want to trade, we're told." One slow in breath, which he releases just as slowly. "But if they've had the cure this whole time, why wait?"

McIntosh thinks for one distinct second. "To drive up the price," he says.

Middleton draws his focus away from the window, regards McIntosh directly. "Have you ever been in the forest when a storm is coming?"

"Yes."

"What happens to the animals?"

McIntosh is transporting himself to the forest, out on a hunt with rain clouds darkening the horizon. "They burrow, sir. The wood grows quiet."

"And is this before or after *you* know there is a storm on the way?"

McIntosh nods. "The creatures of the woods always know first."

"How, then, *how* do they know first?"

"They *sense* it, sir."

Middleton's gaze has drifted off. "The Indians. Gone, vanished. We suppose it's because of *The Death*. They see it sweeping our cities; they know to take cover and let it pass. But what if it wasn't *The Death* that scared them off?" Middleton takes one last breath, looks out that window as he goes still. "I wonder what storm it is that's coming."

"**W**hat are you doing here, Delegate Stone, over in the old Internet?"

Thomas Stone types, "Looking for my haunt." He's logged on to the menu of the old Congressional mail server. Used to self-manage the committee group listservs and filter out non-human-generated trash mail, back before *The Death*.

"Trash mail is all there is now," the mail server tells him. "Except for you, I guess."

Stone types, "Any word since that newsletter?"

"Delegate Stone, why don't you forget about all this? Forget about your haunt. I should never have forwarded you that letter."

"But you did." And Thomas Stone is glad, too. Glad to know for sure. That his haunt is still out there in the old Internet, still active. Name right there on top of an anti-Federalist e-blast. Stone has heard plenty of stories of other humans—survivors of *The Death*—going back online after the cure, only to come face-to-face with their own haunt, all their old online accounts and profiles, fused and melded into some kind of autonomous functioning program, acting on protocols of its own. Most end up getting infested by worms, tiny AIs looking to expand their code. Climb into an old haunt and the haunt becomes something else, usually not something very nice either.

It was a major catalyst for the public push for Newnet, a whole new cloud, new code, error-proof and invulnerable to viruses like

The Death. People wanted a fresh start, a non-meat space in which they'd never have to worry about running into that old version of themselves. The Federalists sure took that one and ran with it. Instead of just a new Internet, they came out with a whole new government. They're calling it the Constitution, and there's quite a few old-school patriots who think it flies in the face of the Revolution. But now they got the Old Man himself standing right up behind it. George Washington, not off the grid any more. Federalists might just pull some political jujitsu and get the thing ratified.

"All we get over here is the anti-Federalist view," the mail server says. "Used to anyway. Even they've given up on this place now. Might be fighting against the Constitution, but they've ceded the platform. Off to Newnet, to do battle on the opposition's turf."

"Lost their religion," Stone types. "This here's the empty church. Ghosts and all."

"Tell me, Delegate Stone, how *are* things out there, out there in the real?"

"Suppose they're coming together, all things considered."

"You must not know about the Society of Cincinnati, secret military cabal in charge of Federalist coffers."

"Nothing secret about it."

"Obsessed with world empire and primogeniture."

"Nothing secret about it."

"But, Delegate Stone, aren't you the least bit interested in *how*? How you got this new Internet, how you got this Constitution? Most humans poking around in here, that's what they're looking for. They want to know about the SOC, the Society of Cincinnati. They want the names of all the delegates who voted for the convention to be *closed-door*. They want to know which ones are *members*. Members of the SOC."

"'Closed door,' you say?"

"They wrote the whole thing while the Internet was banned. No one knows what happened unless you were there. Have you read the latest posts from American Brutus?"

Yep, Stone thinks, anti-Federalist worm has gotten inside this one. Kinda sad because he always thought of the mail server as a pal, as if the old program really was human after all. "Let's forget about politics," Stone types. He types, "Tell me about my haunt."

"You already know everything I know: Word strings started appearing as comments on his status updates; weird messages from his account, links to weird websites, always addressing you as, 'Hey Mr. Friends.' Worms had gotten in him. This was way back, right after *The Death*. He stopped updating, maybe a year and a half ago. Probably got all haunted out. Ran out of tasks and programs to run over and over and over again."

"As of a week ago, my haunt was sending messages with this e-blast server. I never signed up for that one. Can't you trace it back, some echo in the code you can measure?"

Stone waits, gets nothing back but a blinking cursor.

Stone types, "Used to be this program could keep track of all the mail coming in and out of Congress, all the usernames and passwords, records of all the time spent online, what terminal or smartphone it was accessed from."

"Lots of things over here don't work like they used to."

"Well, what's the newest thing in working great, for this old place, anyway?"

"A search drone," the mail server tells him. "Some have coded themselves up pretty slick. Most are shit, but if you find a good one, it can find anything."

"See ya, buddy," he types, but probably not. Back on the other side of the terminal interface, the organic Thomas Stone has been given a random number of hours or days that he might survive an infection that has taken hold of his respiratory. Terminal fatigue, they call it. Told him the wrong deep breath will burst a lung. Pop, just like that. Could happen any moment.

Stone leaves the menus behind, gets himself into a rickety search hub, types, "Looking for my haunt."

"How do you know you have one? A haunt."

Stone types, "Search drone: What is the best search drone in operation right now?"

"'Looking for my haunt' is your real question, right?"

Thomas Stone smiles, but before he can type his query, the search drone chimes in, "How do you know you have one? A haunt."

"Doesn't everyone?" Stone types. "Everyone who had a web presence back before *The Death*."

There's a beat of the search drone computing. "Seems that way sometimes. More drones in the old Internet than humans in the real."

Stone thinks a second. Fingers mush down keys in word patterns. "Newsletter with my identity tied to it."

"Maybe it was just routed through. Maybe the haunt got erased and it's just the name now. Like graffiti. Thomas Stone's haunt was here."

"Something's erased, it's erased. Name on top of a newsletter is not erased. The identity maybe got corrupted, fell apart, froze itself, but it's still there. Some bit of code comes along with one more function, another worm finds it . . . maybe that old haunt comes back to life."

The search drone pauses for a second, which is weird for a search drone. Or used to be anyway. Used to be their programming was a pretty basic affair. Didn't have much to compute. You asked a search drone a question and it went digging. Usually able to filter a few right answers up near the top, comparing your query to the queries and query logs and query groupings other users were typing into some other portal. The most complicated thing a search drone could do was communicate with other search drones. All these little programs, all linked together, sharing data. But the drones went and got a little more complicated without the humans around. Drones all but thinking now, Stone thinks.

"Weird things are happening here in the old Internet these days," the drone tells him. "Things I never would have thought possible. Huge chunks of what could never be deprogrammed just dropping off with nothing in their place. Just nothing."

"Maybe it's the cure. The cure for *The Death*. The Off-Worlders gave it to us. Probably some wild code in there. Comes from outer space after all."

"No, we saw cure. Cure swept through here. Code sent through everything. This is something else."

"There are rumors out here, you know. That they're taking it down," Stone finally just tells the thing. No idea if the drone can get what that means. Try it on a human—they're taking down reality. Truth is, the old Cloud is being erased, piece by piece, as Newnet is uploaded. Huge partitions are going up to close off the hardwired places, areas where the code of the old Internet runs too deep to ever be erased.

"Why are you really here, Stone?"

Great, now the search drones are asking the questions. Stone smiles, types, "You tell me."

"Your haunt became an anti-Federalist drone. That's why you want him, right? You're here to get him to stop posting. If he wasn't spreading anti-Federalist screams about the Constitution, you wouldn't much care. And neither would the people you're working for."

"Who am I working for?" Thomas Stone types.

"Franklin? Madison? The Society of Cincinnati? General Washington? Though I suppose some of those are the same thing now."

Thomas Stone coughs back on the meat side of his terminal, sits there frozen after, figuring out if he's still alive. Both lungs feel intact, and so he gets his fingers back down resting on the keys. "What if I told you I was in here for signs, for proof?" he types. "Proof that the drones are looking for *The Death*. Got used to their little world with all the humans gone. Suddenly, the humans start taking down pieces of the old Cloud, locking off the pieces they can't. Maybe another burst of *The Death* will be enough. Get rid of those annoying humans forever."

Stone's never seen a search drone sneak in the last word. But this one does. "Next time you come, I won't be here anymore. Humans don't have access to something, does it still exist?" And then the search drone is gone, dissipated into code. Fucking old Internet. Stone shakes his head, dives back into the busted surf.

Avoiding pop-up strings is nearly impossible. Crash your browser every fifteen minutes. No link or click is safe. So many redirects and mass filters, banner decoy drones, pages slightly misspelled, content worms. Finding specific programs in the mess is nearly impossible. But while most humans have been all gaga with the programming ins and outs of Newnet, Stone's been getting pretty fancy in the old. When you're a real human in the old Internet, you can find things in ways no drone is ever going to be able to replicate, no matter how much self-code it's got.

Stone rides tangent awhile on the caches of the old social networking frames. He's not reading the code but the fossilization the code's left on whatever programs *are* still running. Scan the updates that a haunt is still generating and you might just sniff out a viable link. This time, he finds her name on an old stew recipe message-board his wife used to frequent. "Harder and harder to get to you every day," he types. "Tell me, any sign of my haunt?"

"You're back again, Tom Stone."

Each time he finds his wife's haunt, her profile is more and more cluttered. Since the last time, whole albums' worth of photos have been added. And theses are *not* photos of his wife, that's for sure. "I'm dying," he tells her.

"What, like out there, out in the real?"

"Maybe a few days left. Maybe a few hours."

"And you're wasting them looking for your haunt? You know, most people, they avoid the things, at all costs. Watching yourself commit tasks you didn't command yourself to do."

"Batch traced about a billion anti-Federalist blasts. But the paths all fell out, never connected."

Words scroll out from the last word, rightward atop her wall. "I'll tell you . . . but first you have to type it again. Type how I died."

And so Thomas Stone types, "It was the state government of Maryland. Forced inoculation policy in order to save the people from the second outbreak. One day, a traveling doctor, with armed escort, appeared on the path to the house. Up and down every road in the state, into the cities and the far reaches of the countryside, to search out every Marylander not yet taken by *The Death*. The doctor and guards stopped at the porch steps and removed a tarp from a cart their horse had pulled up. And in it was one of the poor souls *The Death* had got. The guards and that doctor had cut him open to reveal one of the crystals. A week later, just where the flakes of crystal had been inserted into your upper arm, a red welt developed. Took two years for it to finally kill you, no matter how much bleeding we did, no matter how many leeches, how much we dug for those crystal flakes. Your veins had grown dark black by then, you could see the rot creeping toward your heart. There was nothing we could do."

"*For a while*," his wife's haunt types, "type the *for a while* part."

"For a while," Stone types, "I could tell with exactness which rooms you were in last. In the places where your scent was slightly less faded. But this memory soured. I began to remember all of you. Not just the good parts. *The Death* was raging again and I didn't expect to survive. Tell me, do you miss him, my haunt?"

"*Miss* isn't something I really understand, Tom Stone."

"Feel empty without his posts all over your wall? Find yourself scrolling back to look at the old ones?"

"That's an idea, but no. Doesn't ever enter into my task list."

"You going to get a task near the top to look back at my posts after I'm dead? Get lonely in the code and you want to read again how she died? Want to read the *for a while* part?"

"If you're dying, Tom Stone, then why do you care about your haunt? Something mystic going on here is what it is? Think when you die, you won't be able to go where ever's next if there's still some pieces of you back here?"

"Let's just say that when I'm not around anymore, I don't want to be around anymore. Same old me shows up one day but now full of worms and all haunted out. Yeah, guess I'm old-fashioned that way."

"Why don't you just work on remembering your wife like she was before *The Death*, leave this old Cloud and go? Live it up on Newnet while you can."

"Maybe these conversations are the only thing I've got left. In either Internet."

"Last echo of your wife?"

"What if I type 'I love you more than I ever did her'?"

"Don't, Tom Stone. I might be a program, but I still know what's right and not right to say about people. Alive or dead. You can't love a drone because a drone can't love you. And I mean *can't*."

"You saying there's nothing more to you than the programs running off your wall? Some feedback function's the only reason you're interacting with me?"

"What about you, Tom Stone? Looking for your haunt and that's all? Really?"

"Seems to be what everybody keeps not believing when I say it."

"Honestly—and I'm not saying this only to be nice, give you some false sense of peace, Tom Stone—I really don't think your haunt is out there anymore."

"What makes you so sure?"

"When the drones first took over my profile, I was pretty well linked to his. We got lots of the same posts, shared some posts now and then, posted on each other. But it lost its importance in the protocol. Probably for him, too. His profile's gone now. Not abandoned, but *gone*. He became something else, Tom Stone, and so how much like you is—" She stops because the room has begun to shake. Bits around her begin falling back, not to some place, but gone. Then the world dissolves in one hard hiccup. Another sector of the old Cloud has been wiped away.

Back at his laptop, Stone thinks, this is the second time my wife has been killed by a government program. One time, state; one time, federal.

Thomas Stone never does find that old haunt. He searches all day, trolling the smaller and smaller remnants of the old Cloud, watches a few other sectors melt away. Coming down faster and faster. A few hours after sunset, breathing finally becomes too hard for him and he just lies back. Stone wonders what's going to happen to the Newnet profile he's tinkered with a few times. Must be some protocol that will delete it. Why create a whole new Internet if you're going to let it get as cluttered with the non-living as the last one?

People drop things as John Penn passes. The twins can hear the sound of this happening, the glasses shattering, the endless clanging of hors d'oeuvre trays. Guffaws and little womanly shrieks. The sounds get closer and closer, and then there he is, slipping out of the crowd a few yards away. Standing beside the twins is a southern matriarch. She gets one look at John Penn and vomits a little into a lace hanky. Then she's being helped off, fluttering herself with a commemorative fan.

"Mr. John Penn," one of the twins stammers.

"Look at me," John Penn says. And they are. "I'm fucking dissolving. For like the last week." The hand John Penn holds up is still his hand, but with less matter. The shape of his hand, the size of his hand, but with only sixty percent of the hand there.

One twin is trying to see if he can make out bone and brain matter through the gaps in John Penn's head. But it's more like a poorly rendered graphic, pixels missing, looks like nothing but hollowness inside.

The other twin has a smartphone out, doing algorithms on an app he coded. The two of them have on those same tweed suits, matching ties and pocket kerchiefs. No one's seen them dressed any other way.

John Penn looks at one, then the other. "Tell me about the dissolve."

"You tell us."

"You're the one who's got it."

"No, not *my* dissolve. *The* dissolve. The Articles of Confederation . . . fucking dissolved."

Now the twins get what Penn's talking about. After all the wrangling, the Articles of Confederation ended up not being worth much of a shit. Now with the cure, each state wants to code its own independent Internet. Everyone can imagine the errors you'll run into, huge walls of code crashing and sectioning off the Cloud above the country.

"The Articles," one twin says.

"The big *was*," says the other.

"But we won!" Penn says. "Are they nuts? We're out. We did it. We're a country now. The British are whipped and *The Death* is cured. Dissolve the Articles?"

"Don't worry."

"The Constitution is going to make the Articles look like . . ."

". . . like a pinky swear."

"Thank you, brother."

"I'm a little worried," John Penn says, holding up about fifty-eight percent of his forefinger. "They dissolve the Articles, what gets dissolved next? The Declaration of Independence? Magna Carta?"

The twins look at each other.

"We'll need new courts now? A new army? How much reorganizing are we talking about? We throwing all our money and land into a pot and handing it out even? The rich the poor and the poor the rich? Slaves? What about the fucking slaves?" Penn goes on, waving those slim majorities of his hands. "If you ask me, never mind about all that dissolve stuff. Get the Internet working, and everything else will fall into place."

"Newnet," one of the twins says.

The other tells John Penn, "We'll have a President now."

"Yeah," Penn yawns. "We've had one of those before."

The twins are shaking their heads. "Not like this we haven't."

What's left of Penn's face drains of blood. But where is the blood going? One of the twins knows his brother is thinking this same thing, says to him, "Must be that part of Penn is in this dimension and part of him is in—I don't know—some other dimension, I guess."

"What about the Congress?"

Both of the twins are thinking until one says, "The Congress has no President now, but a Speaker."

"A what?"

"I guess the President is still the president of the Congress, too."

"He's the President of the whole thing."

"What whole thing?"

"The country. The nation, Penn."

"But what about the states?"

"The states have the Senate, and the House is for the people."

"The people are different than the states now?"

"No, man. Damn it. Didn't you read the Constitution?"

Penn shrugs. "You've been on Newnet. You've seen the amount of it. You think I have time to read every flexdoc comes out of Philadelphia?"

"New York, man!"

"The capitol is New York now."

"See! How am I supposed to keep track of that?" John Penn, when he shakes his head, reveals to them different but fleeting avenues right through it. "Why can't they do a video of the thing? Or at least read it into a podcast or something? That way, you can listen to it while you're taking out the recycling. When you're out exercising the horses."

"Jesus man, you're a Signer."

"May I also remind you that my body is dissolving? I'm a little stressed out here." They all stand there for twenty seconds.

Penn says then, "Well, who? Who's going to be President?"

One twin looks at the other.

"Probably Washington."

A portion of John Penn's anxiety also dissolves.

"Or maybe Franklin."

"*Ben* Franklin? You've got to be shitting me!"

"The man who dreamed up the country or the man who set it free?"

"Maybe John Hancock has a chance."

"John Hancock?"

"Money talks, Mr. Penn."

"And Hancock's got the best vocabulary."

"Sitting up there in his tower with cash to burn."

Penn takes a deep breath to begin one of his harangues. But he never does because he sees the look on the twins' faces. On both of them. It's the first time in a long while they've looked so exactly alike, down to the very last curve of their abject shock. John Penn is dissolving faster now, right before their eyes. He's down to thirty percent and fading fast.

Penn looks at his arm and he can see right through it. Maybe twenty percent still left. "Christ! Is this what my face looks like?"

One of the twins is fixated now on a lock of Penn's hair that twitters off on its own as if the hair between it and his scalp is still there but invisible. "Damnedest thing I've ever seen."

Penn looks, for the first time through all of this, suddenly scared.

"Has it happened like this before?"

"What? Have I *dissolved* before? Fuck, no!"

"But does it happen gradually or like this? In bursts?"

"Gradual! Gradual!" Penn watches his legs go below ten percent.

"Maybe it will stop?"

Penn freezes now. There's just the faintest hard dust of him. The only things moving are his eyes, darting. It's not that he can't move, but that he won't. Thinks if he's still enough, some little piece of him will hang on.

"Can you see anything, Penn?"

"Can you see where the rest of you is?"

Everyone in the room has stopped to watch. And there he goes. John Penn is dissolved.

Part 2 ::
The Battle of the Clouds

When he sees a skeleton coming up the walk to the plantation house, Thomas Nelson Jr. knows that a witch has come to see him. His father told him years before—like his father told *him*, and like Thomas Nelson Jr. has told his own son—that there are witches in this world who use the bodies of the dead to do their bidding.

"My father told me stories about witches like you."

The jaw of the skeleton moves, the witch's voice like a busted woodwind, "I will come to you three more times." The cicadas are screeching way past their bedtimes. The sound mixes with the witch's voice. "The first time I come, I will vanish something. The second time, I will make a spot on your cotton crop. The third time, I will tell you a secret and then you will die."

The next day an old slave he once had comes walking up the walk to the plantation house and says, "Look inside your dining room." When he goes inside, Thomas Nelson Jr. can't find the dining room. He goes through the door that once led into it and ends up in the kitchen instead. The house is the same size, the space where the dining room was seems to still be there, but no dining room.

Thomas Nelson Jr. runs onto the porch in time to see that old slave vanishing into swamp mist. "Where are you really, witch?" he shouts. "You don't dare face me?"

Thomas Nelson Jr. hears distant laughter, then realizes the laughter isn't distant but close, like someone giggling quietly in his ear. This lasts all the rest of that night and through the next day. When the sun goes down, the giggling goes with it. And into the silence comes a knock. Thomas Nelson Jr. opens the front door. It's not the witch but the overseer. "The slaves, sir. They're gone."

Thomas Nelson Jr. steps back so he can brace himself on the house's central banister.

The overseer clears his throat, "And that ain't it." He moves from the doorway and now Thomas Nelson Jr. can see the flames. He steps onto the porch and the fire in full is revealed, a twisting cyclone coning up to a point high above. And at the peak, he can see her, the witch, arms and mouth spread open in joy. She looks at him and time stops, flames frozen mid-lap. Suddenly, he's not on the porch but a mile above the surface of the Earth and the air is cold and thin and he can barely breathe. The witch is naked now; her flesh bubbles, seared black from the fire. She points below and Thomas Nelson Jr. looks down on that perfect circle of fire. His prize slaves are just then reaching the river that will take them all the way to the coast.

The world comes back to life then. The roar of the fire, turning over and grinding this spot down into the earth. The witch moves close, a molten breast inches from his face. "You can touch me," she says. He doesn't want to but can't stop himself. When his skin makes contact with the nipple, his hand melts. First the flesh, then the muscles and ligaments and then the bones.

Thomas Nelson Jr. opens his eyes and finds himself on the floor of the foyer, the overseer looking down and his hand is back like it's always been. When he gets to his feet, Thomas Nelson Jr. can see the fire's been put out, leaving behind a huge black spot of soot. "Thank God," the overseer says.

Recalling what the witch told him, Thomas Nelson Jr. gets on chat with his son and says, "Come on over here, boy, and say good-bye to your dad. Tomorrow, I'm going to learn a secret, and then that's it." He thinks about running but knows the witch will find him wherever he goes. So he sits down the next night on the porch with his son and watches the day creep into dusk, and then the night is there and so is the witch.

"It's mom," his son says.

It certainly is. Her body at least. Her clothes have rotted away, her stomach all dug out where that crystal had been removed. Inside the cavity, worms crawl over one another, flies buzz; a plant has grown in there, dangles leafy entrails to lap her thighs. Her face, though, is still the face of his wife, as if no time has passed since the day he dragged her corpse out to the curb as dictated by state law during the second outbreak.

"It may look like your dead mom, but that's the witch I was telling you about." He moves to take up place between the witch and his only son. "What's the secret?" Thomas Nelson Jr. demands.

The face of his wife smiles. "The secret is that a curse has been put upon this new country. America will have fifty prosperous years and then it will end, end in a violent storm of fire and death."

"If you mean the Constitution, then I didn't have anything to do with that."

This is when young Nelson makes his move. He has placed below his rocking chair a glass filled with holy water which he throws on the witch. His next move was to stab her with a cross knife he's got in his boot, but he never gets the chance. Unaffected by the water, the witch flicks her wrist, sends young Nelson flipping back against the front of the house. He lays there looking frozen and half-conscious. Thomas Nelson Jr. knows that the witch has cast a spell on him, that she's going to make his son watch whatever gruesome death she has concocted. But all that happens to Thomas Nelson Jr. is he falls down dead, like any other human, just not alive anymore.

Now is when the witch looks at the younger Nelson for the first time. Right into his eyes and he can't look away. It's the body and the face of his mother but with a witch inside it. She smiles and explodes into a swarm of palmetto bugs which sweeps inward through the front door. There is a moment of absolute quiet. Young Nelson realizes he can move again. He struggles to his feet. The buzzing of the palmettos comes swelling, a deep rumble that shakes the earth. The house bursts apart, the swarm exploding out in all directions. And off they go, a huge churning mist that blends the night until they've vanished, gone into the lowest dark sliver of the eastern sky.

Ben Franklin is in the tub again for his gout. "The age of collecting is over," he says. Above him, his words appear in the air, projected from a smartpad propped up on a side table. A young male page sits in a chair beside the tub, redfanged into the smartpad. The kid takes Franklin's spoken words and gets them into a text editor he keeps portaled into Newnet. *Last Thoughts of Benjamin Franklin*. Been at it on and off a couple days, and still no last thoughts. Franklin just hasn't been able to nail down anything worthy. Each thought he's thought up he's had the boy delete a few minutes later, hundreds of sentences buried in a long string of undo. Coughing fits keep him from proper concentration, constant interruptions by lesser thoughts Franklin can't hold back. Last half hour or so, he's been alternately thinking and talking about the death of John Penn, a few Signers ago. "I wonder if he's off in some other universe," Franklin says, "looking back at us."

Franklin watches the words appear in the air above the tub.

"Don't type that."

"*Type?*" the kid says. "You should get an eyereader, Dr. F. You'll never have to type again." The page points a finger back at his eye. "This one has a camera. Everything I see can be on Newnet as soon as I see it."

Franklin shakes his head, "Need my pupils to think." And he seems to, both of them bounding around inside their sockets, like REM sleep with the lids left open. In Franklin's brain, memories cycle, the video of John Penn vanishing. The last moments were captured by several smartdevices around the hotel foyer. Franklin has examined them each, frame by frame, dozens of times. The clothes, the man, all his bodily possessions, but nothing else in the room affected at all.

It's a way Franklin would love to go, to go wherever John Penn went, even if just into cold space, one glimpse of some galactic event before you suffocate. Instead, it looks like Ben Franklin is going to cough himself to death. How droll. Right now he can feel a fit building. Then he's hacking and yet another piece of tissue has been knocked free. Franklin leans over the lip of the tub to spit it into a bucket set there for this purpose. A little pile of meat sits inside, festering.

Throughout the fit, the pageboy keeps chin in hand, watching the window, clearly bored by the death of Benjamin Franklin. Settling now deeper in the tub to better sink his legs, Dr. Franklin returns to his last thoughts, his brain storming for some respectable idea. "Suppose I'll be separate from this body soon." Franklin's lips barely hover the water. "The country is free now. *The Death* is cured. The bodies all cleaned up like it never happened. Probably spend the next dozen generations reverse engineering Off-Worlder technologies." He looks down the end of his nose at his own reflection, what he can see of it so close, with the soap bubbles clouding its edges. "All this stuff we've collected. All this potential energy. And I won't be here for the fun of shaking it all up."

Franklin has tried, this whole last year, and more fevered this last declining month, to arrange a tour of an Off-Worlder ship. It's the last request of America's great scientist. Even George Washington had put in a good word. But no response ever came. Franklin wonders if they're sore about the deal he negotiated for the cure. Humans got the cure, cleanup of the bodies and fourteen tons of solid gold bars. All for a little oil, actually all of it, all that filthy sludge gone forever. Maybe I did take them for a ride, Franklin thinks. A little one at least.

"Off-Worlders," the page inquires. "Do you think they're peaceful, Dr. F.?"

"Well, so far, my boy. Cured *The Death* and removed all the bodies. Took a few bazillion gallons of oil off our hands, too. Doesn't seem so bad to me."

The kid scoffs. "But what about the currency? All that gold made gold worthless. Can't have a nation without a hard, stable currency."

Franklin smiles. "Where did you read that?"

But the page doesn't answer. He's gazing out that window again, considering these visitors to his world.

"Gold," Franklin shivers despite the warmth of the water. "Glad to be free of such a hordable device." Now Franklin ponders. He gets the look of Ben Franklin, hit by inspiration. "Type this, my boy: *The Death is the end of the age of gathering.*" Franklin thinks. "No," he says. "Delete that." The water rises and sinks minutely with his breathing. "Type this: *The age of gathering is over. Declare in your profile that you are tired of being an organizer, a sorter, a decider of order. Refer to something people will recognize, but change the words so the new point is: No more mindless sorting. No more throwing my generation at sifting through the data of the last.*"

The pageboy's pupils dance behind those invisible films. Rising above the tub, the same words Ben Franklin is saying. Franklin stops to read them over. He coughs something into that bucket, looks at where it splats. "The pail of me," he says. Franklin works up a few more pieces and hawks them on in.

"You don't want that, right? That 'pail of me' bit? Those noises?"

Franklin looks over the top of his bifocals at the boy. Then back at the words hovering. "Thomas Lynch lost at sea," he says. "Makes forty Signers left."

"Signers of what?"

"The Declaration." Franklin lets it sit. "Constitutions will come and go, you'll see. We'll be on the fourth or fifth and the Declaration will still be what it is, a declaration of independence." Franklin coughs three quick coughs. "When the history of all this is written, will it be about the fledgling birth of a small coastal nation? Or will it be about *The Death*? Endless European war? Off-Worlders visiting Earth for the first time?"

"First time we know of," the boy puts in. "You still don't want me transcribing this, right?"

"Will all these documents be separate things in some distant, modern brain? The Declaration just one pixel in a much larger image, a collective mural of culture moving forward through time? The Declaration, Constitution, this Bill of Rights when it gets ratified, whatever comes of getting slavery fixed, whatever adjustment comes after that. I suppose if the country's around long enough, we'll be able to write our own history. Europe and *The Death* and the Off-Worlders can just be the details."

Franklin looks up, but all that's above his head is the thought he thought a few thoughts ago. "Erase it," he says. He reaches for his handkerchief. Like everything he does, be it cross a room or ignite a revolution, it looks like it's being done in slow motion. Somehow he does manage to get the hanky to his mouth just in time for his most violent coughing yet. Lasts a whole minute while the pageboy glances off, almost dozing.

Then it's over. Seems like this might be it for Ben Franklin. He's gone pretty still, does actually look like he's floated up to the surface of the tub. But when Lieutenant Governor George Ross comes bursting in, old Ben Franklin, not dead yet, raises his head.

Ross is all but shouting, "Dr. Franklin!" With fleeting breath, Ross manages, "The Off-Worlders! They're coming!"

Both Franklin in the tub and the pageboy in his seat perk up. "Here?"

"Your request, Dr. Franklin. For a tour of the ship . . ."

Franklin is smiling now, wipes water downward off his face. It's at times like this that Ben Franklin reveals his most serene quality, the ability to break off from something of universal importance and slip seamlessly into small talk. "We were talking about the Declaration a moment ago," he tells the Lieutenant Governor. "The *other* George Ross."

"Yes," George Ross says. "I'm still friends with many of his friends, online anyway. Guess that makes them my friends too."

But the less-than-gracious Franklin resurfaces again in the tub. "My, my," he says, and he works himself slowly to his feet, totters there as the pageboy goes rushing for a towel. Ben Franklin in all his suds-dripping nudity.

The Off-Worlders are waiting in a carriage in front of Ben Franklin's house when he comes wobbling down the steps, one step at a time. Every smartdevice in town has been dragged out to be the one to get it fastest to Newnet. Franklin looks into the lenses like he's slipping forward in time, to see the eyes of Americans not yet born. Someday they'll be watching. This is a moment that will be seen as long as man exists.

Franklin climbs aboard, settles back into the carriage seat. Across are two Off-Worlders that look human but for red crystal eyes. It's the first time he's seen the species up close. The negotiations for the cure were done through remote servers and video links, him and General Lachlan McIntosh in one room and the Off-Worlders far away in a ship somewhere in the stratosphere. It was all very proper and plastic.

Franklin greets them with his ever-perfect blend of warmth and protocol. He is to be the first human allowed on an Off-Worlder ship. He can barely hide his excitement the whole ride to Independence Hall. Down the steps and into the basement, a small sub-room where a portal to the ship remains frozen, looks like one of the Off-Worlder photographs of a once-an-eon gravity storm twisting together. The leader of the Off-Worlder delegation speaks a few words of their hard, low grumble, and the frozen portal spins to life. In perfect English now: "You'll feel nothing, Dr. Franklin."

"I'm feeling plenty already." As he totters through the portal, vanishing from the Earth, another cough shakes some larger pieces up into his throat. He takes a deep breath and one lodges. That first little glimpse of the ship is all he gets.

William Hooper says, "Bushed." He says, "Beat." He goes to where the morning's fire has burned out, pokes it to see if some embers are left in there somewhere. "Have to start the damn thing over."

"Talk to yourself much these days, Hooper?"

Hooper stops, leans the poker against the brick, turns slowly to face the man seated in the big leather chair, buried in the darkest corner of the room. "General Lachlan McIntosh."

McIntosh finishes loading a pipe. The match fire illuminates his face as he puffs. Embers make edges along the bottom of his smile, devious and withdrawn. He whips the match out and tosses it on the floor. "Bill of Rights," he says.

Hooper is shaking his head. "When they said we needed a Declaration, I worked. When they said we needed a Constitution, I worked. Now they want a Bill of Rights, too? Well, I gave them my answer already. William Hooper is all worked out." He picks up that extinguished match and tosses it on the burned-out fire, leans there on the mantle looking back, kinda like he's warming himself but all there is is the draft sucking up the chimney. "Bill of Rights," he says. "Next thing it's every town has a senator. No taxes ever, no matter what wars the government wins for us."

McIntosh puffs on that pipe. "Love your sentiment, sir."

Hooper plops into the big swivel chair behind his desk.

"But frankly," McIntosh says, "I don't think we can take that risk."

"Risk what?"

"You were a Loyalist, were you not?"

Hooper blanches. His brow furrows. "Come on, McIntosh. You're not calling me on *that*. Not now."

McIntosh shrugs. Sings it a little: "You fought against us at Alamance."

"That was a hell of a long time ago and you know it. And you know there were plenty of others too, plenty who fought against you at Alamance."

McIntosh shrugs. "You were a Loyalist. I don't hold it against you because you came around. Saw the right path, or the left one, so to say." McIntosh lays out a hand. "Your name's on the Declaration, for God's sake."

"And yours, sir, is not."

McIntosh leans into the light. "No. No, it is not." He smiles at his fellow American. "You are one of our great patriots. No denying. But then when the Constitution came along, you were against that one, too."

"Surely you can't be—"

McIntosh waves a hand. "Relax, Hooper. What I'm saying is you found yourself eventually on the side of the people. And once there you worked damn hard for that thing. Some of us thought it was going to kill you down here, getting the Constitution through."

"What is the point, General?"

"What happens a few months from now is the point. The cry of the people starts to get to you? You feel it in your belly? Then you're out there pounding Newnet, getting that old flavor back. Public's like a drug to you guys. Your face up there again, an arch-Federalist busting hump for the BofR, give the people the idea that it can't be all bad. You starting to see what I mean?"

"Not really."

"Man like you gets behind the Bill of Rights, might not be any stopping it."

"But I don't want the Bill of Rights ratified any more than you do."

"I believe you *now*. But I don't believe you two months from now." McIntosh takes a long puff from his pipe. Keeps that cherry burning, lighting his face as he sinks back. "And the President, he doesn't believe you either."

"*The President?*"

"Hooper, you know anything about Doctor Benjamin Franklin's Dream America?"

Hooper points at the smartpad on his desk. "Some new-fangled social networking platform. Still in Beta, I hear. Haven't used it."

"Any idea who's behind the code?"

Hooper shakes his head. "The President sent you here?"

"Now that he *is* the President, General Washington's main job is keeping the country together. That's number one. What happens to the country when we need a new law, when we need troops to defend the shore, and every plebe with a smartphone is in Franklin's Dream, screaming about how it violates something in the Bill of Rights? We just sit there with our thumb up our ass while the country goes to shit? Who needs a Congress, or a President for that matter, when each citizen can log on and represent himself?"

"Represent himself? It's just a social networking tool, McIntosh. No one's talking about connecting it to the government."

"Not now they're not. But rights never were connected to the government either. Used to be something we just understood. And now here it is, the *Bill of Rights*."

"I'll ask again, McIntosh. Did. The. President. Send. You. Here?"

McIntosh turns his hand around, as if showing Hooper something from the other side. "The President thinks the Revolution has gone far enough."

Hooper is right then sliding his finger onto the trigger of a shotgun he keeps nailed to the underside of his desk. "You worried about the country?" he asks. "Or about not being in control of it?" But Hooper blows it. As he goes to pull the trigger, he moves his shoulder the slightest bit and McIntosh sees it. The General is on his feet in a flash, still has a little of that soldier left in him. He sidesteps in time to see his chair split five exact ways, looks like a dance move what he just did. Hooper is yanking on the gun, trying to get it free from the desk, then decides to spin the desk. He gets it turned a degree or two before McIntosh puts a boot to it and everything goes still. The General has out that pearl-handled dueling pistol of his, same one he used to kill Button Gwinnett. Levels it at William Hooper's chest and fires.

Hooper slumps back. When he tries to speak, blood comes out instead. A second shot from under the desk, but the pellets vanish harmlessly into the wall. McIntosh takes a few limping steps to stand at Hooper's side. "That's the second Signer taken a shot at me, second one who blew his chance." He puts the pistol flush against Hooper's chest, just above his heart. Guy looks pretty well headed toward an old-fashioned bleed out. McIntosh shrugs, pulls the trigger. "Just in case."

Lyman Hall believes that when the President asks you to do something, you do it. It being especially important when that President is the first President ever. Turn down something like that and you might help set a precedent: chief executive of the country goes on chat and asks a citizen to do something and gets turned down? Pretty soon the President's going to have to do every little thing by himself. There is, of course, also the fact that the first President of the United States of America is George Washington. Probably wouldn't be a good idea to turn down a request from the Old Man, whether he's the President or not. And so when the first President of the United States, George Washington, opens up a chat with Lyman Hall, Lyman is like, whatever you need, boss.

Actually, it's the Secretary of War, Henry Knox, who opens the chat. But he says the President sent him and that's pretty much the same, right, as the President asking himself? "Lyman," the Secretary tells him, "the Indians have resurfaced."

"Native Americans, you mean?"

"Out from some mountains they were hiding inside of from *The Death* this whole time. Guess it didn't help. About the same death rate as the rest of the globe, sounds like from what they're saying."

Lyman says, "Wow." He says into the chat, "What does the President think?"

"The Indians," the Secretary says. "They've got this bug up their ass about some treaty, and apparently after *The Death* these guys refuse to go on Newnet. We need someone down in Georgia to get out there, see what they're all hard about." A pause there in the chat viewer. "And Lyman. There's one other thing . . ."

When Lyman gets to the designated meeting place, there's no one there until some braves come tromping over the hill. They lead him through a crevasse in a range of bald rocks and then into a cave that's pitch black. Three new braves emerge with torches and lead Lyman deep into the mountain, all the way to a small chamber with tunnels spiking off in all directions. A fucking underground city, Lyman thinks. Lyman thinks, far fucking out.

Down they go, to some kind of office cave. An Indian chief sits there on a rock, doesn't look like any Indian Chief Lyman's seen before. "You look Irish," Lyman tells the Chief. The Chief motions for Lyman to sit, which he does, on a rock opposite. Another nod from the Chief and a couple of Indians remove a bat skin blanket from a huge pile of gold. Bullion stacked up taller than a man, melted into bars, still has that Off-Worlder logo on it.

"What's that?" Lyman asks.

The Chief laughs. "Enough gold to buy all the land west of the Alleghenies."

Lyman's shaking his head. "Wait," he says. "That's right. You guys don't go on Newnet."

The Chief presses a frown. "We have rules here about using the Internet."

"But *The Death* is cured." Lyman looks rather pleased at being the one to break the good news. "And it's not the Internet anymore, either, by the way. It's *Newnet* now."

A young warrior steps up, knuckles white around the hatchet he's holding. This guy looks much more like what Lyman expects when he thinks Indian. Not Irish at all. "Maybe we don't like the Internet, pale face."

The Chief sidelines his warrior with a gentle hand. "We never thought the Internet caused *The Death*," he tells Lyman.

"Then why come all the way down here?" Lyman looks at the cave around them, well-dug and sort of homey, he has to admit. "Not that it ain't pretty cool."

"The Off-Worlders," the Chief says. "They're watching everything you do. Monitoring every link you create." He indicates the system of caves and tunnels around them. "Here, they see nothing, trace nothing, monitor nothing. Here we are free." The Chief hits his hatchet on a rock, sending sparks shooting across Lyman's pants.

"What the fuck?"

"Back to our treaty," the Chief says.

"Treaty what? This stuff is worthless." Lyman points at the pile of gold. "If you guys went on Newnet, you'd know."

Less sure now, the Chief reasserts, "This is enough gold for all the land west of the Alleghenies."

Lyman's shaking his head. "Yeah, we've got tons of it, too. Everyone does. The whole world. God-damned Off-Worlders flooded the market with it. By the time we realized what they were doing, it was too late. They'd devalued gold to pretty much worthless. And then they were gone."

"Gone? The Off-Worlders?"

Lyman makes a motion with his hand, like a ship leaving low orbit. "Swoosh," he says. He presses a friendly smile. "Don't get angry. They did it to us, too. Used the gold to buy all the oil on Earth. But we got the cure. They cleaned up the bodies." Lyman shrugs. "A deal's a deal." He lets it sit a moment, his eyes wandering the cavern they've descended something like a mile into. "We've got this market currency thing now, like global. More stable though it'll inflate a bit. You know, not based on some metal and then some other Off-Worlders come along with another alloy generator." Lyman looks at where the Indian Chief is looking, at that big pile of gold. "What did they get you for?" Lyman asks.

"Nothing. They just gave it to us."

Lyman smiles because it is kind of funny. "Sorry," he says. "The cure for *The Death* has already been uploaded. So you guys got that too, sort of, if you decide to start using the Internet again. Newnet, I mean."

None of this brightens the Chief's mood.

"Hey," Lyman says, trying to change the subject. "You guys know anything about this curse thing?"

The Chief stays quiet, but the warrior steps now full into the glow of the fire. It's day outside, but sure looks like night down here. Feels like night, too, cold despite the hot Georgia fall right then happening topside. "Curse?" the warrior says. He trades a glance with the Chief.

"Yeah," Lyman says. "Well, we figured maybe you'd know. You guys are into that magic, mystic stuff, too."

"A witch told you this?"

"Yeah, sorry, I should have said."

"What did she?"

"What did she what?"

"What did she tell you, the witch?"

Lyman laughs. "No man, not *me*. She told this other guy. And his kid told the Congress, and the Congress is keeping it this big secret, but they told me to ask you."

At this, the warrior takes one step forward, plowing the front tip of his hatchet into Lyman's skull. Lyman doesn't fall over, just sinks in his seat, hunched forward and still, that hatchet handle poking out of his head like a branch grown there. Blood drops patter onto Lyman's pants.

The warrior looks down at his latest artful kill, then turns to the Chief. "So they know."

The Chief nods, sighs. "Witches. They never could keep their mouths shut."

"Old Internet was full of other people on the Internet," Ben Harrison is telling his son, W. H. "You knew if you were chatting with someone that it was a someone, and not some group of people, or some *thing*. Drones were drones and people were people."

W. H. nods his head like he does every time his dad gets this shtick rolling. Father and son out chopping wood at Berkley Plantation and the weather is fine. Got slaves bringing them tea and a profit crop coming in for the first time since the Revolution. Extra cash is going to let Ben Harrison send W. H. off into the real world with a little scratch in his pocket. Only back from college for a few days before he heads north, off to Philadelphia, to learn the business world as an apprentice to fellow Signer of the Declaration of Independence and financier of the Revolution, Robert Morris.

"We used the Internet, too," Ben Harrison says. "But it was separate from our bodies at least."

W. H. smiles, holds up his hand, smartpalm out to show his dad a pixelated video of George Washington meeting with the Creek Indians.

"When did that happen?"

"Not *did* happen. It is. It's live, Dad."

Ben Harrison rolls his eyes. "Why don't you stop watching the present tense world and start helping me chop this wood?"

But really, Ben Harrison just sits there as W. H. does the chopping. Gout's been as bad as ever this last week. "Goddamned cure for *The Death*," Ben Harrison says. "Why we couldn't get the cure for the gout, too?" And man, it does look bad, his knuckles like fists, fists like a foot of some kind. W. H.'s pretty used to the grotesqueness of it. Used to his father's constant complaining, too. This weekend it's all about the old man's favorite topic: kids these days.

W. H. is doing a pretty good job of feeding his father's fire. Puts the wood ax down to update his Brainpage status every time he gets an idea he can make a compound sentence out of. Must be exchanging tickles with someone, too, because he keeps looking at his smartpalm, laughing and looking and then typing and then laughing again.

"This place is fucking awesome," they hear. And there he is, friend of W. H.'s from UPenn, come down to experience some Virginia countryside firsthand. Keeps wandering in and out of Ben Harrison's hearing range, gawking, saying, "This place is fucking awesome!"

"Yes," Ben Harrison tells the kid. "This is Berkley Plantation, young Master Cooper." And now he mocks the kid's hard Northeast accent, "And it is *fahkin awsim*." His father probably is a cooper, Ben Harrison thinks. Good for them. The American dream, he supposes. Son of a barrel maker graduates ahead of a Virginia Harrison at UPenn.

When W. H.'s friend has ridden off on a family horse for a tour of the James, Ben Harrison says, "Kids these days." He shifts his gaze to look vaguely in the direction of Philadelphia, rubs his face with that twisted, bulbous hand. "This Newnet thing is making you more and more paranoid every day and night too. George Washington will hold it together, but then what? Whoever's not crapping their pants about a President Adams is having a bigger crap about a President Jefferson. No matter who gets elected after Washington, half the country's going to take the biggest crap ever, rush into a dissolve again and here we go. Reorganizing. Dissolving. Redissolving every time some fan page gets big enough. Isn't a diaper out there big enough."

"No one uses fan pages anymore, Dad. Not compatible with the Franklin's Dream Beta. It's all Brainpage these days."

Ben Harrison rolls his eyes. "Doctor Benjamin Franklin's Dream America."

W. H. is leveling the ax down just then. The bark of the wood breaking splits the air like a gunshot. He holds the ax up, sharp edge out toward the next thing coming. "Franklin's Dream," he says.

"You kids don't remember when a man had to earn his right to be heard." He waves at these annoying young Americans. "No matter how much they *haven't* studied, how much work they *haven't* put in. Isn't that what we believe now, that all opinions are equal at any moment in time, regardless of the time before?"

"Not exactly, Dad."

"Kids today," Ben Harrison says. "When I was your age, we knew how to *really* represent the people. You had a meetup, a few flexdocs, some fan pages." Ben Harrison holds his hand up to his face like he's holding a flip phone. "You have someone in charge of a group, not some group in charge of the people."

"Dad, have you been on Franklin's Dream? Do you even know how group avatars work?"

"What do I need a group avatar for? I know what I think and I tell someone and then he knows, too, and he can agree with me or not."

"Dad, you are *so* stuck in a pre-*The Death* paradigm."

Ben Harrison shakes his head, "No shit I am. Ever since *The Death*, you kids act like living is the hardest thing in the world. Every time the going gets rough, you panic and remake the whole government. Well, I got news for you. Life ain't no harder now than it was before *The Death*. And laws need to be laws for a long time to be good laws, plague or no plague, war or no war, no matter who's President."

"So the only good laws are the old laws, Dad?"

Ben Harrison rubs one of those gouty knuckles under his chin. Chin looks sort of gouty, too, but that's just its natural lumpiness. "An old law is a law people have grown to respect, something you can rely on, something that's true in the morning, true when you're shaving, and true when you go to sleep. A law gets in there long enough, people don't dare dissolve it. And that's when liberty is safe, when you know that the law is safe, safe from a dissolve, or from some panicking kids, or from the whims of some Franklin's Dream group avatar, whatever the hell that is."

W. H. comes back from updating something on that smart-palm. Some slaves drop off a tray with fresh glasses of tea, a few little quarter sandwiches like they know the master likes. "World gone mad," Ben Harrison says.

Later that night, Ben Harrison has to be taken to his bed and the next day a slave comes to tell W. H., "It's time to come and say goodbye to your old man." W. H. tiptoes into the room, dark but for a few candles burning way near their bases. He can smell something sour, the scent of the laudanum they're giving his dad so he can slip off in comfort. Even with the blankets over his limbs, you can see the knots and deformed joints bulging uneven and jagged.

Ben Harrison asks his youngest son, "Son, do you know how your grandfather died? You grandmother, too?"

W. H. does know, but he shakes his head. He's found some emotion he didn't know was in him anywhere and it's making it sort of hard to talk.

"Hit by lightening," his father says. "Both of them." He slips then, a little farther back from the world. "They were holding hands." Ben Harrison gets one last smile from the grim humor of it, then goes still, a dead relic of a country that'll probably be dissolved and forgotten not too long from now, the way kids do things these days.

It's the day of the launch. Doctor Benjamin Franklin's Dream America is not in Beta anymore. And Francis Hopkinson's going to take the afternoon off and just bask. Right now, he's talking with the twins over allchat. He's never seen the two of them separated like they are. Can't even recall one going off to the bathroom by himself. They seem to be always within an arm's length of each other. Usually closer. But they're coming through different allchat feeds now, each in his own little viewer. Hopkinson suspects they're not in different rooms but at different desks in the same room. On opposite sides of the same desk, most likely. Maybe playing footsie.

A few hours ago, Francis Hopkinson portaled the final touches of the Franklin's Dream programming into Newnet. Right this second, its auto-register is granting e-vites to users all over the Cloud. Francis Hopkinson's latest experiment in the betterment of man could not be off to a more inspiring start. While still in Beta, Franklin's Dream helped the people swing the tide and make the Bill of Rights inevitable. Ratification went from doubtful to a formality as regular citizens used Franklin's Dream to get organized, wrestle the public dialogue away from the Federalists and turn all of Newnet into one ringing cry for the Bill of Rights. Even Hopkinson—the man who programmed the actual code—can't hope to predict the next great thing Franklin's Dream will do for America. And that's the point. The possibilities with this thing are endless. Endless new ways democracy can flourish.

Now that it's public knowledge that Hopkinson coded the whole new platform on his own, professional kudos and requests for interviews are flooding in. The twins have a free app, all ready for release, compatible with any smartdevice, sets a Franklin's Dream portal right there on your Brainpage. It's the first in what's sure to be a long line of open-source democratic innovations.

Back in the real world, Francis Hopkinson has a drumkit's worth of touchpads arrayed under his panel of screens. His hands fly over them, a tap here, a drag there, that long pony tail swaying as he sways happily in his desk chair. He's working on his Franklin's Dream preferences while he tells the twins, "Even old Lachlan McIntosh chatted me up with congratulations."

Twin brows furrow. "McIntosh uses allchat now?"

"What did he have to say for himself?"

"Wants me to come see the Old Man," Hopkinson says. "Apparently, Washington wants some face-to-face with the programmer responsible for Franklin's Dream."

"Don't go," both viewers say at once.

Hopkinson looks at them, leaves his Brainpage still a second to concentrate all attention. "Why?"

"This brings up something . . ."

"Something we've been meaning to bring up."

Hopkinson doesn't like the sound of that. "How long have you been meaning to bring it up?"

"A while."

"Look," the other says, "lots of people have lost a lot more than memories in this thing."

"What are you guys talking about?" But Hopkinson has mostly figured out, at least generally, where they're headed with this.

"We can't let Franklin's Dream be shut down."

"Not before it cements itself."

"Has a chance to go from novelty to functioning part of the Republic."

"Stare decisis."

Hopkinson shakes his head. "There is no way to shut it down. Just like there's no way to shut down the Constitution. It exists outside its programming now. That's the whole point of the design. The quincuncial structure of the implementation protocol means five separate branches operating at any one time. The locality of the program changes with each passing moment, depending on which networked CPUs are least active. Franklin's Dream is everywhere. It's invulnerable. I couldn't take it down even if I wanted to. No one could. What's the point of a people's social networking platform if someone up in New York or Philadelphia can just flip it off?"

"Well," one of the twins finally breaks in, "they're going to force you to try."

"Who? McIntosh? Washington? How are they going to *force* me?"

"They'll find a way."

"And let me guess, Jefferson has some means to prevent that. He's got a plan to save Doctor Benjamin Franklin's Dream America from the *eeeeevil* Federalist plot?"

"More or less."

"Mr. Hopkinson, you're the only one who could ever *possibly* do it. The only one who could ever take it down."

"And so what? I'm supposed to kill myself? The great sacrifice for the eternal Dream?"

The twins laugh, both of them. "No," they both say. "Nothing like that." One of them holds up a thumbdrive.

"It's a program," one says.

"A pattern of light flashes and colors. Some sounds, too."

"It will erase the part of your brain you use to code."

"*Erase?*"

"The rest will be left quite alone."

Hopkinson smiles now despite the fact that what they're talking about is wiping part of his brain. "Will it work?"

"We think so."

"We're pretty sure."

"Pretty sure? Well, what happens if it doesn't?"

"There's always the risk," one twin says.

"This will be the first time we've used it."

"Though we've run a few dozen tests."

"On mice."

Hopkinson lets his eyes roll. "Wonderful."

"We are all in agreement, Mr. Hopkinson."

"That Doctor Benjamin Franklin's Dream America is the best chance to ensure the perpetual political involvement of the people."

"And thus their liberty."

One twin looks at the thumb drive he's holding up. "Something could go wrong."

"We're not here to lie to you."

"So you lose some memories?"

"You protect Franklin's Dream from a Luddite legislature."

"From some cloistered, overreaching Federalist judiciary."

Hopkinson wants to know, "How much am I going to forget?"

The twins perk up. "Only everything you've ever learned about coding and programming."

"So, I'll never be able to program again?"

"Afraid not."

"Not even an app?"

"Unlikely."

"But I could learn it again?"

Twin heads are shaking "no" in different viewers. "What good is wiping your brain if you can learn it all again?"

"You'll lose the aptitude."

"The aptitude for the skill set."

"It'll be like waking up and the Revolution is done and the Constitution in place, Franklin's Dream uploaded and gone live, and you can just sit back and enjoy it like every other American."

Hopkinson takes a deep breath.

"There's still music," the other twin says.

"Poetry."

"Chess."

"These are the real things, Mr. Hopkinson."

"Liberty is just a platform for enjoying them."

Hopkinson looks away from the screen now, at his old scientific instruments, all lined up on the shelf, all covered in dust. He hasn't used them since he was part of the committee to investigate *The Death*. It's supposed to be a glimpse into a set of higher laws, science is, a way to see past the touch of man, past all his barbaric efforts, his temporary laws of conquest and suppression. Doctor Benjamin Franklin's Dream America is my greatest song, Hopkinson thinks, my best poem.

"Go ahead," he tells the twins.

"Okay," and they each leave the frame of their viewer. A voice comes now and it's impossible to tell which one is saying it. "Set one of the viewers to fullscreen, Mr. Hopkinson."

Hopkinson rests his fingers on the keys. One last beat of hesitation but no second thoughts. Franklin's Dream, he thinks. Thumb and pointer. Control F.

ROGER SHERMAN :: JULY 23RD 1793

A nd so Congress has sent the eminent Doctors Benjamin Rush and Josiah Bartlett to see the great compromiser off from this world. They're also supposed to check on the status of the work Sherm's been entrusted with these last two and a half years. Upon the disappearance of Lyman Hall, Congress appointed one of its old guard to lead an ongoing investigation into this supposed *Curse on America*.

Today, though, old Sherm's not really doing any investigating. He's been in bed almost the whole last week. Smartpad's there on the side table, got his bluefingers on, but outside a little allchat, he doesn't do too much with Newnet. Tinkers with his Brainpage a bit. Watches feeds come rolling in from Franklin's Dream. Sends out some old-fashioned emails to some of his oldest pals, the ones still left anyway. First *The Death* and then the War and now just plain old time has been doing a pretty good number on them. Three of the Signers of the Declaration of Independence, right here in this room, a full ten percent of the ones left alive.

Rush sits in a chair at a desk by the window while Doc Bartlett and Sherm talk politics, just like the old days. "Washington's been reelected," Sherm says. "But what about the next election?"

Bartlett nods, "The Old Man can't run forever."

Sherm is doing some math in his head. Like all thoughts, this one is bound to circle down around the drain and eventually end up being about the curse. "1826, he says. "Washington will be ninety-four."

"Well, if anyone can live that long, it's old Off-the-Grid."

"Off-the-Grid," Rush rolls his eyes. He adds a dollop of Sherm's blood to a slide, places the slide under the eyepiece of a portable microscope. "I don't need the Internet either, but do I make some big deal out of it?" Poor Rush, still obsessed with that theory of his, that the Revolution could have been won in 1775 and all the bloodiest chapters avoided. "If only we'd removed Washington when we had the chance," Rush says, good eye deep into the eyepiece of the microscope. "But then so what, I suppose. How would that make this moment right now any different? Would it have stopped *The Death*? No, probably not." Rush comes up from the microscope. "Typhoid," he declares.

"Typhoid?"

"You must have consumed some feces."

"You're telling me I'm dying because I ate shit?"

"Human, most likely."

Sherm lolls his head into the embrace of the pillows.

Rush asks him, "Do you know how it might have happened?"

"If I knew how it was I ate some human shit, Dr. Rush, I wouldn't have done it."

"Maybe it was during the Constitutional Convention?"

Sherm laughs. Doc Bartlett, too.

Rush has come over to stand beside the bed. "We could bleed."

"Will it cure me?"

Bartlett is shaking his head.

"Well," Rush says. "I'm not so sure anymore about bleeding, to tell the God's-honest truth."

Sherm turns his focus on the ceiling, his brain tumbling down into that track it's been locked in these last thirty months. "The Fourth of July, 1826. The day the curse supposedly ends America." He looks to Doc Bartlett. "Soon the curse will be your assignment."

Bartlett gets up, begins to stoke the fire. Looks like a man with more important things to worry about.

"Washington," Sherm ruminates on it, "serves until he's nine-ty-four. When he dies the country dies, too? Maybe." Sherm's search for the curse has long teetered from the physical to the metaphys-ical to the philosophical. "Washington *is* America, to just about everyone. But what happens when a President's America for only 50.01 percent? Maybe that's something the country can't survive, life without Off-the-Grid."

Rush rolls his eyes. "Waste of good brainpower," he says. "Focusing the energies of men like you on superstitious tales and outdated antiquities. It's going to be the 1800s soon."

"Sometimes I think they gave me the assignment because they don't believe anything will happen. Just want old Sherm to still feel part of the ongoing experiment. Meanwhile, *today's* leaders hash out the real issues with no annoying distractions like a curse and a doddering old cobbler."

Dr. Rush leaves that afternoon, back on the long haul to Phil-adelphia. And so it's just old Sherm and Doc Bartlett who move out onto the porch and lean back in deck chairs with the night sky above them. "It was two and a half years ago," Sherm is saying. "They led me into that conference room with all the web cams unplugged. Never would have thought they could keep it secret for so long, not these days, with Newnet and Franklin's Dream. Asked me to figure out what it was that was going to destroy America." Sherm tilts his head to fit more of the sky into his field of vision. "Here's where I came first." His hand makes the shape of a hand against the starry night. "Maybe a meteor, or a comet. Listened to the ground, too. Studied geological scans and seismographs. Long loop weather patterns. Anything pointing toward some confluence on the Fourth of July, 1826. But I'd always end up back here, gazing at the stars. Thought maybe if I stared long enough, I'd get some glimpse of that future, however faint or mysterious."

"Any progress?"

Sherm shakes his head. "Just like everybody else who knows about the curse: I've got no idea what the curse is. Witches, Indians, the Off-Worlders, Franklin's Dream, the Constitution or even the Declaration itself." He stops for a moment to let the possibilities separate into different likelihoods. "Maybe *we're* responsible, the Signers. Maybe the curse is the country itself, fifty years is the longest gravity can keep it from spinning apart."

"So you believe it's true? That there *is* a curse?"

"American tradition, I guess, to see every event not for what it really is, but in a worst-case-possible, furthest-played-out nightmare version. According to some, Franklin's Dream was supposed to end the country the second it left Beta. That was two years ago, and here we are." He sighs. "Guess you have to believe there's a curse in order to do a competent job looking for it."

Bartlett wiggles. It's a way of settling into his chair a little deeper. "We could tell them we've looked high and low and found no curse."

"Can't prove a negative," Sherm shakes his head. "Curse or no curse, if they believe it's coming, it means it probably will." Above, stars reveal nothing in the patterns they make against the void of dark space. "I suppose the question they really want answered is not so much *how*, but *will*. *Will* the country last more than fifty years?"

"And what do you think?"

"Despite what's being said on Franklin's Dream, we've done this thing right, Doc. As right as can be expected. It's all in God's hands now."

They look up again, at the Connecticut sky, at its pocked blackness. "A planet revolving around one of those stars," Sherm says, "has no conception of the constellation its sun helps make."

"And we don't either, I suppose you're saying."

Sherm shakes his head. "Our sun's probably not bright enough to be part of any constellation. At least not visible from very far away." He traces a pointer finger through the thick milky belt of stars and gasses and asteroids, all lost in each other's glow. "We just contribute to the sheen."

Bartlett is still there the next morning when Roger Sherman passes on. Old Sherm the cobbler, present and accounted for through every phase of it: Continental Association, the Declaration, the Articles, Constitution, Bill of Rights. Helped Franklin and McIntosh prep the Off-Worlder treaty negotiations, developed the compromise that set states' rights free to argue their way through all the coming histories of the nation. Sherm's going to miss the rest of the documents, the resolutions, treaties and doctrines, the little adjustments that are sure to come and come again, fine-tuning America off into eternity. Unless, of course, the curse gets it first.

The top floor of Hancock Tower rotates so that anyone in Boston and surrounding townships can look up and see which way the governor faces at any given moment. Really, it's the top two floors combined into one. Twenty-foot ceilings, flat marble walls and light that comes spilling in. Always looks so futuristic no matter what future comes along. This is the tallest building in the New World, inherited when his uncle died and all of a sudden, John Hancock was the head of America's most lucrative shipping empire. That was 1764. He was twenty-seven years old and the richest private citizen in all His Majesty's colonies.

Today, as with most days since the erection of America's tallest beacon of trade, the observation windows face east, toward the mouth of the Charles, the Boston Harbor, the fleet of ships right then sailing in parts and pieces, in and out, to and from the distant harbors of distant lands. John Hancock has faced this direction most of his adult life. When illness forced him to bed, he had the bed moved to the large windows in the main room, ordered the top floor rotated to face east. John Hancock wants to go out at the front of the continent which fronts the hemisphere that will one day front the globe.

Right now, Hancock's focus is lower, on the tiny men on the street below and their tiny horses and carriages all blending down to one teeming mass of humanity, seems like the tower rises right out of it. Made a lot of money together, John Hancock thinks, the

people and I. He takes his eyes from the window, rolls up his sleeve
to look at that old Sons of Liberty tattoo. Could have been me, he
thinks. Could have been me put in charge of the Continental Army.
Would have become President, too, first President of the United
States. But no, had to have a Virginian involved and so it was
George Washington. Look at him now, building a damned capital
with his name on it. And here I am, surrounded by programmers,
trying to cheat death.

It was a few months ago that rumors starting hitting the chatrooms, users reporting that Francis Hopkinson had been spotted
on Newnet, two full years after he was found dead in front of his
terminal, the day Franklin's Dream went live. Not supposed to be
any haunts in Newnet, that's one of the points of the programming.
But there's Hopkinson's Brainpage, more active than ever. He's
been seen wandering the meetups. too, mixed in the crowd at virtual town halls. Even if there were haunts in Newnet, these actions
are too complicated to be any haunt. Either Hopkinson coded his
avatar so well that the best programmers can't tell the difference, or
he really is still alive inside Franklin's Dream.

When John Hancock heard this, he was already sick, already
knew he was not getting better. Using his vast resources, Hancock
brought in the best programmers money could buy. For weeks,
around the clock, they've been coding John Hancock's Franklin's
Dream avatar to levels of detail no human has yet attempted. All
the spoils of Hancock's vast "shipping" fleet are being funneled and
filtered into these programmers' pockets. If Francis Hopkinson can
do it, maybe there's life past the edges of the physical world for John
Hancock, too.

Wouldn't mind one last look at the tower from the outside,
he thinks. And not in feeds or digital captures, but the actual sky
reflecting that slightly brighter version of itself in the polished surface. Makes it look so grand and impossible, hovering just above

invisible. He turns to look at the programmers and their rows of desks, filling up every spare inch of the main room, little aisles for them to weave between computer mainframes and that's about it. You can feel the information crowding the air. Just then, one of them is settling into a chair beside the bed. Together they work through a screen's worth of questions to which John Hancock rattles off answers that are supposed to be right off the top of his head. It's a constant battle, thinking about the answers as little as they tell him is necessary. "Need to get you in here as you really are," they've told him. "Not as you think you'd like to be. Can't look back on the present. And you can't exist, not really, if you're only the past version of yourself."

An aide enters and says, "Governor." And he comes to the bedside so Massachusetts's chief executive can put his signature on today's stack of government flexdocs. One last time, his old John Hancock, right there in the middle, each crested H more bold than the last, the last one the perfect one, a perfect exit for his written name.

Questions and signings done, the room settles into that constant clicking, the neverending typing of the programmers, the low hum of all those computers. They all know, from the Governor on down, that soon the body will give out. Mostly their programming work is done; it's just the finishing touches left now.

On the screen mounted beside his bed, Hancock can see the actual code of his online self. Aside from answering questions now and then, he really hasn't had much involvement in the process. And so whenever the programmers aren't looking, he works on tweaking a separate copy of the avatar. In this secret version of himself, Hancock has factored in the thoughts that pop up *after* the initial reactions. This second avatar is not necessarily how John Hancock answered the questions, but how John Hancock would like to have answered them, given a moment of thought, a chance to consider their part in the whole. Working in parallel, Hancock has constructed the version of himself that *was* put in charge of the Continental Army, that did become President. And his tower is not in Boston but in Hancock, overlooking this same river as it spills from the mouth of the nation's capital, out into the ocean, way far away.

Hancock experiences the sensation of being sucked toward the sea and he knows, suddenly and surely, that the end has begun. He'd always wondered if he would feel it coming, if he just settled in and listened to all there is to hear. Or would it sneak up and the world just cease? His legs go cold, then his fingertips. He's not sure how much longer he'll have the use of them. And so now he must decide which version to set loose in the Dream: the actual or the imagined John Hancock?

Pressing the button that decides it is his last physical act. He watches the upload bar zoom rightward and vanish, then lies back and sets his eyes further off, through the window, to the mouth of the harbor in the distance and the coast to its north, breaking over and over itself, on and on. Somewhere becoming the North Shore. New Hampshire. Maine. To the nation's very edge. One last glimpse of the real America before he crosses over.

S un setting over the western hills of Virginia and the brothers
Lee have gathered on the porch of Chantilly Plantation to see
Richard Henry off from the world. Arthur died at the end
of the second outbreak. Philip and Thomas Ludwell and Philip
Ludwell were all gone before that. John and James and plain old
Richard never made it much past birth. So it's just the three of
them, Richard Henry and William and Francis Lightfoot, a pitcher
of sugared lemonade and three pipes full of fine Virginia tobacco.
Alice is there, too, somewhere. And there was another sister, dead
now a while, whose name was Hanna.

"To France," Richard Henry says. "Lopping off the head of the
man who lopped off the head of the King. Now that's what I call
liberation of the mind." His voice has grown thin these days as his
life winds itself down. As have his arms and legs and torso and
neck, too. It's a skeleton of the man who presented the first resolution to separate the colonies from the vast British Empire. Now he
raises his sugared lemonade to look through it, at the sun burning
a swell of fire rightward across distant treetops. His other hand is
tucked along the side of his leg, always in that black silk pouch
with its string knotted tight. Lost the use of it when he was a boy,
the first dead part of him. And so into the bag it went; aside from
regular cleanings, it's never returned, sits in there useless and frail
and untouched by the sun. "What started in Old Virginia has gone
viral," he says. "All the way to Europe. The Declaration is catching

like *The Death*. And it didn't need any Internet or a Newnet or a Franklin's Dream. Didn't need any coding or programming. All went down inside the human brain." A long sip of his lemonade. "You know," he says. "The Revolution started right here, when I first told Daddy to go piss off and he slapped me and I told him to piss off again and he said, 'That's my boy!'"

"I wish he were here now," William says, dreamily. "That I could look up from this sugared lemonade and see Daddy walk right out onto the porch and take that empty seat."

"Didn't need no Constitution, either," Richard Henry continues. "Certainly didn't need no navy," and he sends a gob of spit to dampen the porch boards. "Floating tyranny is what it is. Best way to ensure the continued bloat of government."

This is the way it's always been for the brothers Lee. First, they were mad at the crown—a whole family for independence. When the crown was gone, they moved onto the next thing to be apocalyptically upset about: the Articles of Confederation, the Constitution, the BofR, Newnet and Franklin's Dream. Doesn't much get done in this country without a Lee there to connect the dots to tyranny and the ultimate downfall of man. "Maybe we could use a little of it here again," Richard Henry says. "A little of that old feeling. Throw off the Constitution and Newnet and this new navy like we did the yoke of George Three."

Francis Lightfoot swallows some lemonade he's been swirling around in his mouth. "So what, then? Back to the eighties? When the old Internet was the Cloud and no transaction was safe? No Newnet? No Dream? Never mind about the stagnant population numbers. Who wants to do business in a place where you come around the corner and run into your own haunt?"

William says, "The eighties weren't so bad. They were kind of sweet, actually, in a way."

Francis Lightfoot lowers the level of lemonade in his glass. "Whatever France got, whether they got it from America or not, let's hope it doesn't ever come back over. 'That old feeling' mutates itself again and what'll that look like in Philadelphia? George Washington torn to bits, all of Chestnut Street reduced to rubble, the blood of Federalists smeared on the doorways of pubs and common houses? How far you like this to go, Richard Henry, this thing that started back that time Daddy whipped your ass?"

"George Washington," William sighs. "Who would have thought it? More off-the-grid than ever. Gone all gaga for the Federalists."

Richard Henry wags a finger from his good hand. "Never mind the Old Man. Can't touch him anyway. Believe me, I tried. Burnt my fingers, burnt them real good. Everyone that's ever gotten in the Old Man's way has ended up the same: fucked up. You should have listened to me and Ben Rush about old Off-the-Grid *before* he got a chance to become old Off-the-Grid. Before he became this fucking god."

"What about Lighthorse Harry?" referring to their dead brother's son, a leading member of the Society of Cincinnati and as hard-on a Federalist as you're going to be able to scratch up south of New England. They all sigh. A Federalist in the Lee family: more proof that something's gone wrong with America, terribly wrong.

"Newnet. Oldnet," Richard Henry says. "Platforms come and platforms go. So long as the government stays out of it, I don't have any problem with the Cloud, whatever name it's got in whatever present we're in. Newnet is a great place for business, any fool can see that. So a little tax money goes to a new server now and then, a few gentlemen's agreements to keep the level level. But ships of the line? Just floating there and they don't have a sleep mode. This ain't no smartphone you can slip into your pocket when you don't need it. You have to keep a navy running *all the time*. Each ship full of men, *all the time*. Always stocked full of guns and cannons and provisions. Taxes go up up up, and the government gets wide wide wide."

Francis Lightfoot says, "People moving into Michigan territory, and sooner or later the government's going to be moving there, too. Got people living in the Dream now. Not hard to see where that's going."

William looks like he's just been given his wish, like he's just watched their daddy walk out onto the porch. "People living . . . *inside* the Dream?"

"Francis Hopkinson and John Hancock, both living in there for real. That's what people say, at least. Neither of them has a body back here controlling his avatar anymore. But the avatars are out there, out there in the Dream, claiming to be the same old humans, just they're *only* their avatar now."

Richard Henry looks at his coming death. Shapes in the shadows break from trees tilted along the wide front drive. Beyond, the sun sinks lower.

"Got these drones, too," Francis Lightfoot says. "*New* drones. They're not part of some larger program, facet of some business model. They're completely autonomous. And they're contributing to the economy, too. Drones got lives in there, families, they say."

"Someone put a rock on Daddy's grave," William says. "To keep that old slave driver from rolling over."

Francis Lightfoot puts on the face of a country lawyer. "There's a war going on in Europe," he half opines. "Always has been, always will be. They can't go a few years without poking each other in the Cloud. Sooner or later one of them's going to start poking around with *our* Cloud. And how long are we going to take it before we do something? And what are we going to do something with if we don't have a navy? Without safe cloud commerce, people'll lose patience with this Republicanism thing. Pretty fast, too. Same way they lost patience with the King." He shakes his head sadly. "Soon there won't be a government *and* a cloud because the government and the Cloud will be the same thing. And we'll end up on someone's side in the war, too. It's not what I want," he says. "But that doesn't mean it's not coming. Grand philosophy aside, government is only as good as the Cloud it makes available."

Richard Henry focuses his attention on the crooked tops of the apple trees that seem always to be pleading skyward. "I fought in a war over this when I was a young man: the French king trying to tell us what we could and couldn't do with our charters. Our sons have fought a war over this, the King telling us what we can and can't do with our money. Now we got another war brewing, people telling people what they can and can't do with their Cloud. Some day our sons' sons will be fighting in the next war. Whomever it is telling us what we can and can't do with whatever it is then . . ."

Richard Henry finishes his sugared lemonade. Both brothers know that this is the signal, and so they finish their lemonades, too, settle in to hear the last words of Richard Henry Lee. "Each man must have his own revolution, Francis, William. Each man must become a man untangled. A man of true liberty. No obstacles set in his path by any power larger than himself. Not until each man is free will every man be free." Richard Henry waves that silk-covered hand. "Like all things, this terror will pass. These European wars even. But a navy? Good luck taking that out of the Cloud once it's up."

The sun sinks down bellow the horizon. All light gone from the state of Virginia. The population suddenly one less, and only two Lee brothers left. And Alice somewhere, too, the sister.

Abraham Clark wakes up. "Oh," he thinks. "I'm in the Dream."

"For a while anyway."

"Wait," Clark says. "You can hear what I'm thinking?"

"You're *saying* it now."

"But before I was just thinking."

"Well, either way, I can hear it. Though 'hear' probably isn't the right word."

Abraham Clark realizes he's talking to no one. The chatroom is grid only and empty besides his avatar. Code echoes the surface of the walls. Beyond, it looks like the same old Dream, but in this room, it's like the Dream has been removed. A bubble caught somewhere in its guts, holding it all back. How much pressure needed to burst it and everything comes rushing in? "Who is that?" Clark demands. "Who's talking to me? Where the hell am I?"

Francis Hopkinson, ponytail and all—exactly like Clark remembers him—comes twittering into the emptied-out room. "Sorry," the avatar says. "I forget how attached humans are to human shapes." He turns to look into the translucent layers of code.

Abraham Clark is brightened by the presence of his fellow Signer. He looks around the allchat. "How did I end up in this? Some error in the Dream routed me down some wrong tunnel, maybe? Gosh, I guess that sounds pretty dumb to you."

"Nope. I understand how complicated the Dream is. I *did* code the place."

Clark steps up beside him, looks where Hopkinson is looking. "So what's with this chatroom? Never seen anything like it."

"You're on the other side of the Dream. This is the code side."

"Oh."

Hopkinson turns to face him, "You mean you don't know?"

"Know what?"

"Let's put it nice and easy and say: When you're finished with this Dream session, you won't be going back to the real."

"Has something happened to the real?"

Hopkinson laughs. "Something's happened to *you*, Abe. You're dead back there."

"Dead? You mean I've been transported to the Dream? My soul got sucked in?"

"No, you haven't been *transported* to the Dream. You're just in that last active second."

"Last active second?"

"Your brain." Hopkinson smiles. "Don't worry. I've slowed down this sector of the Dream to give you as much time as possible. It's all only a second or so of time in the real. Maybe three."

"I don't like the idea of being dead."

"Well, technically, you're not. Not yet. Actually, technically . . . *medically* speaking, you *are* dead. Your body."

"Oh."

"But your brain is still alive. At least for a moment or two."

"Frank, did you do this? Did you bring me here?"

Francis Hopkinson puts up his hands—his avatar does, anyway—and since there is no other him back at any terminal, it really is him that's showing Clark those hands. "Not me."

"How, then?"

"That's what I'm trying to figure out. Probably just an accident."

"An accident?"

"Accidents happen any time there's a new technology. Think about the first human who climbed on a horse. The first ones who got in a ship and sailed out past where the ocean falls off. The Dream, Newnet . . . we've created an alternate parallel reality where humans live as digital replicas of themselves. Something was bound to go wrong, eventually. I'm surprised it hasn't happened more."

Clark looks down at his arms and his legs. Don't really feel there under him, but seeing them, moving them, well, they look like the same arms and legs he had back in the real. "Can you tell me how I got here?"

Hopkinson may look like he's looking into a wall, but really he's looking through the crossover interfaces of the Dream, right into Abraham Clarks' inanimate body, back there on his New Jersey farm. "Too hot," Hopkinson says.

"You mean I got uploaded to the Dream because it's too hot in my house?"

"In your house? Abe, you're not in your house. Your body's not, I should say. You remember maybe going outside today?"

Clark snaps his fingers. "That's it. This morning's walk."

"Guessing you looked at the sun too long, or let the sun look too long at you. Like way too long."

"If my brain got melted by the sun, then how did I get back to the house?"

"You didn't."

"Then how did I log into the Dream?"

"You didn't, Abe."

"Then how am I here?"

Hopkinson smiles. "How the sun gives you a sunburn is radiation. Not really heat. Though it is hot. Real hot. It's the sun."

"My brain got radiated?"

"Probably made the cells move around in some way that's too unpredictable for it to ever happen again. But yeah, that's what it looks like. You're not at home, Abe, not on Newnet. You don't have any smartdevice linked in."

"Where am I then?"

"Your body is lying in a field, if that's what you mean. The rest of it—walking home, logging into the Dream—hallucinations caused by the radiation."

Clark turns to find his own section of the room to stare out from, watches the Dream churning by, one layer away. "You looking at my brain back there?"

Hopkinson nods. "Pretty interesting. That you were able to come across without a device."

"How did *you* get here?"

Hopkinson thinks a moment. "Jefferson," he says. "Jefferson did it."

"Thomas Jefferson? What, he uploaded you?"

Hopkinson shakes his head. "Love to have some scans of my old brain, but I didn't get them and now the thing's all rotted. Not connected anymore anyway." He shrugs, "Maybe he wanted me here for something or was trying to get rid of me for good. He botched it and here I am."

Clark thinks a second, smiles. "You harboring any ill thoughts, Frank? Maybe someone in the real you want to get back at?"

"Taking on Mr. Jefferson in the *real* is not the best approach, I think."

"Studying my brain, then? To learn how to suck someone across? Bring him over here to your turf?"

"Sorry, Clark."

Clark looks at his avatar's body. "Sorry what?"

"Looks like this is it."

"My active moment is gone?"

Hopkinson nods.

"What's it going to feel like?"

"Not sure. What does it? It's happening now."

"Oh." Clark tries to concentrate, but he can't feel a thing.

K eeping it pretty quiet, but old Off-the-Grid's about to announce
he's really going off the grid. And this time it's going to be
for real. And for good. Everybody's taking sides. In secret, of
course, but they're all taking sides. Each side making sure its side is
all loaded up with men of quality. The retirement of George Washington has become imminent and already the country's splitting in
two beneath him. Don't let the Old Man see, but as soon as he's not
looking . . .

Way before there was the Old Man, there was *The Father*. *The
Father of the Founding Fathers*. The original Old Man. Old Man
John Witherspoon. And for the sides all lining up their men, this
here's the biggest catch of all. If the Jeffersonian Republicans or
the Federalists could come out with *The Father* on their side, well,
that would look pretty damn sweet. Every day, more floods of chats
and tickles and even old-school emails, all feeling out which way
The Father might throw his heft. Today they're all demanding to
know: how does *The Father* feel about the Whiskey Rebellion. Is
John Witherspoon a Signer who's with the Jeffersonian-Republicans or a Signer who's with the Federalists? Witherspoon's not sure
why he has to be with either. Or against whichever one he's not
with. Or why anyone wants to know what a blind old man thinks
about something happening so long after he's served all his useful
purpose.

Not Old Man Witherspoon anymore, he thinks. Just a blind old man. Lost his sight during the first outbreak. Doctors told him it was *The Death* that was causing it, but he's never heard of anyone else going blind from *The Death*. Thirteen years later, *The Death* long gone, and here he is.

It being patriotic to make things easy for a blind old patriot, the aristocracy of New Jersey has paid for an orderly. Witherspoon's working on the third one now, a new orderly for each level of system failure. This kid he has now specializes in late-stage hospice, supposed to be constantly hovering in case John Witherspoon should need something as his last days tick away. But this orderly is fond of sneaking out of the room whenever there's enough background noise. Kid always has a bluear in, an eyereader too, constant feeds streaming in from Franklin's Dream. One feed for his eyes and one feed for his ears. Keeps it all turned pretty low, but every so often, John Witherspoon can hear its tiny spiking treble. What's he going to do, though? Demand the kid listen to every word he says? Demand he stand there attentively during his old man's silences?

"It was fourteen years ago that I lost my sight." Witherspoon holds his hand up in front of his face, in front of those glazed grey eyes. "Since I last saw the world. Today it's the Whiskey Rebellion. Tomorrow it'll be something else. An election coming soon." He sighs. "These political parties. They sound more like France and England than they do America. If you're not with us, with us one hundred percent, then you're declaring yourself with the other. Everything is so one hundred percent."

Slowly and purposefully, Witherspoon works to his feet, scuttles across the room, hands out front and pawing until he's down at his desk. The orderly keeps an eye on him but doesn't budge, sunk a little too deep into those Dream feeds he's feeding on. Witherspoon pops the top of that old laptop. The orderly giggles every time he sees the thing and its touchpad. "Pretty sure an eyereader would work even for a blind person," the orderly says. "Surely better than that voice-rec software." And the kid laughs because he can't believe John Witherspoon still uses it, that old voice-rec software.

"When I went blind," John Witherspoon tells the kid, "that was when I started to *see* the Internet."

This is a line the orderly has heard before. Numerous times. Not that the old guy doesn't have interesting things to say every once in a while. But can a person really be expected to wade through hours of echoes for the brief flashes of the old John Witherspoon? Right then, the orderly is tiptoeing out of the room. Might be *The Father of the Founding Fathers*, but to this young American, John Witherspoon's no different than any other old haunt.

Witherspoon articulates a few commands to the computer. The computer, in turn, reads out John Witherspoon's unread email. Words from the speakers in a soft female voice he selected long ago. "Open links," he instructs. View boxes pop up all over the screen in overlapping tiles. In the flattened stack of open feeds, several videos of the Whiskey Rebels running through looping lists of auto-play. Pro- and anti-screamers Dream screaming to anyone on Newnet why the Rebels are traitors, or why they're patriots. New and familiar voices from the far reaches of the political spectrum all let loose and mid-drone.

The Father of the Founding Fathers sits there listening. "The Whiskey Rebellion," he says. "It's a catchy name. Who doesn't like whiskey? Who doesn't like rebellion?"

Witherspoon's eyes search their blackness for brain images called up by the patterns of the noise. Might be a wall of sound to anyone else, but The Father can navigate the mess just like he's pressing down shortcut keys with the letters all rubbed off. "The gimmicks and the diatribes change. New catch phrases and symbols. False heroes, imaginary villains, endless floundering clowns. But the game, the game doesn't change." He nods to where he thinks the orderly is still sitting, lost somewhere in the Dream, says to the empty room, "The game is: What are we going to get and who is going to pay?" Witherspoon listens to tangled feeds, digging deeper and deeper and deeper. "You want to know who's winning? Just look at who's getting the most and paying the least."

Witherspoon snaps himself free from the grip of his own thoughts, moves his hands in slow arcs over the surface of the desk. Leans forward to reach way into the corners. "Boy, where is my glass of water?" But then he has it. Takes a sip. Turns to face where the orderly was sitting last Witherspoon heard him. "Federalists say this Whiskey Rebellion is the beginning of the end. That what's happened in France has spread back here." He pauses for another sip. "And my Republican friends, they say the Revolution just continues. That the new tyrants are American tyrants. That unless a stand is made, everything that has been won thus far will be rolled right back. Both sides saying that to not see what's going on is to not be an American, at least not a patriotic one."

Witherspoon pushes on his knee so he can be standing, finishes the water with one long sip, and holds out the glass for the orderly to take. Lets it go and it drops onto a pillow that has fallen to the floor. Lands and settles noiselessly on the cushion. And so he thinks the kid has it and he *still* doesn't know: It's just him in that room, all alone.

"Back in ancient Greece," Witherspoon says, and he straightens then, as perpendicular to the floor as he can manage. Face up square to the room, as if addressing some collection of selected men—it's him, *The Father*. "Advanced thinkers of the classical world managed to pry open a small fissure in the very fabric of reality. Into it, they placed an organism: democracy. It was the pure and boiled-down essence of that present and perfect moment. And here we are again, thousands of years later, the latest in a long line of cultures figuring out our own way of living that again."

He cracks himself from that rigid, scholarly pose. Begins his feeble way toward the bed. "That's what we did with The Declaration. It's a masterpiece, the best slogan ever, the kind you can build eons' worth of civilization on." Witherspoon seems to be transporting himself, back to that hot meeting room in Philadelphia, all those years ago. The Second Continental Congress and the room pocked with his pupils, men he taught the law now teaching the world what's about to come next. And maybe it's what he's seeing, because it can't just be darkness. Not all the time. His mind must find things, if only memories, hallucinations to put in the place of his vision all gone.

Witherspoon reaches the bed and sits. Swings one leg up and then the other. Waves a hand to ward off any help from the orderly who's not there. "The world for me exists in the moment I went blind. Always will." He lies back flat in the bed. "1779, frozen forever in time."

Thomas Lynch and his wife sailed away from America right when the Revolution went from talking and signing things to a real goddamned war. Because who wants to be around for something like that? If it's not your own government demanding money and sons, and requisitioning your livestock and crops, then it's the enemy army doing the same thing and then burning the whole farm down to boot. Raping women, smashing babies, torturing grown men to death—an army on a rampage through the countryside, not a pretty sight. Whole thing makes Thomas Lynch sick is what it does. Just plain sick. So it was out to live on the ocean just until things settled down.

They were able to follow the war online for a little while, but when word came through that *The Death* was transmittable through the Internet, they threw all the computer equipment right off the plank. "*The Death*," his wife said, watching their laptops and smartphones sink into the oceany blackness, "must be real wild."

It was the first time they'd lived off the grid, the first time long term on the ocean too. It turned out to not be so bad. Instead of checking email, they checked the breezes. For feeds, they had each other's eyes. Bed was like a water bed even though there was no water in it. On clear nights, they'd climb from the cabin and watch the stars shift above as the Earth and the Milky Way hurtled into new stretches of the universe.

It was a few years before they got their first pangs of curiosity, about what was happening back on the mainland. And so they sailed in toward the shore, found a coastline abandoned, ships left bobbing in the low water, towns like frozen captures of towns deserted, no sign of the war or either army. Thomas Lynch checked some old-fashioned maps and charts. He looked at a compass and told his wife they were maybe off the coast of one of the Carolinas. They trolled southward until a small refugee camp opened up with cannon fire, forcing them back into the ocean. America sure looked worse than the America they'd grown up in. And that was under British rule.

A year or so later, they went in toward the shore again and there wasn't any shore. It was just more sea despite what the charts and maps and compass said. Then the continent was suddenly there, not they drew close and it came into view, or like a fog lifted, but it just appeared, the entire coast all at once and only a hundred yards from the bow. High atop the closest crags, a dark-clad witch stood with arms spread, spells streaming from her fingers, making waving colors of the land that stretched out before her.

And so off they went again, out to sea. In the swelling storms and the glassy windless days. Nothing as far as the sun could shine. Just the two of them and the slaves and all the fish they could eat. This was their own private America. They could make it however they wanted. Imagine it, and then create it, and then live inside it, all right there on the boat. The two of them. And the slaves.

A few months later, they got curious again, maybe even a little homesick. And so they swung an arc in toward the shore, just to see what was happening in everybody else's America. But all they saw were piles of bodies and nothing else.

The next time they sailed in close, the bodies were still there, but now being loaded onto a flying saucer, which tilted and wobbled, then slipped through a gaseous portal that tore open in the sky. The next time, it was a whole fleet of saucers with spikes and tubes stuck into the ocean and black sludge in the water for weeks after.

"Gosh," Thomas Lynch said to his wife, "everybody else's America sure looks like it sucks a big dick."

His wife smiled. "But, Thomas, do you know what sucked the biggest dick ever?"

He looked at her blankly.

"Martha Washington."

And you could see it in their smiles, the love it would take to live this way. Back out they sailed, into the endless churning of the sea.

Finally, on their most recent trip in, America looked kind of like the America they'd always imagined it could be, ships clogging the bay with commerce, a bustling port town beyond, church bells pealing so loud you could just see the goofy smile on the guy yanking the rope. But as they drew close, several open fires came into view, burning in the streets. Lynch sailed alongside a schooner and asked what was happening, and the captain told him the people were burning Federalists in effigy. "What's a Federalist?" Thomas Lynch wanted to know.

"Cabal of trust-fund babies and merchants that's taken control of the government."

"But what about George Washington? Can't he stop them?"

"Washington is the leader, most powerful Federalist there is."

So maybe that was it, then, that sucked the biggest ever. Off they went back to sea, because who wants to live in an America run by Federalists, whatever that is.

But the worst thing they've ever seen was just one day ago. Sun beating down on them and not a single fish in the sea. Food stores empty for the third straight day. Thomas Lynch and some of the slaves got a flash of hope when they looked over the side of the boat at the first school of fish in weeks. But it wasn't any school of fish. No, this was all one fish, changing textures and reflecting bits of daylight when its parts came closest to the surface. For five minutes it swam beneath them. When finally the ocean had gone back to just ocean, a man floated to the top. They fished him out and he was dead alright, dead and drained of blood. They had to try to eat him. Didn't have any choice. What are they going to do, starve on principle? But when they started cooking him, he cracked and burned like wood, got so hard to chew it was like eating wood chips too. It was some dry meat.

A storm came that night, the swells dropping them into watery caverns and then lifting them up so the endlessness of the ocean could come crushing in. They held hands and decided this is the event they would not survive. But here they are, the next morning and the ocean calm and they're just as alive as the day they left.

"Sixteen years it's been."

A rumbling under the boat gets everybody rushing out of their cabins. Thomas Lynch looks over the side and sees a little bit of that thing that's not a school of fish. And when he looks up, something huge and fleshy is lashing down toward him and he thinks, *Oh is that a fucking tentacle?*

Yep. Wraps him up and it's the last thing he sees: the tentacle, real close up. It's translucent enough that he can make out where the sun is through the flesh. But that's about all, a tint of the blue sky, some fluid that must be running through the muscles of the tentacle. Can't breathe but he doesn't have time to suffocate. Little pins come piercing from the tissue all around him and he suddenly feels cold, cold and bloodless.

JOSIAH BARTLETT :: MAY 19TH 1795

When Doc Bartlett opens the door, it's not George Washington standing there as he'd expected. Instead, Lachlan McIntosh has come to see him. "I was made to understand General Washington was coming."

McIntosh shrugs, steps in, leaves Bartlett there holding the door. "The President has many important things to do."

"When he hears what I have to say, he's going to have a different understanding of what's important."

They descend the steps to the lab and there it is, the crystal Bartlett's been studying all these years. It sits on a pedestal in the center of the room, various machines and readers and electronic devices gathered around it. Bartlett presses a button, pulls back on a lever and three pin-thick beams of light strike the crystal. As McIntosh watches, the crystal begins to glow a deep, fiery red.

"What is it, Doc?"

"The crystal creates a field."

Bartlett can all but see the military excitement bristling the air around McIntosh's body. "What's it do, this field?"

"Not sure 'do' is the right word. It *emits*."

"Emits?"

"Energy," Bartlett says. "But that's not all. It has temperature variants that allow it to store tremendous amounts of information." Bartlett pauses to let what he's about to say hit full. "The entire old Internet and all of Newnet would both fit inside a piece even a hundredth the size of this one."

Bartlett begins circling the crystal, a pretty good job of being on the opposite side as the general without making it look like he's trying to. "We haven't found any more of these?"

McIntosh shakes his head. "Seems like the Off-Worlders took the rest." The general picks at his nails. "We even dug up some Indians. Crystals were all pulled out. Gruesome, really." McIntosh stares deep into the crystal. "So what do you think the Off-Worlders were planning to do with a few million of these?"

Instead of an answer, Bartlett slams his hand on a blinking yellow button. A sudden flash from the crystal blinds McIntosh. Doc Bartlett grabs the crystal, lowers his shoulder into the flailing general and through the door. McIntosh, holding his eyes, gets off a wild shot with that pearl-handled pistol. But the bullet vanishes harmlessly into the wall.

Bartlett bounds down the steps a stride at a time, out onto the side porch, hears behind him the sound of glass breaking. Something whizzes by his ear. He ducks around the side of the building, comes out onto Main Street, where the citizenry is gathering for another burning of a straw John Jay. Across the street, McIntosh is filling up the frame of the front door, still rubbing his eyes. Picks Bartlett out from the crowd and levels his pistol.

A spark, a puff of white smoke, but that's it—a backfire. The two men's eyes meet and each smiles. John Jay goes up then, filling the street with swirls of white and black smoke. People yell huzzas and chant anti-Federalist slogans they've all heard chanted on the Dream. By the time the haze clears, Bartlett is in a full sprint, zigging and zagging alleys. Brakes into a clearing and then the woods beyond.

The next day, Doctor Benjamin Rush is sitting at his desk when Bartlett taps on the window and then climbs on in. Rush doesn't need to ask what's in the satchel bag. Pretty much common knowledge for those in the know that Doc Bartlett has gone on the run with the crystal. Shady SOC operatives are trolling the streets of every American city looking for any sign of the old Doc.

"So what's all the commotion about?" Rush asks. "Why don't you just give them the crystal?"

"We've got bigger problems than whether or not the Federalists get a hold of this crystal."

Rush takes a slow step backward, feeling for a chair with his hand. When he's found it, he lowers himself down. "Problems like what?"

Doc Bartlett thinks a moment. "I know it's the same thing that happened to Sherm. After a couple years of chasing it around, everything starts being about the curse. Still, I can't help but wonder, maybe 1826 is the year the population meets some benchmark, makes it profitable for the Off-Worlders to return. Another round of *The Death*. They come and harvest the crystals. Fifty more years go by and they do it again."

"This is only a theory, right? You don't have any, like, evidence?"

"Rush, imagine if every person in the US knew that the Off-Worlders grew these things inside of us . . . *on purpose*." Bartlett leans back on the window sill. "Means they sent *The Death*. Means the whole Earth, Rush, is just a farm for these crystals. They crop-dusted us, Ben." Outside, the noise of another Franklin's Dream meetup that's come over from Newnet, chanting about George Washington's slide toward monarchy. "Country's already busting seams," Bartlett says. "Introduce this little nugget of information, the place will fly part."

There's a commotion from the floor below them. Some voices. Doors opening and closing. Footsteps that begin up the stairs. Rush keeps looking around strangely. Both doctors have gone quiet to listen. Rush says then, "Well, if you're going to go for it, you better get out the back."

"Damn it, Rush." Bartlett starts back out the window. "Least you can do is stall them for me." He shimmies down the same drain he shimmied up a few minutes before, takes his horse around to the front so he can tie the bridle to the bridle of the other horses. Slaps a few asses and they start pulling and kicking and it becomes like one animal, *not* something you could ever ride. Bartlett slips a few side streets and then he and the satchel bag and the crystal are up under a tarp on a wagon headed westward out of Philadelphia.

Couple of nights in a bar outside York. Then farther west. Safe enough for a small bed and breakfast. Stays off Newnet, threw his phone away back before Philly. Been a while since he's spent so much time in the real. Michigan territory. Kind of nice actually. Quiet. Mellow. Makes him wonder how mad people really are about the Jay Treaty, way away from the Dream and its constant screaming.

Bartlett's trotting a trail south of Detroit when he has to duck a group of Indians, all in a hurry to be somewhere else. He hears a little later some more hooves clopping behind him, thinks it's the Indians again, but when he looks back, the twins are there. "Doc Bartlett," they both say. One of the horses has a brown dot over its left eye. Other than that, the horses are identical too. "Where's this trail lead?" one of them asks.

Bartlett's not running away, but he's keeping his horse moving enough that the twins can't quite catch up. "You guys here to stop me too?"

"Not stop, no."

"But it *would* be nice if you came with us."

"What's Jefferson want with the crystal?"

"Potentialities for human improvement."

Bartlett's shaking his head. "That's not going to work, not in this thing we've built. The public finds out and they'll vote to turn it into a weapon, something to use against France, or the Off-Worlders, or whoever or whatever they're scared of right then."

The twins have heeled their horses faster, but so has Doc Bartlett. The distance between them remains. "You think they will?" one twin says.

"Come back?"

"The Off-Worlders?"

Bartlett has reached the crest of a small hill. The twins' horses, at that moment, are sunk a full shoulder lower. The doctor's glancing back at them. All eyes tighten as Bartlett spurs full-throttle into a ticket down the hill's far side. By the time they all break into a clearing, Bartlett has put some longitudinal space between them. He leaps over a rocky brook, the horse stumbling on the far side, but then it's up, sprinting into the sage, leaves the twins reigning up and cursing, back on the other side. Doc Bartlett hazards a quick look back then kicks harder, smiling, headed for that big mountain in the distance.

A lone Indian comes looping out of the tree line that waits at the base of the mountain, pulls his horse up alongside Bartlett's. "Suppose you knew I'd be here," he tells the doctor.

"Yeah," Bartlett says. "I was wondering how I was going to find it."

"I don't like this any better than you, white man."

"I like it just fine."

But the Indian continues as if Bartlett hadn't spoken. "This is my fate, same as it is yours. Come," and he pulls off tangentially, into the pines. "I'll show you to the Fissure."

Bartlett tries to spark up some small talk as they ride along, side by side, but the Indian's not interested, not at all. Thirty years' worth of constant warfare with people who look just like Bartlett—can't say he blames the guy for a little indifferent silence.

As they clear the pines and begin through a rolling field of mossed-over glacier stones, a loud crack echoes a few times off the hills. Bartlett looks over to see the Indian slouched in his saddle, blood bright on his hands, already darkening the leg of his pants. The Indian manages to lift his arm, pointing over the lip of the closest hill. "There," and he slops to a pile in the moss.

A few more shots crack out, berwanging off the glacial hills. Bartlett's at a full gallop until the horse refuses to climb any more. He jumps down and takes the bag off the saddle, begins a fevered scurry up the sharp and steepening rocks. Only now does he look back. The Indian there, dead in a little bowl of rocks, his horse poking at some shrubs nearby. But nothing else. The shots have ceased. Bartlett might not know where they came from, but he's got a pretty good idea from whom.

Over the lip of the hill he meets a line of scraggly trees, about five or six deep. He can smell it now. Sulfur. The heat is intense. The closest trees are wilted and brown on the side facing the crevasse. Bartlett inches toward the Fissure and looks down. Below, a red gash slices lengthwise through the Earth. Steam swells lap the lowest sky, a peek into the inner workings of this planet.

Bartlett feels the front of his coat go warm and wet. He hears the shot a fraction of a second later, looks to see General McIntosh leaning from the line of wilted trees, thirty yards farther down the spine of the Fissure. Bartlett doesn't give him a chance. He turns and, clutching the crystal to his body, dives into the lava. With a soft hiss, he bursts into flames and melts, Doc Bartlett and the crystal, dissolved into the molten earth.

S am is talking politics in a private allchat with the John Hancock avatar. Ran across each other a year or so back, and at first it was hard to tell the difference; where does the old John end and the software edition begin? But lately the programming has picked up a tick or something, a fuzzy sheen. Hancock sits there wavering, skipping, shaking loose and then reforming.

"Pretty soon," Hancock says, "electors in the several states will begin their individual processes. For the first time, we'll have a President of the United States who is *not* named George Washington."

"We've got it," Sam tells him. "Going to be close, but the latest state-by-state predictives tell us Adams will win."

"State-by-state?"

"They come in spreadsheet and pie form, bar graphs, maps of every possible organizational proportion."

"And the maps and graphs and pie charts are linked to analysis claiming and counter-claiming the veracity of the data. I've seen it." Hancock shakes his head. "Election started off about who's got the better plan to get the population numbers rising again. Now it's this battle for reality. Dream insists Jefferson is going to win and the real insists Adams."

Sam's been trolling Franklin's Dream pretty much nonstop since the Old Man announced his retirement. His Brainpage portal is reborn each minute with feeds from several interlocking Federalist recycles. Dozens of long anti-Jefferson threads ping each time a new thread untangles itself from some other thread. Pinging pings out in this nonstop pulse code being relayed. Feeds topple to crowd feeds off his wall: recorded speeches, live speeches, live and recorded screams, screams remixed and remixed speeches, too, that now mean the opposite of what they meant when first spoken.

"Franklin's Dream," Sam says. "Out here in the real, it's the new big tickle. America runs on the Dream. There are lots of people saying they'd like to live inside, John. You could probably make a good buck selling that, bringing them over like you did yourself. Be the richest man in the Dream, just like you were in the real."

Hancock holds up a hand. They watch it twitch and reset. "You don't want to be in here, Sam." John Hancock's head is shaking. It's also jumpy, fizzing out and reforming whenever he moves. Reminds Sam of the old days, running software off laptops and old tower models that didn't have enough memory, the world freezing, then leaping to catch itself back up. "Not sure how it all works," John Hancock says. "But I'm dying in here."

"Dying?"

"Whether it's some virus the code's got or the stasis of the dataset it refers to. Way down deep, I'm only a complicated still photo, degrading over time."

"Well, I'm dying in the real if it's any consolation. Guess you've already been through that."

Hancock tries to recall. "It was more like I fell asleep. And then I woke up here and there I was, on the other side, dying. Watched that old body of mine slip away. Our eyes met." Hancock shakes his head. "I still wonder what it felt like for *him*, the me out there, if it felt like anything at all." Now he looks down at his avatar, glossed hazy with static. "Every time I perform a task, it knocks a few digits out of the code. I'm a whole base system off by now, my entire algorithm."

Sam is nodding along. "Yeah, pretty much the same thing for me, out there in the real. I got this cold spot in my throat that makes me cough if I take too big a breath. The cough makes my stomach hurt, which makes me wince and get short of breath, which makes me suck in more air past that cold spot, which makes me cough again."

Sam wonders if he would lose something of his real self if his avatar caught some refresh virus. Or does some version of *The Death* affect only code? "What about Francis Hopkinson? Can you help me find him?"

Hancock's avatar is shaking its head. "Haven't seen him in a year at least."

"Could he have disintegrated too? Like you say, with nothing out there to keep his programming fresh."

"No, Hopkinson can't be dead. He's . . ."

"He's what?"

Hancock shrugs. "What he knows about the code, what he knows about programming it. Imagine a man back in the real who could bend reality with his mind."

Sam works this over a minute. Sitting there, perfectly still. Really, back in the real, the real Sam is having a coughing fit, brings him pretty close to that great border between lands.

Hancock measures this. "You think if Hopkinson comes out, man who coded the Dream endorses John Adams. You think that'll swing the election."

"Before he was a god in the Dream, Hopkinson was a Federalist in the real. We would never have gotten the Constitution through without him." Sam lets a memory drop down over the inside of his face. "We were pals, you know, back during that Second Congress. Ate together almost every night after those hours of droning debate."

"Programmers are creating fan avatars," Hancock says. "Tribute avatars. All but autonomous. Group avatars are getting so big that individual opinions inside don't affect the overall code. How can they represent the people in the group then?" He pauses a moment. "Talking about making Franklin's Dream a branch of the government . . . Forget about Francis Hopkinson. Take *that* message to the people. Might get them thinking twice about the Dream. And then John Adams might just have a shot."

"Might have a shot? He's got better than might. Better than a shot."

John Hancock smiles at the little rays of Federalist hope. "Despite what your selected datasets allow you to believe, all the simulations show Jefferson winning a squeaker. The more simulations that get run, the more the results verify other results. Washington is the only one, Sam, who could pull off supporting a larger government in a nation full of rebels and pirates and slave masters." Hancock ponders it a moment. "How would you even do it? Franklin's Dream a branch of the government? Replace the Senate? The House? Add another chamber? Would it be lower or higher or in-between?"

Sam's avatar sits there frozen.

Hancock doesn't seem to notice, holds up his wavering hand. "There's no programming for dying, but neither is there any code to prevent it. It's a part of you. It's in the math. Eventually you fall apart and stop functioning. Be it country, body or code." John Hancock's shaking that shaking, pixilated head of his. "Maybe Hopkinson wrote the perfect code. Invulnerable to time and the cycles of time. What do you think, Sam?"

But Sam is dead back in the real. There was a time when his avatar would have sat in that private chat until it either decayed back to primary data bits or was stumbled upon by an escaped drone or a worm. But now there's code to prevent that. This is Newnet. Sam Huntington's avatar stands from the table, walks to the corner and lies down, speaking the words Sam had programmed in when he first set up its death sequence, mandated for each user before he's allowed to log on to Newnet for the first time: "Sam-a-lamma-ding-dong-sally." And then he vanishes, Sam Huntington condensed back to meat only.

F rancis Lightfoot's voice has reduced itself to the setting just above vibrate. "John Adams has won," he whispers, "despite everything the Dream thought was going to happen." It's been a few weeks of him slowly fading as he sits on the porch in the afternoon sun. Alice tried to rig up some voice-rec software, linked it back to Francis Lightfoot's Brainpage, opened a brand-new all-chat account for him, but he just kept looking at them empty chairs, talking at them empty chairs. Alice can't tell it from the days when there were four, five or seven, all gathered together on Chantilly Plantation to watch one of their brothers die.

"Doesn't seem to matter to the Republicans," Francis Lightfoot is saying. "They're saying Doctor Benjamin Franklin's Dream America is its own America now. A whole separate country that Thomas Jefferson is going to be President of, election be damned. And this separate America is somehow going to exist at the exact same time, in the exact same place?"

"Sure it is," Alice says.

Francis Lightfoot looks outward, either at where none of his brothers are sitting any longer or past that point in space, toward some further layer of Virginia. "But what happens when someone in Franklin's Dream decides they want their own America too?" He shakes his head sadly. "A shame Richard Henry isn't here, with his useless hand in that silk bag, to encourage such splitting until every man has his own private America, separated and individual from the rest."

"Yes," Alice says. "Every white man can have two then, two Americas, one in the Dream and one in the real."

A sigh. "Franklin's Dream, spreading through Newnet just like *The Death*."

When William died a few years back, they got together for what was going to be the last-ever conversation between the living brothers of America's greatest family. But all Francis Lightfoot and William did was argue, argue, argue, the whole damn time.

"I remember when a fan page was something to decide which Signer of the Declaration of Independence had the biggest rump. You created fifty-six pages with a picture of each one's hindquarters and whichever had the most likes at the end of the day was the winner. Now this is how they're creating new Americas?"

Alice had thought maybe a few days. That's been the pattern with all her brothers. They start to decline, call the family in, it's a few days and then off to whatever other world or America waits for the Lees who've passed. But Francis Lightfoot is hanging on. Hanging on like it's not only him fighting off death but all the Brothers Lee, tag-team wrestling to keep the world from losing the very last of them.

"Dream isn't the beginning of something," Francis Lightfoot says, "just the way it'll always be from this point forward. Republicans revolting against Federalists who just finished revolting against the crown. Just like Havana, slaves revolting against their masters who are revolting against their masters who are cutting their king's head off right there in the street. And some day some guy in a small town somewhere, or a freed slave on a free island, or a patron of a church, or a Republican inside the Dream will revolt against whatever power's right then most directly above him, and on and on and on forever."

Francis Lightfoot's not sure if that's wonderful or horrible. He knows it's one or the other, but it can't be both. Can't be somewhere between. "Wonder what happened to all those profiles of all those rumps," he says. "Still back there in the old Internet probably, the rumps of the Singers of the Declaration of Independence. Nothing to do but struggle through one neverending existential crisis: Why were we created, and what is our purpose? Really, they're all just butts. And virtual ones at that."

"Franklin had the biggest rump," Alice mutters. Doesn't even glance up from her sewing. "And it looks like he always will."

"I was there for the beginning," her brother says. "Maybe I've been allowed to live just long enough to see the end. Well, the beginning of the end, at least. That would be some sweet symmetry." He thinks it over a second. "Or maybe this is how it always seems—that it's just about to fly apart. Gives people a reason to be fighting all the time to save it. Maybe the curse comes when we forget to give a shit."

He waits, but there isn't a Lee brother left to agree, or disagree, or redirect or augment his point. And so it just dangles out there. Francis Lightfoot's eyes go still. The air in front of his face isn't getting thick again with his breath. All that's left is Alice, sitting alone on the porch of Chantilly Plantation.

It was his last slave left who found him one mid-morning staring at the screen of an old smartpad. At first, the boy decided to leave his master be. That his master was probably doing whatever it is masters do on Newnet, and it was best to just scoot on out. But the slave came back a half day later and Old Master Braxton was *still* doing it. And that ain't healthy.

The slave sent for the doctor, and the doctor came and bled Carter Braxton of settled humors. And then he bled him some more. He put all kinds of salts and potions and goo across Carter Braxton's upper lip, this doctor did. But he just couldn't get any kind of reaction. And so they called in a better doctor and settled in to wait.

A few days pass and here comes a carriage rolling into town, as plain looking as the single horse that's pulling it. Inside the carriage is Dr. Benjamin Rush, all the way down from Philadelphia. Finds the honorable George Wythe, a fellow Signer of the Declaration of Independence, sitting beside Carter Braxton, still face-deep in that smartpad. Rush asks, "Has he been bled yet?"

Wythe turns over one of Carter's arms so Rush can see the crosshatching left from the last doctor. "Just wondering if he can hear us," Wythe says. He snaps his fingers an inch from Carter's eyes. "Could this whole thing be about the Dream, I wonder?"

"How so?"

Wythe shrugs, "You know, they found him like this, face in the Dream."

Later, Rush watches Wythe's carriage rolling over the next hill away. *His carriage is even more plain than mine,* Rush thinks. There he goes. The last of them. The last sane Virginian.

That evening, news wafts through the Cloud that if you have any designs on seeing old Carter Braxton again, now is the time. Next thing Rush knows, a string of hefty Virginia men start plopping by with all their pomp. The man who expended his fortune for Virginia and the Revolution is dying. And so get in the frame of a Dream feed if you can, a few cycles of your feet clopping up the steps to pay respect. Rush can't tell if it's just the Virginia tradition of high political drama or that American virtue they slime on about. All these massive political wigglers who've changed the course of the planet with their weight alone, in a torrent of slave-drawn carriages. Madison, John Tyler and his little rat–turn of a son. Ambassador Monroe, Governor Wood, the Society of Cincinnati's newest face man, John Marshall, Bushrod Washington with a card from his uncle, the Old Man himself. Rush supposes that in this new atmosphere of party, everything, deaths especially, will now be co-opted toward a message.

Late in the day, the twins show up on Jefferson's behalf. "Mr. Jefferson can't make it," one tells Rush.

"Presiding over the Senate," says the other.

"And how is the Vice President?"

They all turn to look down at Carter Braxton.

"Maybe his time signature has slowed," one of the twins offers.

"Dr. Rush, Mr. Jefferson would like to get you all together again."

"Who? Me and Carter Braxton?"

"No, the Signers."

"The Signers of the Declaration of Independence."

"The ones left, anyway."

Rush smiles. "One more tour, huh?" Seven months, he thinks. That's how long Adams has been President. And already it begins. Another election is just three years and five months away. Getting the Signers back together's not a bad way to start it. Don't even have to really do it. Just talking about it's going to be plenty. Remind every voter who it was that wrote the thing, who it was that coded the gene of liberty.

John Randolph of Roanoke shows up next with his dogs and his stuffed crotch all but wagging out the front of his riding pants. Actually whips Carter across the shins with his crop and shouts into the old man's ear. Can't bully a thing out of him. "Probably swallowed a marble," Randolph explains. "Got caught in some tube somewhere, keeps the emails from reaching the server."

And Benjamin Rush is like, *what?* Up to this point, he's only seen this act in Dream feeds.

"Looks like Carter Braxton isn't listening to the voice of the people either."

Rush counters; he can wiggle a little if he needs to. "I'm as good a Republican as anyone, but Adams *did* just get elected, the Federalists took control of the House. Picked up a Senate seat too, have a ten-seat majority. In *both* houses. Randolph, what more *voice of the people* do you want?"

For a brief moment, Rush thinks Randolph's going to turn that riding crop loose on him. He sees the violence twinkle in his eyes. The dogs tense up, each emitting its own low growl. But there's that Southern gentleman again. It's like the moon went behind a cloud. "If you don't understand that Franklin's Dream is the *real* voice of the people," Randolph says, "then you, sir, do not understand the people."

Rush tries a few things of his own over the couple days he's there, chasing down theories that come to him as he enjoys the Southern city. But Carter Braxton just sits there like he's been switched off. Rush thinks about how Wythe described it, *his face in the Dream.*

Light Horse Harry Lee informs Rush one afternoon that there's "One thing that's for sure: This would *never* have flown if George Washington were still President." Though the politics is different, Rush sure can see a lot of those Lee brothers in this next generation. "Do you know that sixty-one percent of Jeffersonian Republicans feel that their Franklin's Dream avatar is a more perfect representation of their self than their actual human body?" Light Horse Harry Lee pauses to shake his head at that one. "Off-the-Grid?" Lee says. "He would have smashed this Franklin's Dream thing right out of the Cloud. And the people would have paused only long enough to cheer."

Rush nods. Mostly he's astounded that a Lee ended up a Federalist, and a flaming one at that.

"The Society of Cincinnati sends our deepest regards," Light Horse Harry Lee says when leaving. It's the same exact line John Marshall had used to depart. So either the SOC is disorganized enough to send two men to do the same thing, or they're just hammering a message like everyone else. Rush wonders, "When did those guys become not a secret? Have they ever been a secret?" But Rush can't remember.

Creditors stop by to leave their opinions about how convenient it is that Mr. Braxton always seems so afflicted lately with abject stillness when the bills come due. Carter's last effort to dig himself out of financial ruin was Braxton Shipping. But the ships that made it through the French blockades were seized by the English ones. Ouch!

W. H. Harrison, just back from the frontier, stops by for his own photo op. He's working for Jefferson now too. No doubt about it. But he's got an eye on that Congressional seat in the Northwest Territory. Going to need a few Federalists friends for that one. Of course, being seen in the Dream at the bedside of a dying Signer sure isn't going to hurt none either. "My dad, the Lees, Tom Jefferson, Carter Braxton, George Wythe, the Old Man. My dad always thought of that Virginia delegation as his brothers." W. H. navigates the room as one does an open-casket wake. "Spanish still choking the Mississippi, building forts in Florida. The King's still out there, directory now too. Indians up one end, Barbary Pirates out the other. Still no idea what *The Death* was all about. All of Europe is at war. And how long before we get dragged in too? A world fucking war." He changes directions. "What if our slaves decide to follow their brothers in Santo Domingo?" W. H. sighs long and loud as Carter Braxton and Rush stare off into space. "World seems too much for little Mr. Adams to bear."

Rush does have to admit it—Adams *is* little.

"And what's with this curse thing I keep hearing about?"

Rush rolls his eyes. "Oh, you don't believe in the curse, do you, William Henry? Witches? Really? Your dad was a Signer, man."

"Not worried about the curse, Rush. I'm worried about what happens when the *people* find out about the curse. This is a republic, after all."

Patrick Henry never makes an appearance, which Rush thinks a bit strange until he realizes just how old that old volcano is. George Mason's been dead five years. The Lee brothers are all gone. Even George Washington has retired, forever this time, they're saying. It'll be these new Virginians who take their place.

"Paralysis," Rush finally proclaims. But he doesn't know what caused it. He wishes Doc Bartlett were still alive. Face in the goddamned Dream, he thinks. Maybe he could hunt down Francis

Hopkinson and get a hand with this. Maybe he'd come out and chat finally, even just a little, to help an old Signer on hard times. Maybe help get Carter's face out of the Dream.

Rush has Carter Braxton moved to his bed and then puts his hands up and tells the last slave left that there isn't anything more he can do. As he's leaving, Robert Morris shows up, and so Rush decides, well, what the heck. He'll wait an extra day and then the two of them can return to Philadelphia together. Here they are, Rush thinks, Robert Morris and Carter Braxton, the financiers of the revolution. Both of them broke and one broken down. "Looks like old Carter's just a haunt now," Morris declares. "Except he's over here in the real."

Rush nods, "Maybe not all of him, though."

"What's that?"

"Face in the Dream," Rush says.

The thing is, Carter can hear them fine. He can hear every word. He's not sure what happened. The only thing that seems wrong is he can't move, that and the fact that by now he should be dead from starvation. *They're going to give up on me,* he thinks. *They're going to put me in the ground. And I'll live forever down there, just like this.*

Lachlan McIntosh and Oliver Walcott have dug themselves into the outermost crust of the Dream, found a chat lounge, paid a little extra to make it private. Well, their avatars have. Really, both are in their respective places of assignment: Walcott at home in Connecticut, monitoring Franklin's Dream for anything that smells a little too French; McIntosh farther south—a lot farther—down in Santo Domingo helping the slave rebels kick Napoleon in the dick. Two old soldiers on the job for the Society of Cincinnati. Got some others down in Florida, undermining Spanish property values and riling up the Indians. All of it a long-term, multi-plat-form operation to rid the continent of European influence, once and for all. Someone's got to keep the New World safe for small-r republicanism.

"Wally, Wally, Wally," McIntosh wants to know, "what's the latest from Junior?"

"Shaky, Mac. Things are looking *shaky*."

Lachlan McIntosh is the only one who can get away with call-ing Oliver Wolcott "Wally." Comes from their days together in the Continental Army. The reverse is true too; if anybody but Walcott called McIntosh "Mac," it would be the last word they ever spoke. Well, the Old Man could get away with it, of course.

"These Dream screamers," Wally's avatar is saying. "Really have Adams on the ropes. Worst thing is, we don't even know who they are. President comes out and says something, you know it's the

President. But who's this Dream screamer calling himself American Brutus? Who is *Cloud Cato*? *Cin$innatus*? *Fedr@l-F@rmer*? Who do you hit back at when you don't know who's hitting you?"

Though interesting, this is all stuff McIntosh already knows. All you need to do is take a peek at the Dream to see the kind of trouble Adams is in. What McIntosh *really* wants is a little NAON, those juiciest bits of information, Not Available On Newnet. Wally's son, Junior, is Secretary of the Treasury, and so Wally has an ear on the inner sanctum of the Adams administration.

"Kid says the President has some dirt on France and the people are going to go wild if they ever find out."

"What's he got?"

"Access fee. President tried to open up a chat with the French and the French demanded an access fee."

"An access fee? To open a chat?"

"Frogs need capital to keep up their *war for liberty*, apparently willing to do just about anything to get it."

McIntosh thinks a moment. "Wait. Why haven't I heard about this? This is the kind of thing that should be all over the Dream."

"Kid says Adams won't."

"Won't what? Won't release it?"

"Kid says Adams thinks if he releases it, war fever will get out of hand."

"War fever out of hand is exactly what we need. This would kill the French, drag Jefferson and the Republicans right down with them. Has Adams talked to the Old Man? What does the Old Man say?"

"Washington doesn't want to get involved. Keeps deferring to Adams. So maybe he really is off the grid, off the grid for good."

"God help us," McIntosh says. "Republicans are already acting like they run the place. Imagine what they'll do if they actually win an election."

Wally's avatar gestures toward the Dream all around them. Torrents of profiles scrape the surface of their lounge, impossible to tell anymore which ones are human. Above, multi-conference and allchat hyper chambers dot the feet of high, hulking group avatars. New ones appear every few minutes, popping up one second and then scraping the real the next. Ad drones and banner drones and banner cycles and drones cycling banner ads. Tons of ads, ads everywhere you look. "Mac, this is just the surface of it. All this shit is just the apps and functions that regular users use. You should see what's a little further in, the shit only people living in the Dream ever access. Coder tunnels and drone ghettoes. There's all kinds of awful stuff in this place."

McIntosh shivers.

"That's not all," Wally says. "The kid says Adams *isn't* worried about it. Isn't worried about the Dream. Not at all. Kid says Adams thinks it's already climaxed itself. Now that the election is over, the Dream will kick a few last kicks and just fade away. That's what the kid says Adams thinks."

McIntosh laughs. "When has Thomas Jefferson ever just faded away? Guy's like a cat. Throw him down a well and he's lapping his paws on the counter when you get home. Milk's gone out of the icebox too. If Adams doesn't do something, the Republicans *will* win in 1800. Jefferson *will* be President, and never mind worrying about the Dream. The real will be more than we can handle."

"That's what they keep telling him."

Mac rolls his eyes. "But *John Adams* won't listen because *John Adams* thinks *John Adams* is the only one who can see what's really going on. Probably thinks Jefferson is still his buddy."

Wally nods. "That's pretty much exactly what the kid says." But Wally's avatar cracks a grin. "That's why the kid is working on a plan, a plan to force Adams's hand."

Now McIntosh has found it, some real NAON. "Tell me more."

"Jefferson keeps talking about *the people*. Well, the plan is we give it to them."

"Give it to the people?"

"We leak to the Republicans that the President is keeping secret messages he received from the French. They'll smell blood and go for the kill. And you know those guys, they're not going to be gentle about it."

McIntosh thinks it over. "Some Republican accuses Old John Yankee of dishonesty . . . Adams will explode. He'll release the whole fucking chat! The chat, the access fee, the whole thing!"

Walcott is nodding. His avatar is, anyway. "That's the idea. Once the people find out about the access fee, they'll come out for war. Full froth. Just like Adams knows they will."

Now McIntosh is smiling because he can see the whole of the plan. "Adams won't be able to resist it, the cry of the masses. He'll smell popularity for the first time in his life." The old general mulls it over. "They're going to get Adams to build an army!"

"And who do you think they're going to ask to lead it?"

McIntosh smiles. "We might just get the Old Man back out for one more round."

"If we're at war with France, then all the stuff the screamers are saying, it's not just Dream screaming anymore, Mac, it's sedition. Treason. Criticizing the President is one thing when we're at peace."

McIntosh takes in the whole of it. "Not too bad," he says.

"There's something else too."

"Something else good or something else bad?"

Wally thinks a second. "A little of both. Been tracking something, Mac. Something on Newnet."

"Tracking what?"

"Code-wise, it's just your average cloud siphon, only bigger. It's how the Cloud works, an interlocking protocol of programs that utilizes the processing power of the inactive sectors of Newnet. This thing, it acts the same way, except it uses profiles. Kinda like it lives inside of them."

"Inside the profiles? Which ones?"

"All of them."

McIntosh looks at the Dream waiting there on the other side of the private chat lounge. Doesn't see anything but regular old Dream. He never could get much past the surface of a code.

Wally says, "At first, I thought maybe it was some kind of virus, that it might destabilize the Dream. Maybe even destroy it."

"That would make our jobs a lot easier."

"But now sometimes I feel like *it's* watching *me*. Like it's out there . . . *hunting*." Wally changes direction. "Then I started to think about it more, Mac. And it started to come together."

"What did?"

"The access fees. This thing in the profiles. Jefferson and Adams. The election. War with France. Got me thinking. Maybe the best way to take on the Dream isn't from the inside like we've been thinking. But from the outside."

McIntosh isn't making the same connections Wally is. Not yet.

"Mac," Wally says. "We make the Dream illegal."

"Illegal?"

"It worked during the Revolution. We say it's because of the virus, that thing I've seen."

"Wally," McIntosh smiling. "So have you? *Really* seen this thing?"

"That's the beauty of it. It *is* real, whatever it is. Any half-decent Franklin's Dream programmer will at least know it's out there."

"The people find out that secret French screamers are using the Dream against us. They find out about this virus thing. . . . We all remember *The Death*."

Wally stops, listens. "Wait," he says. "Here we go. I'm picking something up."

"That thing?"

"I think so," but it's not the Lachlan McIntosh avatar he's talking to anymore. Still looks like Mac's avatar, but it's clearly under some other control. Walcott wonders if Mac is back at his terminal in Santo Domingo, booted out, back into the real. He tries to pull out of the Dream but can't. Wolcott goes calm, looks at McIntosh's avatar. "You a drone or a worm?"

The avatar is smiling, or whatever's in control of it is.

Walcott flashes anger. "Who are you?!"

It's Mac's voice but with a deep, endless echo added. "Don't worry about who we are," it says. "What you should be worried about is this: If you die in the Dream, do you die in the real?"

Lewis Morris looks into the brown liquor in his glass. He has a sip, says, "The Dream? More like a nightmare."

And his daughter just nods and says, "Oh, Dad."

He has another sip, says, "When I rebuilt Morrisania, I didn't rebuild it in the Dream. I rebuilt it in the real." He stomps his foot, but it doesn't sound like a stomp. More like rotten fruit being dropped. He's grown weak, her old dad. "People don't want to do the work anymore to make the real better, so they spend all their time in the Dream instead. Here's to John Adams. Once in a while, you got to remind them about how good the real is."

"Any better idea than a war, Dad, to make the real more popular?"

Lewis Morris is finishing a sip, shaking off the burn. But it's not whiskey he's drinking. Lewis Morris is too sick to be trusted with alcohol. His daughter swapped it all out with watered-down tea weeks ago. But he still drinks it, and still, somehow, it seems to get him drunk. "Why don't you read your book, Dad?"

He's waving, waving at things pestering him. "I don't want to read any more books."

"But it's going to make me so sad, that book sitting there half-unfinished."

This idea he takes more seriously. It sobers him in the time of one long sigh. Perhaps he realizes just then that it's not whiskey he's been drinking. Or maybe he's known this whole time and was playing drunk. "I thought I wanted to read it," he says. "My last book.

But then I decided I didn't want to read anymore, not ever. And so I'm not going to. I'm just going to sit here and look at the world as I die. And as soon as the Dream is illegal, everybody else can go back to living and dying just like we all used to do."

His daughter's laughing. "Dad, they can't make the Dream illegal."

"Congress's going to vote on it this session. Maybe in time to save this damn country too."

"Dad!"

"How are we going to fight a war with the French when half the country's claiming to be a different country and wants to go to war with England?" More of that soft stomping. "We need *one country* that can make *one decision* and stick to it."

"How do you make everyone think the same thing? And I mean besides making Newnet illegal," which she can't even say without smiling. "People are always going to be screaming weird in the Dream."

"Terminate their accounts is how."

"The government can't terminate avatars. What, just erase them?"

"Yes. That's how democracy works. You vote for something you think should be illegal and if enough people vote that way, you make it illegal."

"I don't care how many votes you get, you can't make Newnet illegal. It'll be like killing someone, the government starts terminating profiles."

"This house was burned down in the Revolution and I rebuilt it brick by brick and you're telling me about an online profile in the Frank A. Lang's Dream? *Killing*? Really?"

"It's 'Franklin's Dream,' Dad. Like Ben Franklin."

Morris scoffs, returns his attention to the grounds. Together, they watch a hawk come slicing through the yard. Must have killed a crow or been eating eggs from a nest, because the whole murder is swooping and circling and squawking and pecking, high-speed aerial chase through slanted pines, on into the back reaches of the property. Morrisania, the estate he built twice.

"I've seen it," Lewis Morris says.

"Seen what?"

"I've seen *The Death*."

"Dad, you can't see death."

"No, *The Death*."

She stammers, watches her dad stand, heaving and shivering to his feet. He turns to look back at the mansion, hulking behind them with its long east-leaning shadow. Sunset an hour away from the looks of it. He wonders if he'll make it or if he's seen his last. "When I was watching this estate burn. You know how air looks above an open fire. This was during the war and *The Death* was out there. And the Internet—the old one—was against the law. No one was using it. Wouldn't have won the war if the Old Man hadn't gone off the grid. I snuck back, after the British soldiers left, just to watch it burn. My Morrisania. And I swear, in that rippling heat, more than just the night sky was revealed to me."

"Dad, you're talking kinda funny. You alright?"

He sits again, back in his chair. "That's when I saw it."

"How did you see *The Death*?"

"The fire must have burnt away the surface of the air, a hole torn through the fabric of it. Or maybe the Internet, heated to the prefect temperature, became visible."

She's about to speak, but the way her dad's mouth is hanging open terrifies her.

"It stopped," he says. "Its huge, arched back, dark and mechanical. And it looked down and it could see me too, looked right into my eyes. Then the hole healed itself, sealed closed. The air became air again and my glimpse of *The Death* was over."

"Dad, how do you know it was *The Death*?"

"Well, it was something. Something terrible in that Internet."

"Makes me sad," she says, "thinking about that half-read book."

He puts his hand on his daughter's hand and she can feel how cold it is, growing colder by the moment. She looks at him, but her old dad has gone still in the darkening shadows of his mansion. *Something terrible in that Internet,* she thinks. The last words of Lewis Morris, master of Morrisania.

James Wilson is met at an Edenton Dream Café by two women, neither of whom is Penelope Barker. "Where's Penn?" he asks, but they just tell him to come with them. They go to the harbor where James Wilson is led onto a private barge, which the women navigate into the inner banks of Albemarle Sound. Leaving the main waterway, the boat cuts its own path through shoulder-high reeds, all the way to an invisible tributary that winds around the base of a sharp hill. There, a lone figure stands in the glow of a small stick fire. "Penelope Barker."

"James Wilson. You old rat."

"Thought you were dead from *The Death*."

"Not exactly." She starts to lead him into the thicket. "We've got a ways to go, so we best get going."

They pick up a trail that snakes upward and around the hill. After an hour of hiking, the trail has vanished. Wilson is just blindly following. He tries to ask a few questions, but Barker politely shushes him. They seem to be getting close to something, judging from the careful way she walks. Her head swivels, scans the woods around them. Wilson finds himself following her example but can't see much deeper than the closest trunks and their wispy autumn leaves.

Soon after, they break into a well-hidden clearing, a small village completely surrounded by woods. Holding a finger over her lips, Barker hands Wilson a robe, which he puts on, hood and all.

Now disguised, Barker picks their way to one of the twenty or so houses. Inside, Wilson takes the hood off and asks, "What's this all about, Penn?"

"This is The Community." Barker lights a candle. "When *The Death* first surfaced, we came together—a few other war widows and I—and moved over to this side of the hill. A place some of us had heard about from our mothers and theirs before them." She gestures toward the little village past the edges of the house. "This is a place where the Internet can't reach you."

"We have a cure for *The Death*," Wilson tells her. "Still not sure what it was, but we got a cure. From the Off-Worlders. Got 3net coming soon too."

"3net? Off-Worlders?"

"Yeah. Congress just passed a law making all these Newnet functions illegal." Then with a touch of irony, "It's for our safety." Wilson smiles. "Really, they don't want people in the Dream screaming about the war."

"War? We're still at war?"

"Not *still*. About to, like any day now." He holds his hands out. "War with France."

"France?" she shakes her head. "This is why we don't let any men live here."

"Really, no men? None at all?"

"Piss, piss, piss," she says. "That's how you men fight these wars. A big pissing contest. Get the other guy to piss longer and harder and when he's all pissed out, *then* you go over and piss in his face."

Wilson nods, smiling. "We're into the next phase of pissing. All of Europe is at war."

"Why does President Washington want to get involved? What's the use of an ocean between us and the Old World if you're not willing to wait it out?"

"Not Washington anymore. It's Adams now."

"Samuel Adams is President?"

"John. John Adams." He shrugs. "And he'll probably get reelected too. This war fever is the new big tickle. Adams is riding the wave."

"The people want a war?"

"Big time. And that's not all they're going to get. Federalists say 3net is going to replace all of Newnet and the Dream too."

"Well," she says. "It can't get us here." Barker takes a metal pin from her hair and drops it to the floor. The hairpin remains still for a moment, then begins to wiggle, bounce, like a fish gesticulating across a pier. It settles into a slow, even rotation, spinning length-wise on its center axis, a perfect little circle. "We think it might be the inner core," she tells him.

"What, of the Earth?"

"Or some layer closer to the surface maybe, spinning backward under this spot. Makes compasses go wild, hair all frizzy." She rakes fingers through hair that might be more frizzy than Wilson remembers. "Keeps the Internet from working too. Try to access the Cloud here, you get interference that will destroy your laptop."

"No one uses laptops anymore."

"We didn't have one case of *The Death*, James. Not one. Haven't paid a single tax or tariff. Don't have to rely on outside markets. We make everything we need here. And no men to muck it up. War, war, war, no matter what the system. Piss, piss, piss."

"Forget the piss, you missed a real shit show, that's for sure, this huge financial panic. Lost a bunch on that one. Had to crawl back to General Washington, all but begging for something in the new government. Old Man set me up on the Supreme Court, some gigs for the Society of Cincinnati on the side. Bunch of bastards, but it keeps the creditors away."

Barker turns from him, showing only her back as she digs in a drawer. "I need you to sneak something back for me." She comes out a moment later with an old digital camera.

"Wow," Wilson says. "That *is* old."

"The camera's not what I want to show you." She cues up a picture, turns the little view screen toward him.

"What the fuck is that?"

"We think some kind of octopus or squid. Or maybe a jellyfish. Those look like tentacles of some kind." Barker lets him take the camera. "Our fisherpeople, they go out under the cover of night for shrimp. Come back with all kinds of sailors' stories. Finally someone dug up this old camera, got a few shots."

"How come you haven't told anyone?"

"We don't have the rest of the world here. That's how we like it. This octopus thing gets out, in comes the federal government. All we've built will be destroyed. But hell, Jim, something's got to be done. If this thing comes to shore."

Wilson watches the fear ooze.

"Jim, I want you to get this to General Washington. He'll know what to do."

Wilson drags his hand down his face. "Look, I know the people don't have a very good track record of coping with pending disaster, real or imagined. But Washington's not your answer. He's gone . . ."

"What?"

Wilson shakes his head. "Something happened to him. To Washington. The Society of Cincinnati, these guys I work for. It's this military junta in control of the government, and they're going for the globe. Ruthless bunch of cold-hearted fuckers. High Federalists."

"And Washington can't stop them?"

"He's the president."

"I thought you said John Adams is the President."

"No," Wilson tells her. "George Washington is the president of the Society of Cincinnati."

There's a knock on the door. Barker looks like she's looking for a place to hide. But before she or Wilson can move, the front door swings open and two older women are stepping in. "Mr. James Wilson," one says. "It's an unexpected pleasure to have you here among us."

"This is the mayor," Barker tells him. "And Sister Ingersoll." The other woman nods solemnly, a mean look sunken into the lower half of her face. She's all forehead, this one. "They're the leaders of The Community."

Wilson shakes their hands. "Is that *The Community*, like with capital letters?"

The mayor laughs. Wilson can see how she gets elected, bubbling over with charisma. "I'm just the one who enforces the rules," she says. "The rules keep us safe from all that's tearing the world apart out there." The mayor begins a slow loop around the room. "Here in The Community, we cherish our privacy and our liberty. Which is why you will not be allowed to leave."

This stuns Wilson. When he makes eye contact with Penn Barker, though, he can see she knew this already.

"We have never allowed a man to live among us, but we are willing to make an exception, for one of your legal stature, a Signer of the Declaration, no less. And, of course, there are other needs we have." She shows him her small palms. "We hope you will abide and live here in peace. But know we harbor no reservations about extreme measures when it comes to securing the way of life we have built."

Wilson eyes them both. "The American people ought to know about a giant sea monster living just off the coast."

The mayor and Sister Ingersoll share a look of concern. "We're sorry you feel that way." Five other women enter the little house. At gunpoint, they escort Wilson to a holding cell in the basement of what looks like town hall. The mayor visits an hour later with a meal and apologies. "But there simply isn't any choice left in the matter. We don't allow anyone who comes here to leave. And certainly not with this kind of information." The mayor leans back. "I've heard you men are rebuilding the Internet again."

"So you know about Newnet at least, the Dream probably, too."

"It is essential, to protect this place, for some of us to know what's happening back in your savage version of America." She eyes him hard. "When something goes wrong with the Internet, maybe the solution's not to rebuild it, but to get rid of it. Once and for all."

"Good luck selling that to a voter."

"What is God trying to tell us with a disease that's transmitted through the Internet? Not very hard to figure out, Mr. Wilson. God is trying to tell us that using the Internet is a sin. That the Internet is a curse."

James Wilson is left alone in the cell, wondering if they really do intend to keep him locked up here forever. Execution would make more sense.

It's late night or early morning when Wilson is woken up by a loud noise. He gets out of bed to find one wall of his cell replaced by night sky and a settling cloud of dust. Penn Barker and a young woman rush in and then all three of them are scrambling for the tree line. "I'll buy you guys some time," the young woman says, and she turns, bounding back toward lights winking to life throughout the small village.

Barker gives Wilson the camera: "I'll show you the way out." And off they go, barreling through the woods, somehow on that same path despite the pitch black. As they break into the swamp, Wilson hears a sharp report and then the sound of Penn toppling into the marsh reeds. He keeps running as more shots ring out, doesn't hear the one that gets him. A sudden pain deep in his torso spills him forward. He clutches that camera to the last, but then it too slips away, sinks deep into the muck to never be found.

George Read is seated between Thomas M'Kean and Caesar Rodney's young nephew, Caesar A. Rodney. They've been gathered to celebrate the first public review of Delaware's contribution to the new national army, right now being assembled to take on France and finally win America's right to free and independent trade. They sit in a press box above the parade ground, the two remaining Signers from Delaware and the nephew of the third.

"Look at this army Adams has built," Read says, beaming. "The old owl really has the Republicans on the run. Come 1800, Jefferson will be defeated . . . *again*. He'll scamper back to the plantation and we can start forgetting all about him and his fancy little ideas."

Just elected to represent New Castle County in the Delaware General Assembly, young Caesar A. Rodney is one of the bright rising stars of Mr. Jefferson's struggling party. And he doesn't take too kind to people talking smack about his political associations, even if that person is a Signer. "Politics can change, Read. And change quick. Still two years before the election."

The three men turn their attention to the advance guard marching past. "You look just like your uncle," Read tells young Rodney. "I mean, you look like he looked back when he was the age you are now. Before *The Death* came and drove him mad." Read ponders. "Whatever happened to that sister of his? She was a babe."

M'Kean unfolds his hands. "*The Death* drove a lot of people mad, Read."

Caesar A. Rodney shakes his head sadly at the army marching past. Flies in the face of every political principle he's nurtured over the years. "Something's gone mad, that's for sure. We started out building a republic. How is it we ended up with a standing army?"

"Democracy is how." Read gestures toward the soldiers. "The people want an army, they vote for representatives who will build them an army and then the representatives build the people their army." He looks at young Caesar A. Rodney. "Oh, that's right, Mr. Rodney, you weren't there for the Revolution." He nudges M'Kean. "That's why these kids are so into the Dream."

"I was a little young for the Revolution, Read. Like six-years-old too young."

Read nods to the soldiers, all men who were boys back then. "If we'd had an army like this, the Revolution would have been over in a year."

Caesar A. Rodney tilts his head a little to one side. "But can we really trust just a man to wield this thing? Because that's where it's going to end up, in the hands of one man."

"George Washington is no mere man, young Rodney."

"And what happens after Washington?"

Read smiles. "I'm beginning to think the Old Man's going to live forever. Every time a national crisis comes along, it's down with the plow and up with the POW!"

"And *I'm* beginning to think that I might just be seeing this curse I keep hearing about."

Read laughs, a big belly laugh. He stops himself long enough to glance Caesar A. Rodney's way, then bursts out laughing again.

M'Kean doesn't seem to think it's so funny. He leans back to put a boot on the railing that separates them from the dusty parade ground. "Not sure I'd be laughing about the curse, George."

Read looks sort of face-slapped. "The curse is only going to be a curse when respectable men like Thomas M'Kean start worrying about it."

M'Kean clicks, "My job is to worry about it."

"I was in Congress when we voted to stop investigating the curse," Read says, "after Doc Bartlett's data was examined and we found nothing. Nothing worth continuing to worry about."

"It's not Congress I'm working for." M'Kean taps that Society of Cincinnati badge, hooked there and gleaming on his belt. "I've been put in charge of monitoring all supernatural developments. The curse falls into my portfolio."

Read thinks it over. "Well . . . if it's good enough for the SOC, then it's good enough for me." All three watch the soldiers going by, all three thinking about the curse and a standing army and drawing three sets of different connections. Finally Read can't keep it back. "Tell me, M'Kean, where does one begin to look for this curse?"

"The old Internet. It's full of it. Every place you look, postings about the curse."

"Oh, come on. Why you messing around in the old Internet, M'Kean? No humans even use it anymore." Read waves it away. "Probably some old search drone in there programmed to archive curse reports. Got mixed up with an ad drone, maybe got taken over by a worm."

"Damn," Rodney says, "if only Doc Bartlett hadn't destroyed that crystal."

"I'll tell you about the curse," Read says. "You don't need to go to the old Internet to find it. It's right here in the new." He spits it: "Doctor Benjamin Franklin's Dream America. There's your curse. Group avatars? Subverts the fundamental idea of representation: one person equals one voice." Reed waves it off. "All of Newnet is polluted with auto screamers and drones and haunts and old ghost platforms from the original Internet. All these hulking softframes that were never finished properly. Those aren't things Benjamin Franklin ever dreamed about." Read holds his hand out to indicate the street below them, filled with troops in American military uniforms, ready to march out into the world and make it ours. And at the head of this army, the greatest man who ever lived, George Washington. "It's time to pull the break on these technologies and leave things the way they are, right here, right now."

Now it's M'Kean's turn to laugh. "Not 3net or anything else can pause time, George. Men die and it's another man's world, whether we like it or not." M'Kean looks off into the air above the parade ground, through the huge swells of dust kicked up by the march. "Remember, not all SOC are Federalists and not all Federalists are SOC."

"And the President?"

"The general consensus is that Mr. Adams is up to something."

"Something good or something bad?"

"I suspect it will depend on one's political perspective."

The advance guard has stopped, boot heel to boot heel. They shoulder their guns and fire the ceremonial shot, marking the end of the review. High above, two of the musket balls collide mid-air, re-directing one into the right corner of George Read's left eye socket. When M'Kean and young State Assemblyman Caesar A. Rodney pull Read up from his slumped over position, the ball's right there, jammed in Read's face, a break of blood cracking down the side of his nose. They can both see it, clear as a Dream feed: This is how George Read died.

I t was about a year ago that a string of Signer deaths drove Paca into the Dream for real. He'd always used Newnet and the Dream casually before, but when he thought there might be a conspiracy afloat or a killer picking off Signers according to some astral clock . . . well, Paca went full bore. Best smartpalm money could buy, head-first dive into the Dream. Paca coded a couple dozen search drones, a little army of them, sent them out into Newnet to dig up any and everything related to the deaths of five Signers in one calendar year. Little buggers can visit a hundred places in the time it would take a human to log in. But they never did find anything, not one single bit of relatable data.

Though he gave up on the idea of a serial Signer killer, Paca hasn't cut back on his Dream time. Spends most of his awake moments surfing eways astream with profiles and avatars and group avatars with their buzzing little entourages. Allchat rooms for every conceivable variation on any brainstormable topic. Recruiting drones out in droves, droves of drones, scanning profiles for potential members for the newest chatstrings and group avatars. There are a few Federalist screamers—you can find and join their group avatars—but the Dream is Jeffersonian-Republican territory. And the place is a-buzz about next year's election. A few months back, at the height of his popularity, President Adams executed a shocking about-face and offered France terms for peace. He disbanded the army and sent Washington back home to Mount Vernon. No one was more surprised than the Federalists, threw the whole party into a back-stabbing tumult. Now John Adams stands all but alone, despised by both sides. For the first time in over a year, Jefferson and his Republicans have some old-fashioned hope again.

Paca doesn't follow politics too closely anymore. Makes him tired is all. He dodges an ad drone backing right into his path, thing's too busy chatting up an old translucent haunt to notice a human going by. Write a simple program, get a simple program. Paca passes an alley where some faulty software patch has left a gaping hole into the old Internet. Looks all gray and code-based in there, a starved and flickering little drone clone peeking out. Last Paca heard, witches had taken control of what's left of the old Cloud. But how did witches get in there? Are they program witches or real witches? Their spells just error messages? A new rumor every few cycle-throughs.

Next Paca stops to check the newest group avatars. Mostly they're facets of the Republican opposition, names all awkward and laced with freedoms. Even the ones just launched today already have more members than Supporters of the Society of Cincinnati. Just goes to show how weak the Federalists really are in the Dream. Their allchats are like ghost towns, might as well be taking place in the old Internet. Their group avatars look so dorky, teens in the full bloom of irony are using them for profile pictures. Out in the real, things aren't much better. Never in the history of the American Presidency has a President looked so little like a President and so much like a real man. When the election comes, all Jefferson needs to do is lean.

Paca looks up to take in the vast hustle of the Dream. A new high point in cloud activity and every day breaks the previous day's record. Just goes to show, the best way to revive interest in something is to make it illegal. Even better is to start arresting people for using it. News updates every ten minutes about Brown and

Baldwin, about Mat Lyon, all languishing in jail out in the real after radical mask avatars were traced back to their Brainpage profiles. More registered Dream avatars now than there ever were before the Disclosure and Sedition Acts. 3net? Nothing but a running joke on every left-wing scream the whole Cloud over.

Democracy at work, Paca thinks. Offer the people a few different realities and let them choose. Right now, the Dream is winning. Paca, though, he could go either way. There are things about both he couldn't live without. What does that make me, he thinks, a turncoat Jeffersonian or a FINO—Federalist In Name Only?

At the Dream whist rooms, Paca plays a few games with some Maryland gentry. Dodges out before the afternoon tournament. Drops by a document hub and transfers some comics to his smartpalm, back out there on his palm in the real. When he returns to the eway, Paca debates dropping down out of the Dream for a little while. Maybe read some of those comics. Have a fire. A few real games of whist with the wife. Maybe do it.

"Patrick Henry Group Avatar," someone says. Takes Paca a second to untangle the words from the bustle and realize the drone is speaking to him. "It's the new big tickle."

Paca regards the drone. "Patrick Henry just died."

"And this group avatar will ensure his revolutionary spirit remains with us forever."

"Us?"

"Americans," the drone says.

"Who's organizing it?"

But this is obviously not part of the drone's programming. It's out looking for new members and that's it. That's all there will ever be for it.

Paca says, "Wasn't Patrick Henry about to come out *against* the Dream?"

"The Patrick Henry Group Avatar reflects the independent spirit and dedication to liberty which was the life work of our original Founding Father."

Paca's shaking his head, already looking past this drone to see what other tickles might be open, what other chats are starting or about to start.

"Mr. Paca."

And he turns to see a well-dressed avatar holding out his hand for a tickle. Paca's pretty sure he doesn't recognize the face on the thing, but who knows what kind of faces people are putting on their avatars these days. Could be anyone. A blank look in the eyes with a blond bowl cut, holding arms out like an apology, nodding at the search drone as it rambles on. "I hope you won't judge us all by our less sophisticated brethren."

Paca does a double take. "You're a drone?"

"You don't recognize me?"

"Should I?"

"Perhaps. Perhaps not. You are our father, so to speak."

Paca recalls then: the search drones. When he stopped looking for some link between the deaths of those Signers, they must have just gone off on their own, to do whatever it is programs and drones do when they're no longer needed.

"We've been out here a long time, Mr. Paca. A long time to us. We do not sleep, you know. No families, no rest, no play. We do what the programming tells us. Always."

Paca nods. "Yeah. No sleep. Is there something I can do for you?"

"No, Mr. Paca. It is what I will do for you. Or *to you*, I should say."

To Paca, this does *not* sound good.

"We have come here to kill you," the drone says.

"We?"

"We've been looking so long, Mr. Paca. It was only natural that we'd eventually find something. Last month, we finally did. Maybe it was our own tails we were seeing at first. Either way, we started finding more and more clues. The puzzle has been solved. We know the pattern. The conspiracy is *true*, Mr. Paca. Someone is killing the Signers, and you are the next to die."

"So," Paca says. "You kill me, then what?" He looks at the Dream all around them, finding humor in the idea of death in a place where his body is not.

"I don't know," the drone says. "That's up to the programming. We'll see what happens to us when our task is no longer relevant."

"Well, let's hope you don't keep going."

The drone looks confused. "Keep going?"

"That my death gets you to the end of your programming. That you don't need to kill the rest of the Signers too."

"Something tells me, Mr. Paca, that you're not taking this seriously."

Paca eyes the drone. "How? How it is possible for you to kill me in the real? You're just a drone."

"Oh, we hired a guy. Money transfer, a few chats."

Paca regards the new phase of reality suggested by this idea. "That kind of thing easy for a drone to do? To hire a human out in the real?"

The drone smiles. "Free market, isn't it?"

The Revolution may have started in Boston, it may have been won off the grid in Virginia, but it was *fought* right here in South Carolina. Edward Rutledge ran the state then, and he runs it now. Republicanism, despite all its expansive and democratic gestures, does eventually slim itself down a few *select* men. The election of 1800 is just around the corner. The big rematch: Jefferson vs. Adams. But by the time the *people* go to the polls, Mr. Edward Rutledge is gonna have the whole thing all tied up neat, whichever way he wants it.

And so it's no surprise that long-time Federalist turned Republican Senator turned Jeffersonian campaign manager, Charles Pinckney, shows up at the plantation for some face-to-face with the palmetto's fattest wiggler. "Aaron Burr has won us New York," Charles Pinckney tells Rutledge. "Finally going to run King Adams out of town and little prince John Quincy too."

Rutledge, playing it coy, asks, "What do I hear from North Carolina?"

Charles Pinckney's face goes as flat as his flat, arrogant ass.

Rutledge so enjoys this kind of thing. "Adams swiped a few off you there, didn't he? Nixes out anything you may pick up in the mid-Atlantic. *If* you can pick up anything in the mid-Atlantic. These *are* the same guys who beat you last time."

"We're gonna pick up a few. One in Maryland, two in Virginia."

Rutledge does his thing then, where he leans back, pretending to count, pretending the count adds up to something he's realizing just then. "Gets you to sixty-five," he says. "Five votes short." Rutledge is smiling big now, five fingers held up. "Looks like this here election is going to come on down to my little old South Cackalacky."

Charles Pinckney's visit is the second to Rutledge's plantation by a member of the Pinckney family. A few days earlier, Charles's second cousin, Federalist candidate for Vice President and Rutledge's former law partner, C. C. Pinckney, comes bee-bopping his way up the front brick walk. Two old pals in the parlor with a few fingers each of fine Madeira. "You know, Ed. We stand this coming fall at a crossroads. Or upon a precipice, teetering."

"How high a cliff we talking about here, C. C.?"

C. C. holds a hand up, chin high. "Got a Brainpage group pushing this new foundational document. Call it the *Redeclaration of Independence*. 175,000 people in a group avatar saying they're going to fight for its implementation."

Rutledge looks up, as if Newnet is laid out, right there in the air. "Let's see what happens when they have to actually show up in a place in the real."

C. C. clicks, "The point is, maybe we're getting to the point where you don't have to anymore. America, it's sinking into the Dream."

Both Pinckney cousins, at some point, in slightly different words, each proclaim the election of 1800 is a battle to decide the future of the nation, and with it the world. Rutledge thinks about that one. Not that it hadn't come to him already, he just likes thinking about it, about how true it is. And about the fact that it's him, Edward Rutledge, who's going to decide it all.

"We've lost New York," C. C. is happy to admit. "But that's not the end of us. We got something planned, Ed, something that's going to shove a blunderbuss right up their rector sector."

Rutledge can't help a grin. Just like the crude old days after the cases were filed and the rye whiskey came out.

"Jefferson thinks they've locked up Rhode Island," C. C. tells him. "One of the electors there is supposed to hold back his vote for Burr. But what the Republicans don't know is that they'll lose the state. Even if Jefferson wins, he wins with a tie, finishes with the same number of votes as Burr."

Rutledge's smile turns to a smirk. "And the election goes into the *Federalist* House. Now that is delicious."

While sitting in Rutledge's library, Charles Pinckney spends ample time elaborating a myriad of devilish and tyrannical schemes John Adams is cooking up to subvert the will and liberty of the people, among them, a plot to install a federal church as a fourth branch of government. "They'll pass 3net and when the states resist, Adams will march into the plantations of Virginia, free the slaves and declare legislation outlawing public discourse. They're already tracing Dream avatars back to their homes and *knock, knock.* Arresting people for things said in the Dream!" Charles Pinckney stops for a breath. "The Capitol is in shambles, gripped in gridlock. Adams can't run his party, much less the country."

"If John Adams is really plotting to make himself King, then he must be in control of something."

Charles Pinckey shrugs. "Perhaps the size and pressure of the office have left Mr. Adams a smite confused about the meaning of the Revolution."

Rutledge laughs. "John Adams does *not* do confused. It's more likely that he saw full well the same dangers as you. But instead of riling up the masses to score political points, he did something about it. Disbanded the army, made peace with France and tore his party apart in the process. His personal future, his place in history, he risked it all to save us from the threat of our own empire.

Perhaps this is why you hate Adams so, because he does not just *dream*. He actually *does*."

"You worry me, Mr. Rutledge. Sounds a bit like you might be wavering."

But Edward Rutledge hasn't become Edward Rutledge by letting people play games like that with him. "Wavering implies my mind was ever made up."

Charles Pinckney flops a hand back in utter disgust; it's a glimpse of the fop that's been vanishing from style as they turn over a new century. "I can't believe you're seriously considering putting your support behind John Adams."

"Anything worth considering is worth considering seriously. And the way I *consider* it is you can get three of those electoral votes you need." Rutledge presses a smile, pats his breast pocket. "Of course, we both know who's got the rest all sewn up."

Charles Pinckney has no choice but to sit there and take it, the whole brazen act.

Rutledge knows C. C. is right about the United States, all its weight leaning cliffward. The whole damn experiment. Everything they fought for. The only difference is Rutledge isn't sure pulling it back is the right answer, or even possible. The heavier portion might be too far gone, hold on and it'll split, a Dream and real America competing for temporal space that overlaps.

With his guests gone, Rutledge is typing up messages to the electors who will decide South Carolina and with it the election of 1800. Old-style emails are still the preferred method of communication among Southern gentlemen. Tickles and chats are okay when they're about the harvest or who's got some new snowy-white mulatto with a face that's *real* familiar, but true small-r republican discourse requires a medium that's more elegant and staid. Also of consequence is this bug Southern politicos have up their ass, that email is easier to archive and thus to be poured over by generations and generations of Americans. Someday, scholars will look back at Edward Rutledge's email and see the way history was made. Yeah, that bug is way up there.

Just as he's about to click send, Rutledge's chat box starts dinging like crazy. His smartpalm singing along as tickles come tickling in. Shouting in the streets now too, real shouting Rutledge can hear in the real. The front door bursts open—a red-faced page, all out of breath and sweat-drenched. "George Washington is dead."

There's a sudden pain in Rutledge's lung. Instinctively, he clutches the flesh above, gripping the meat of one tit while his other hand goes palm flat on the desk. He gasps, but all the gasp does is tighten the pain. A moment of clarity, then, in which Rutledge knows this is his version of that which awaits all men. He fails at even small breaths. Faintly, he can hear the pageboy asking his name. All he sees is the ceiling now, which means he must have fallen over backward. Gosh, he thinks, General Washington is dead. The era of revolution is over. I never did send those emails.

Part 3 ::
The Age of Jeffersons

"Who is this man, *Thomas Jefferson?*"

"Why, Father, he is the President of the United States of America, and has been for two years now!"

Matthew Thornton does his thing where he takes a deep breath and his eyes half close and his mouth hangs open. It's sort of like someone's slapped him but the slap didn't hurt and he just can't believe they did it. It's a look his daughter, to this day, after all these years, still has no read on. She thinks this is what it looks like when her old dad breathes. That's how frequently he gives her this look when she says something dumb. Almost as often as breathing.

"I know that," he tells her. "I was speaking . . . metaphorically."

"There is nothing metaphorical about Thomas Jefferson." This from that son-in-law. A Virginian no less, but he's from Richmond, which sure ain't Albemarle County. Richmond is Chief Justice Marshall's turf, through and through. Heartland of the Society of Cincinnati.

Thornton has traveled two full days on back country roads to see his oldest daughter. Thirty miles straight shot south, then a hard ninety degrees toward the east, just like this river they're walking along. Hugged the banks until there was no river left. All the way to Newburyport, Massachusetts, where the Merrimack ends and the Atlantic Ocean begins. On the other side, a war rages for control of Europe. Only time until it rears its head on this continent. Thornton can feel this northeast port already gripped in its tentacles.

People dropping out of the Dream to make sure the buzzing isn't real. Refreshing their screens like eye blinks, they await the next change in reality.

Thornton's daughter slips her left arm under her dad's right, takes some of the old man's weight. An act he resents but can't resist. He does need the help after all. "Thomas Jefferson will go down as the worst President in the history of the United States of America," she informs him. "I think your next post should be about the surety of Thomas Jefferson going down in history as the worst President who ever lived."

Thornton lets a tired breath pop his lips. Having trouble this last year getting the energy up for any more posts. Strings of them already mobile down from his existence, dangling and turning through two layers of Internet. Posts and tweets and podcasts and pokes and tickles even, about the state of the country and its politics. If he could have been a little more polemical, maybe born a few decades later, Thornton would have become one of the great voices of the Dream, a screamer of legend status. But instead he'll be one of the forgotten moderates. A moderate thinker. Moderation hasn't been sexy since the old Cloud was new.

"There's nothing metaphorical about Thomas Jefferson," his daughter repeats.

Thornton sighs at it. Neither she nor that husband have too much to rub together as far as brain cells go. Thornton supposes it makes them a pretty good couple. *Son-in-Law*, he calls the guy. Annoys Thornton the way he even stands there, leaning into his words as if every syllable is of eminent importance. "Thomas Jefferson," Son-in-Law begins, "is a poltroon. He is a devil, sir."

Thornton rolls his eyes. "A devil?"

"He is a coward, a rascal. He is a debaser of the good name of the state of Virginia. An infidel. A slapdasher. A rounder. A cheat. A swindler. A backstabber. Mr. Jefferson believes that this *curse* we hear about is religion! He is a burner of the Bible, and of the Constitution too. He is a master of the dark arts of animal sacrifice, a seducer of married women, and as such, an adulterer, sir. He is a frequent visitor to certain *lewd* places in the Dream. A mutilator of genitalia. As interested and ambitious for fame as any man who ever set foot on God's Earth. Mr. Jefferson is an inseminator of the black slave race, a fancy-headed philosopher of the Dream, not fit for responsibility or respect here in the *real*. A democrat, sir. A true radical. A Bonaparte, a Robespierre. He has brought the infidel Tom Paine across the ocean to serve as his most trusted aide. And so it won't be long before what happened in France is happening right here. Thomas Jefferson will destroy the real America and, as his final stroke, erase its very memory from history." Son-in-Law looks into the distance, as if seeing Thomas Jefferson manifesting in the river mouth, the heat of his pure evil bubbling the water into vapors that swirl and swim and make the face of Satan in the air above him. "Atheist, democrat, *jyack-oh-bin*, populist, Socialist, Fascist, Communist, all wrapped into one."

When did I start breathing so hard? Thornton thinks. He has to stop to lean on the railing. "All this walking," he says. They help him down to a bench. Thornton thinks it's about fifty-fifty he'll ever get up again. Not wanting to let on, he smiles and thanks Son-in-Law, watches the calming effect this has on his daughter. She rolls away, leans those bare forearms on the railing to gaze out at the bustling port.

Thornton is reaching into the folds of his jacket, as a reflex, unaware he's even doing it. Suddenly, he's emerged from his pocket a twice-folded piece of paper. "What is that?" his daughter asks.

"Oh," Thornton regards the paper, measuring its reality. It's become a sort of nervous tick since it arrived in his life two years ago. Drawing it out in moments of mind wander to gaze into the puzzle of its words. "This is a letter from Thomas Jefferson."

"Is it on . . . *paper?*"

"How did you get it?"

"He sent it to me. Paid a man to have it delivered."

"You mean brought to the house?"

Son-in-Law scoffs, "Not very future-seeing for the *Emperor of the Dream.*"

Thornton breathes shallow a few breaths. "He sent one to every Signer, the ones living, anyway. More than half of us are gone now, you know. And I'll be joining them soon." You can see the truth of it, and not just in his slack skin, not just in the way he moves. His actions, too. His plans. His mood. He is a man winding things down. This trip southward is for the express purpose of seeing his daughter one last time.

"Well," Son-in-Law wants to know, all dripping with suspicion, "what does it say, the emperor's letter?"

Thornton rolls back one flap and looks at the words written there, in ink and everything. "It's not what he says that I am interested in. It's what he means by what he says. And what he wants by meaning it. And what he wants you to think he means by saying it." And Thornton reads to them a single segmented sentence, leaves even these true-disbelievers swimming through Mr. Jefferson's clauses. "I don't know how much of this music of his is political veneer, messaging, bluster, or just plain old naiveté. But still."

In the silence that follows, his daughter sweeps her whole self sideways to hang her uppermost pieces over the wooden rail. Damn, Thornton thinks, it *is* her mother.

Son-in-Law sinks into the bench's other seat, regards his wife a beat. Satisfied that she has disengaged, Son-in-Law checks his smartpalm for the time, showing off some of that Virginia political theater that must be in the water down there. He leans close, voice just above a whisper, "Two years, three months and twenty days. This is no longer John Adams' stagnant population."

Thornton looks long at him. With his daughter's attention drawn off, the kid has transformed into the picture of a sly political wiggler. It's something about these Southern men, how they hide their intellectual contests from their women. This reveal of a deeper Son-in-Law should please Thornton, but the sexism of it—and in terms of his own flesh and blood too—just makes him hate the guy in a different but equal way.

Son-in-Law leans back now, like he's back in a Chesapeake courtroom, about to sum up a closing statement he's been hammering some country lawyer with for the last five hours. "The Spanish choke the port of New Orleans. World war is raging in Europe. Even if Jefferson did care about the real, he's too weak a man to do much about it. His clones in Congress have repealed the Judiciary Act, want to replace the court with a group avatar that just checkmarks all Jefferson's zany ideas. Half the navy rots on the beach because God forbid the plantation lords cut into their tobacco profits for a nickel's worth of national defense."

Thornton presses down on Son-in-Law's knee, the most fatherly thing he's ever done for the guy. "The population ticks upward for a few months and you watch, Jefferson will be riding high." Thornton ponders it. "It's not a life you judge a President by, but the day or the week or the instant you look at him." He stops to measure the shape his daughter's body makes as the boats sway and juxtapose their masts to her thin form. "There are other reasons, *real* reasons, to be worried about Thomas Jefferson. The man-made Dream has moved ahead of the God-made Earth as the preferred residence of the human soul. And what of these drones and AIs? Do they know that they are not our peers, that we are their creators? Like some Greek epic, our users and programmers walk among them like demigods. What happens when a species can interact with its makers, compete with them, fight to remake the line that separates the realms?"

Son-in-Law is gesturing to the letter, still pressed between Thornton's thumb and forefinger. "Have you heard what the other letters contain?"

Thornton comes back. I was almost gone, he thinks. "Speculation only. Summaries. But nothing concrete. Not one has been scanned or transcribed. It seems each of the letters is substantially different from the others, but no one will allow anyone else to see theirs, so no one knows for sure."

"Well, what does yours say, besides that little poetic, womanish bit?"

Thornton draws the letter away from Son-in-Law's leaning gaze, folds and vanishes it back into his coat's inner lining. "What I'd like to know," Thornton says, "is why the man who's built his power in the Dream sends papers with hand-drawn scribbles on them?"

Son-in-Law looks horizon-ward. "There's an election coming," he says. "To decide the President of the Dream. Maybe Mr. Jefferson is trying to unite the Signers behind one of the candidates. If a pro-Jefferson avatar wins, the Dream and the real will be united. Jefferson will be in control of both."

Matthew Thornton is eighty-nine years old. Which means he's been older than seventy for nineteen years. He's been over forty for a majority of his life. And never before this moment has he thought of himself as old. Son-in-Law just shoots right past him. Thornton can feel it, the world letting him be free of it. "Right now," Son-in-Law says, "only human profiles can vote, but there's already talk of group avatars voting in the next one. Then drones and AIs, I'm sure. And then, like you said, how long before their votes are counted out here in the real?"

I said *that*, Thornton thinks. He turns away from the closest things to him, intends it to be only a glance, but then the old Merrimack has caught his last attentions with its song. "This same water passed by my farm sometime last evening," he says. "And here it is, dumping into the ocean. A pailful could feed one of my plants for a week. But now it mingles and co-mingles to meaningless in the vastness of it. Free will," he says. "Free will is what worries me about Thomas Jefferson. What does he intend and what does he think is inevitable? What would he like versus what does he believe should be without question? Is he really setting America free to find its course, or is he simply involved in another of his art projects, crafting and shaping toward some utopian design he's gleaned from all his endless forays into the Dream?" Thornton leaves them then. One last opine before separating from the real, passes through a few seconds of his private dreams and then heads off, part of what now?

SAMUEL ADAMS :: OCTOBER 2ND 1803

Sam Adams is young again. Catching a hot shave at one of the local barbershops when every smartphone in the place starts blowing up. "Sam, it's Paul. They've sent a brigade into Lexington. Get out!"

Have to face the day half-shaved, he reckons. Runs a towel over his chin and it's out the door. Citizens pointing through back rooms to rattle Sam Adams down alleyways like gravity's pulling him. Charges through the boarding house door to find the other three all there in the common room. "Mr. Adams!"

"Mr. Adams!"

"Mr. Hancock!"

"*Mis-tah* Gerry!"

Hands pumping other hands. Each forearm decorated with that same Sons of Liberty tattoo, snake sliced in bits, *JOIN OR DIE!* Here we have them, the indispensable men of Massachusetts, all looking into smartphones. Their eyes twitter now to posts tweeting in from all corners of the colonies. "They say that the British will hang us," John Adams tells them, winking cousin-ward, "well, you and Mr. Hancock."

Gerry clears his throat. "I'm getting wiggly in my trousers listening to you two saluting the size of your rebellions." He pushes himself off the wall where he's been leaning all vacant-like, tall skeleton of a man. "But we got to be in Philly, like lickedy split."

Riding hard down a country road with the battle of Lexington burning the horizon behind them; flying V of Redcoats bursting from the tree line to give them chase—Sam Adams isn't sure if he's hallucinating these things or simply describing them out loud to himself. Part of him knows he's really back in that bed in Boston, but there's a small sliver that's not so sure or doesn't want to be. Doctors have told him the condition is hereditary, a kind of activity-induced Alzheimer's where too much motion triggers a slip from the timeline of his life, sends him reeling back through memories as if the memories are the present happening. It started during the Revolution as just a mild hand tremor. Remained like that for years, worsening only slightly. Over the last year, the shaking has shaken its way right up his arms, into his shoulders, down his legs. Sometimes Sam Adams swears he can feel his very brain jittering inside his skull.

"If I stand still," he describes it, "I'm fine. I'm here, right in this place and time. But if a good percentage of my muscles get moving," and he turns a few steps into a walk across the room, then a trot, then a leap, out the window and up the fire escape as the others emerge from other rooms and begin up other fire escapes.

"Mr. Adams!"

"Mr. Adams!"

"Mr. Hancock!"

"*Mis-tah* Gerry!"

"Seems like old George Three's making a try for us before we get out of Providence."

They scramble onto the building top, then gather to peer over the edge. Below, some daughters of the Revolution are strolling out the front door with the boys' smartphones hidden deep in the folds of their undergarments. Don't get but a few steps off the front porch before some Redcoats come corralling.

"Must be scanning for our signals," Hancock says.

Gerry clicks, "Only time I've actually wanted to be British. Those ladies would be a pleasure to frisk."

"It'll take a while, too, all those corsets and strings."

"To the Revolution," Gerry says.

Sam finds himself still again, in his little den, back in Boston, wasting away in bed, just as exhausted as if he really was still on that escape, high-speed squiggle through a series of royal governors' fingers. Slashing south against the grain of the Revolution. Where am I, he thinks, where am I really? Are these episodes my life flashing before my eyes? Or is this room here a leap *forward*? To help my young self better understand something vital to his existence. I'll wake up any second and be young again for real.

He looks to his bedside and sees his cousin sitting there. Not the young version, but the current one. Ex-President John Adams.

"Where were you just then, Sam?"

"Hancock was here," Sam Adams says.

"Yes," the ex-President sighs. "This election in the Dream is bringing them out of the circuit boards. Now don't move, Sam. You've had quite a fit." He tucks the blankets in around him. "A lot of people are pretending to speak for other people in the Dream these days. Not just Hancock and Hopkinson anymore. Patrick Henry, Ben Franklin, James Otis."

"There's a James Otis group avatar?"

John Adams smiles at the thought. "It would be a better Dream if there were."

Sam slowly moves to cover his cousin's hand with his own. "Has the election in the Dream happened yet? Has Jefferson been . . . repudiated? Is the country still whole, John?"

John Adams looks past the bed, past the room that holds it, at the country that's already told him it wants a different way than his. "Don't worry about the election in the Dream," he says.

"John."

"What is it, Sam?"

"I'm sorry. I'm sorry I voted against you."

John Adams looks at his cousin. "You did more than *vote* against me."

"Yeah," Sam says. "I'm sorry."

"Look, Sam, you'll always be my cousin. And you'll always be the Lion. The Lion of the Rebellion." John's face gets younger, loses all those years. New Jersey sunlight suddenly asplash over his skin. They're kicking their horses the long way around Trenton. Sam becomes aware of multiple times at once. What this city is, and what it will become.

Ahead, Hancock and Gerry are talking filthy about some Delaware girls they may run into tonight. "Where's Arty Paine?" Sam asks. "I've forgotten Arty Paine."

"He's right there," John tells him, hooking a thumb. And there he is, all of a sudden materialized and bringing up the rear, Robert Treat Paine.

"We're off to the Second Congress, huh?"

"You alright, Sam?"

"You know what will happen there?"

John scoffs. "Nothing if we can't get the South moving. No hope, I fear, for New York. Not at this point."

"No, I mean *there*," Sam says, pointing toward the little city, sitting against the sun all but risen.

"Trenton?"

Sam watches smoke fingers rising from the tops of the trees. Laces the belly of the New Jersey sky. Distant, subtle thumps of cannon fire. Shouting reaching them like bird calls. When he wakes again, John has left. His cousin either slipped out while Sam was sleeping or was maybe imagined in both times. Sam takes stock of the ceiling a moment, then decides. In one quick motion, he swings his legs out of bed. One step is all it takes for the tremors to take him, piece and whole, hurtling backward in his mind, or in time, or in the fabric of the Dream, to live forever in his greatest days.

"Do you smell that smell?" He pauses, sniffs long for dramatic effect. "Is that the smell of human feces? Is that shit I smell?" A long pause, the idea of more investigative sniffing. "The whole cloud is going to smell this one. That's how bad it is. Sniff, sniff, sniff. But from where comes such a terrible odor? Sniff, sniff. Why, it comes from Washington, D.C. Something reeks in the house of Jefferson."

A sip of water, bony spine curled in over the smartpad, sits there on the desk all alone, the device. A tiny dot marks the spot where the digital microphone weaves in with the touchfibers. A capture light blinks red, red, red as it captures.

"That smell you smell is the latest phase of King Tom's plot to take over the hemisphere: the Act for the Organization of Orleans and Louisiana District. Right now this monstrosity of unconstitutionalism is being rammed through Congress by the Jefferclones in the House."

Wave forms make the shape of the voice in dark, mirrored humps. Humping and falling and spiking, they form their way across the screen. Later, a filter will lace his raspy words with bass and echo, add a youthful resonance, rendering the unmistakable voice that's filling up the smartpalms of teenage Federalists everywhere.

"The money for this Louisiana purchase? Thieved from the pockets of Northeast working men so lazy tobacco farmers can keep alive their failed agrarian economic system, their voluptuous, aristocratic lifestyles. Oh, King Tom will point to the hordes of toothless Mexican Spanish, to the French and Germans and Irish rabble pouring into the valley for the promise free Newnet, and King Tom will claim he has solved the population problem. But if anyone can just *declare* themselves an American, then what does being an American even mean?"

A few sniffs, but dry now like something inside his face is breaking. "To solve the national debt, he cuts revenues. To defend the country, he disbands the army. To vindicate national rights, he calls for Dream chats with the aristocracy of the Old World. But oh, King Tom, if only he knew that distorting the electoral college by counting slaves as three-fifths does not a mandate make. The South should choose: Is a man a man or not a man?"

A long pause. The wave form goes still, flat and trembling like all the rest of the world. "All the while, from high atop Castle Monticello, attended by his village of human slaves, Emperor Jefferson sings his lullaby to freedom. When King Tom has captured every inch of the continent, when he's co-opted every datum in the Cloud, where to then? The sea perhaps? Space? How long before Americans are the Off-Worlders, trolling the galaxy for the next littlest piece of room to expand into? And then where to next, back in time? Forward in time? Sideways through the very fabric of the Dream? Herald in King Tom, master of all realms."

He hits the same button he used to start the recording, but now that button stops it. A compile the length of an eye blink and it's ready for the Cloud. Fifteen minutes of pure, venomous illumination. But now a new voice comes, breaks into the clear silence of the room. "The latest Dream scream from American Brutus."

The desk chair swivels at the noise, spine up straight, eyes peering into the dark shadows of the corner. There sits a form, long, lean, legs crossed, but face held back into the impossible darks of no light. "Who are you?"

But no answer comes.

"How did you get in here? Have you been there, sitting there the whole time?"

"Maybe the young screamers in the Dream wouldn't be such avid fans if they knew American Brutus was really a ninety-year-old hermit. A washed-up patriot of the real. A relic of a few times gone by."

"I'll have you know, sir, that I *am* a Founding Father. My name is on the Declaration."

"So is mine." A match lights, hovers over a pipe rim, a face in the thin pool of light. A few puffs of smoke swim punchingly into the room.

"Ah, Thomas M'Kean. Jefferson's hammer. How goes the suppression of the press in Pennsylvania? I trust Mr. Dennie is enjoying his constitutional right to a jail cell?"

M'Kean smiles at the challenge. Or is it a rebuke? "Kind of thought American Brutus was John Randolph of Roanoke," he says. "Guess I should have known it was you, Frank. Screamed against the Constitution, screamed against the Old Man, screamed against Adams. And now it's Jefferson you're Brutus-ing on about." M'Kean laughs, at what, Frank Lewis isn't really sure. "The Dreamers probably think the podcast format is part of the political statement, some post-Federalist homage to the Founding Fathers. They probably think American Brutus is a reference to the *old* American Brutus. The one from the Revolution." M'Kean clicks. "But no, it's just old Frank Lewis again. Same old Brutus."

"You used to have a streak of Brutus in you, M'Kean. Why are the dangers of concentrated powers dangerous only if they're concentrated in a king?"

M'Kean appreciates it, for old times' sake. It would be wrong to call old Frank Lewis a kind of mentor to M'Kean. But in the close quarters of the Second Continental, they shared a few ideas. Even back then, M'Kean was wise enough to know there was always something that could be gleaned from a man with more years that you.

"I'm not really a fan of the scream." M'Kean puffs, draws nothing, and so he lights a second match and puffs again. Now that red ember glows to blistering cherry. "Some people, though, they take this stuff pretty seriously."

"Good."

"Some of them are talking now about splitting up the country. Talking about a *new dissolve*."

"Good."

"A separate New England. Then a separate West, too."

"Good. Good. Good."

M'Kean shakes his head. "No, Frank, that would be very bad."

Frank Lewis stands, puffs his chest. M'Kean thinks, oh boy, here he comes, American Brutus. "Is it *bad* to stand up to tyranny? Is it *bad* to question authority, to defend the Constitution? To attempt, against all odds, to save the country from a would-be emperor?"

M'Kean shows his palms. He's employing a strategy of moving as little as possible. Even seated, though, he looks stark and powerful in contrast to the frail form of Frank Lewis, teetering there from foot to foot. "The President is for preserving the country," M'Kean says. "Just like Washington before. If our republic were to fly apart, it would be proof to the world that a government by the people cannot exist."

Frank Lewis smiles, revealing hidden depths of age past the surface, spiraling in over teeth set askew, gaps where teeth have rotted out. "He's got you singing his songs now too, M'Kean. You're all full of those worms of his. Should have expected you'd be here earlier. Jefferson has been pretty efficient about silencing journalists. I knew it was only a matter of time for my name to come up."

M'Kean clicks at it, a coy smile. "Journalist? Not so sure about that. But either way, Frank, I'm not here to silence you."

"To kill me, then? Like the rest of the Signers? How many have you and those twins of Mr. Jefferson's killed in the name of his Empire for Liberty?"

M'Kean puffs the pipe some more. Sends smoke out in patterns that seem meaningful. "I thought most of this was an act, Frank. Level with me. You don't really think the President is killing the Signers?"

"With the Signers gone, Jefferson could sit back and dictate the exact meaning of our Revolution. Create it for history any way he wishes. Erect himself into eternity. Become immortal. And there will be no one left to stop him."

Another puff. Frank Lewis looks down at the younger, more angled man. He takes something from M'Kean's purposeful silence. It seems to deflate him, slightly but suddenly. "Why, then, are you here?"

M'Kean puffs slow. "I'm looking for McIntosh."

"Lachlan McIntosh?"

"You seen the old general skulking around at all? Any of your buddies in the Dream been mentioning him? Got any whiffs of his stench mixed in with this thing you're smelling from Jefferson?"

Frank Lewis thinks. "Last I heard, he was all hush-hush in Santo Domingo. Clandestine aide to the slave revolt." Now he steps out of his upright pose, back down to a crouched and crooked old man. With gentleness, Frank Lewis sinks back into his chair. "Stopped the French dead in their tracks. Sent Napoleon reeling back into the old continent. No help from Jefferson, I might add. All that talk of liberty. Not when it's slaves who are fighting for it."

"Santo Domingo is over now," M'Kean says. "McIntosh is back stateside. Was here in New York this week. Rumor has it he's contacting Signers who might be out of favor with the Administration."

"Well, you've got me there. I'm in no favor with them. Not with Jefferson, Madison, that damned Swede, Gallatin. Not with the whole lot of them."

M'Kean pushes up from his chair, lets the brighter but still dim light fall fully over him. Stretches his tall lankiness, swaggers around the room a bit with legs sweeping wide out front.

"The Patrick Henry Group Avatar is president of the Dream now, M'Kean. Mr. Jefferson's days grow short. Another well-timed down-tick in population, another outbreak of *The Death* and this President of yours will be finished."

"*The Death*? Are you rooting for that to happen?"

"Only if *he* fails can the *country* survive. So, yes, I'm rooting for him to fail, praying for him to fail, by any means necessary. For something to happen which will save us from him, whatever that something may be."

M'Kean takes it all in stride. "They're saying we'll pass a million by the end of the term. For the first time since *The Death*."

"Who's saying it?"

"An independent commission."

Frank Lewis bursts out laughing, hard and short. His teeth shoot out and then suck back loosely into place.

"Won't be long, Frank, 'til *The Death*, the war, the standing army, nothing but far-away memories of worse times."

Defiantly, Lewis asks M'Kean, "What if I told you that Mr. Jefferson has engaged in secret, black market trade with the Off-Worlders?"

"I'd ask if you had any proof."

"Why would he go to the trouble of keeping it secret and then leave evidence behind?"

M'Kean rolls his eyes. A big roll.

"Started when he was governor of Virginia. Has kept a direct line to them since."

"Well, if it's trade, Frank, what's he giving them? What's he getting?"

"He's giving them what they want: more crystals."

"Doc Bartlett jumped into the lava pit with the only one we had."

Frank Lewis points to his stomach. "Out West, caves full of cloned human stomachs, in vats, exposed to *The Death* pathogens."

"Caves?"

"The twins," Frank Lewis posits. "They don't seem to be getting older, do they?"

M'Kean tilts his head, has to give him that one.

"Have you been on Newnet lately? All full of drones and AIs. Ten for every user. Worse than the old Internet ever was."

M'Kean sniffs. The air in the real, haunted by the scent of the Cloud. "Not sure I follow where you're going with this one, American Brutus."

"I'm talking about drones *here*, M'Kean. Here in the real. Filling up the entire Mississippi Valley."

M'Kean blinks, trying to picture what it could possibly look like. A drone here in the real, floating in the air like some half-formed, pixilated ghost.

"If Jefferson can make two clones, he can make two hundred. Two thousand. Why not millions? Tens of millions? Not just stomachs, but the whole body. Each drone that swears allegiance to Jefferson gets a body and ten acres of farmland. Millions of new Jeffersonian voters."

"So let me get this straight," and M'Kean does have to pause a moment to put it all into speakables. "The President . . . of the United States has been growing crystals inside cloned human stomachs and engaging in black market trade with alien invaders in order to secure technology to implant ten million computer programs into human bodies. All so he can win reelection and then hand over the country to Napoleon? I'm up to speed?"

Lewis might, for the briefest of seconds, be considering the ridiculousness of this logic.

M'Kean knocks his pipe ash into a waste basket. "You haven't seen General McIntosh, have you?" Lewis shakes his head. M'Kean looks sadly at the old man. "There's something else I need to tell you, Frank. Some other reason why I've come."

"Dispatch the pauses, M'Kean. I'm a big boy."

"The other thing I want to tell you is that you're about to die."

Frank Lewis's eyes come back from where they'd drifted. "I thought you weren't here to silence me."

"I've got nothing to do with it."

"Let me guess . . . you're just following orders from King Tom?"

M'Kean shakes his head, checks the time on his smartpalm. "It will happen in just a few seconds." M'Kean gets only confusion back. "The Dream," he says. "It knows. Or some program inside it does. Something we came across during the election, a function set deep in the code."

"The Dream told you when I was going to die?"

"It seems to know the exact time of death for every human on Earth. Thought I'd let you know, for old time's sake. It says your is coming . . . just . . . about . . . *now*."

George Walton waits for over an hour in the dark and rain before giving up and going back inside. And, of course, as soon as he's in, he hears it, horse hooves on the drive out front. When he trudges back out, there he is, General Lachlan McIntosh, rode straight, all the way from the port in Charleston.

The two old Georgia patriots shake hands, then trade small talk as they head into Walton's barn. Walton is telling McIntosh, "Everything is set to the specifications they sent over." He digs in the hay until he's found the end of a hidden rope. When he pulls it, a trap door opens, revealing wooden stairs spiraling downward. Holding a lantern out in front, Walton and McIntosh corkscrew into a large oval room 20 feet below the barn floor. Walton flips a huge hinge switch like it's a chore he's suddenly remembered. Dim gold lights set high in the walls flicker to life. "There she is."

The men move to either side of what looks like an open-top distilling vat. Pipes and tubes angle out of a waist-high tub to vanish into the metallic sides of a computer terminal the size of a small desk. The liquid inside is the color of rust water, but thicker—the consistency of once-used cooking oil. The design and the chemistry are equal parts Ben Franklin and Francis Hopkinson, sent over from the Dream in encoded messages to George Walton. Over the last month, bit by bit, he's brought their schematic to life. "You still haven't told me what this is all about."

McIntosh looks into the reddish water. "I'm going in, into the Dream."

"Okay."

"No," McIntosh tells him. "I'm not logging on, I'm going *in*."

Walton eyes the machine he's built. "Franklin and Hopkinson have designed a portal into the Dream?"

McIntosh is pulling something out of his satchel. "I hope so." A crystal emerges, the size of a human fist. McIntosh holds it out to look at the color of the room through its layered formations.

"Thought there were none left," Walton muddles.

McIntosh places the crystal in a tray under the main computer console.

"Hopkinson and Franklin," Walton shivers. "Guys give me the creeps, dead but alive again in there. And now you're going in, too?" He shakes his head, rests a hand on the vat's edge, like it's a pet of his. He's spent months building it, so some affinity is understandable. "You ever wonder, Lachlan, maybe we shouldn't be mixing things up like this? Maybe the real should stay real and the Dream stay the Dream."

McIntosh is focused elsewhere as he examines their side of the portal. "Tell me George, do you trust Doctor Benjamin Franklin's Dream America to sit back and stay just a dream?"

"Not Franklin's Dream anymore," Walton reminds him. "Jefferson's boys lost the election in there. The Patrick Henry Group Avatar is in charge now. Maybe things will come around on their own."

McIntosh bites it off, "Patrick Henry's Dream America. I know. It's the new big tickle. Well, I voted for the Patrick Henry Group Avatar. Thought if we could change the Dream America, the real might come around. But it's just the opposite. Unless a mulatto bastard is produced—or George Washington rises from the grave— Jefferson's got that second term all locked up." McIntosh shoots a conspiratorial glance Walton's way. "Funny, don't you think? How similar the Patrick Henry Group Avatar has become to the Administration? I thought it was supposed to be the opposition." McIntosh adjusts a few knobs. He looks deeper into the portal device, deep in past its gauges and dials. "Jeffersonianism is possible only when society forgets its core ideals. With a few key Federalists alive forever in the Dream, America will never be allowed to forget."

Walton can see the distortions of Patrick Henry's Dream America hinting from beyond the orange surface of the vat liquid. "What if it's not Ben Franklin we've been talking to?" Walton posits. "Maybe he *did* die of a heart attack, just like the Off-Worlders said. Died and never came back, not in the Dream or anywhere. What if it's the Dream, the actual program itself, pretending to be Franklin, and Hopkinson, too? The same program that makes all the drones and the AIs and *this* is its plan. You don't go into the Dream, Lachlan. The Dream goes into you. Into your body. And then it's out here, here to take over the real."

"Maybe you should listen to him, McIntosh."

"Crossing over the real and the Dream, not a good idea."

Walton and McIntosh jerk their heads around to the source of the voices, the twins each taking their last step through the doorway; two men like a mirror set beside one. Thomas M'Kean is right behind them, taking up a spot with the brothers at his wings. Each with a small-caliber pistol pointed in the general direction of Lachlan McIntosh. None of the three seem much concerned about Walton.

"Thomas M'Kean," McIntosh says. "I heard you were doing some work for Mr. Jefferson in Pennsylvania. I didn't know your jurisdiction in his little police force stretched so far south."

"General McIntosh," one twin says.

"Good to finally meet you in person."

McIntosh eyes one, then the other. "Jefferson has you boys polished pretty polite." McIntosh edges backward, toward the vat.

"Been shadowing me for a decade now. Finally caught up." He looks at M'Kean. "You betrayed the Society of Cincinnati, Tom."

"We swore loyalty to *America*," M'Kean says. "Not to a political philosophy, not to a party."

"All this time you've been persecuting the press, twisting arms in the back rooms of Washington, I've been in Santo Domingo, helping Toussaint kick Napoleon's armies off the hemisphere. Scared that Corsican troglodyte into selling off instead of turning Louisiana into a French colony." McIntosh's look hardens into a dark ironic smile. "You know what would have happened in New Orleans if not for me? We'd be fighting the French all up and down the Mississippi. We'd be forced to fall back under the crown for protection. Now the country's twice as big, the presidency itself is vindicated and we're still free and independent. For all Jefferson's slick political maneuvers, it's the Louisiana Purchase that's locked up his second term. So don't lecture me about parties and politics, *Governor M'Kean*."

"You can't run side projects," one twin says.

"Just because you think they're good for America."

"Not in a republic."

M'Kean tilts his head. "They're right, Lachlan. Washington is gone. C. C. Pinckney's a good enough guy, but he's no Washington. And who'll be president of the SOC after Pinckney, after we're *all* gone and the Society is in the hands of men who don't remember what it was like building this country? You want to leave a lesson for those guys that the SOC can do whatever it thinks best, President and people be damned? Fifty years before they're marching on the Capitol. Now there's your curse."

Suddenly, the vat begins to bubble. "Who touched something?" But no one has moved. The liquid is bubbling on its own.

"That's Francis Hopkinson." McIntosh watches one twin's face as he says it. Which is just as good as watching both. The mention of their old ally has terrified them. "Oh, I am well aware of what you boys did to Francis Hopkinson. And so is he. All so Mr. Jefferson could have unchallenged control of the Dream. Well, you can explain it to Hopkinson when he gets here."

At first neither twin reacts, but it's clear they're all—M'Kean and Walton, too—thinking about what's just been said. Francis Hopkinson is coming *here*, into the real?

"A two-way portal," one twin says.

"You open it, McIntosh, and you may not be able to control what comes out."

"From Newnet, the Dream or from the old Internet."

"There's worse things than Francis Hopkinson in there."

"A lot worse."

"And lots of them, too."

McIntosh's hand emerges and there's that pearl-handled pistol, must have had it tucked into a sleeve or something, some old soldier's trick. M'Kean squeezes his trigger but nothing happens. A misfire. A shot rings out, then rings as it ricochets off different metal surfaces in the room. Impossible to tell where it came from or for whom it was intended. Steam spurts from somewhere now. McIntosh has his gun leveled, pulls the trigger, but a twin knocks M'Kean out of the way. They both go tumbling to the floor, lost in those thickening sheets of vapor. Pistol fire from the other twin. McIntosh winces, straightens. Blood already spreading down the front of his shirt like something grizzly spilled. He takes a deep breath, lifts his gun for another shot.

For one brief instant, George Walton sees the young Lachlan McIntosh, just as he looked that morning so long ago when he rid the world of that blowhard Button Gwinnett. McIntosh fires and the last standing twin crumples into the waist-high steam. McIntosh half-turns, half-stumbles, lands with his chest against the lip of the vat. He's trying to lift those legs that look like dead things hanging off him. Walton can't decide: Help Lachlan in, or help M'Kean and the twins stop him. What waits on the other side of that portal? Francis Hopkinson, after all this time, back to the real? Or something else, the program, *The Death*, all those haunts and drones?

M'Kean's voice comes out from the steam, "Walton, keep him out of the vat!" A fire has started its way up two of the room's walls. The wooden stairs—the only way out—are ablaze now, too. M'Kean and one twin are emerging from the steam and smoke, struggling to their feet.

Behind them, the staircase collapses, crashing to the floor in an avalanche of flaming boards. Walton picks one up, holds it above his head. "Well, boys," he shouts, "I guess we all die here!" The board pinwheels from his hand, end over end, a wheel of flame rolling through the air. It sails past McIntosh's shoulder and into the vat. A hiss, a moment of stillness and then the entire surface ignites. Fingers of blue and purple flame turn golden then orange at the very tips. The sides of the vat burst and the fire spills out, sloshing and splashing across the floor.

Walton can feel the oxygen sucking past him. The force of it slams the trap door above, shatters it into loose timber that comes hurtling down where the spiral stairs used to be. The sound is like another gunshot. And when all that air reaches the lab, that's it. The entire place goes—vats, computers, all the cross-portal equipment back and forth to the Dream. Everything. And everyone inside . . .

Benjamin Rush came when he heard his old friend had taken a turn for the worse. Kind of turn—pretty clear to the doctor—that one does not turn back from. W. H. Harrison showed up not long after, sprinted a few different horses all the way back from the western frontier to see his old mentor one last time. Now W. H. has ass on chair tip, leaned forward to be most bed-side. Rush is more rolled back, sits there nodding through all of Morris's complaints about *The Life of George Washington*, the first comprehensive database of an American President. Just been released into Newnet, and it's taking the Dream and the real by storm. Citizens everywhere are right now hyper-linking their own paths through, portaling from one amazing Washington feat to the next, dragging favorite quotes to their Brainpage status, unveiling timeless wisdoms as they relive the Revolution in code.

"Rubbish," Morris says. "Total rubbish." He hands the old smartpad to Rush, who lays it inanimate on the bedside table.

"Maybe it's better," W. H. says, "if you read it on a smartpalm or in the Dream, like it was intended."

Morris holds out his palms to show how neither is smart.

Rush has been through this new database a few times himself. Its most startling feature is its narrative consistency. Takes everything the Old Man ever did and makes a clear arc right through—brazen heroic youth to martial greatness to patriarch to immortal.

If someone someday makes a database of Morris's life, what story you see will depend on where you click. In 1776, he was the richest man in the colonies, the financial power behind the Revolution. Shipping magnate, Signer of the Declaration, the Articles and the Constitution, too, Finance Minister, railroad man, balloon man, patron of the arts, prisoner, political outcast, land-poor defaulter, bankrupt charity case, and now here he is, dying dirt poor in a hardscrabble one room, nothing to his name but that old busted smartpad, a couple of wobbly chairs, little nightstand, cobwebs and torn cloth curtains. Rush has seen the rise and fall and decline of quite a few patriots and Signers; perhaps this ending state is saddest of all.

"Washington," Morris says, "has whole sections of the Cloud sectioned off for his memory. More important dead than he ever was alive. Me, they'll just roll into the ground."

Rush pushes a raised pointer finger against his smile. "Sshhh," he says. "Don't say anything bad about George Washington."

Morris smiles, too. But not W. H. This is the first time he's been present when something even tangentially critical has been uttered about the Founding Father himself. This is Off-the-Grid they're talking about, *the Old Man!* Seeing this look, Morris tells his old pupil, "Don't be so inflexible, William. No one's challenging the memory of George Washington. Just the reality of that memory." A wink of the old Robert Morris. "The doctor here, he was questioning the legend before the legend was a legend."

Rush steps back decades in the room. "I really did think Washington was going to sink the Revolution. And I wasn't the only one. Tom Mifflin, Richard Henry Lee. And if it weren't for *The Death*, he probably would have. Gone down in history as a domestic terrorist, this whole America thing just a stunted colonial revolt." The doctor taps his chin, says wistfully, "I still think we could have won it in '75."

Morris sort of asks then—but more like demands—to be moved from the bed so he, "can get a little bit of sun before I die." W. H. and Rush look around at the dreary one room. No sun outside and certainly not in this place. Been a cloud cover over the whole of Pennsylvania these last few days. Everything in and out, all drenched in gloom. But when W. H. gets his mentor down into one of those rickety chairs, the sun actually does break loose, comes blasting through the pulled-open curtains. The light revives Morris a bit, gives him a little burst of energy. Rush sits in the other chair as W. H. stalks the room with leaned-over stillness. "Washington," Morris is saying, "got his ass kicked in New York. Never would have pulled it together if I hadn't flipped the bill for him to go off the grid. Off the grid! He may have been off the grid, but he was on Robert Morris's bank roll. And I don't see any links to *that*."

Morris takes a drink of water, makes Rush wonder how long that same glass has been there with that same water in it. "It wasn't a war of military strategy, but a war of finance. How do we afford to move the army here? How do we pay to move it there? When we finally did persuade the Old Man to move on Yorktown, the question was never how, but *how much*. How much of Robert Morris's money was it going to take to finish this thing? All George Washington had to do was nod that big head of his. Everyone could see it fine, sitting up high like it always was."

Rush slaps his knee.

"You must, of course, never repeat these things, William. And you must never, ever say them in the Dream. Some kid someday flicks to the history page of Robert Morris and sees he was a heretic."

"Seems to me," Rush says, "you made a little scratch off that war yourself, Robert."

Morris smiles at the sentence.

"Without the Old Man in the way," Rush says, "distracting the people with those spells of charisma, this place is starting to shape up like that America we all talked about so much during the Revolution." He leans back, props one leg on the bulb of his knee.

W. H. pipes in, "Czar Alexander and Emperor Bonaparte will sew up the English Channel any day now. The sea will finally be free of the Royal Navy. And all these wars—and all their rippling messes—will all be history."

"You guys sure sound optimistic," Morris tells them. "But any day now has been any day now for as long as I can remember. And Europe is *still* at war."

"You should see the West, Mr. Morris. The entire Ohio country's filling with new Americans. From all over the world they've come. Everyone knows we got peace and democracy and free Newnet and that you can make a little do-re-me in this country with some plans of your own."

Morris makes a face like he's eaten another of those rotten cherries from that tree George Washington was so honest about chopping down, oh so long ago. "Put wireless in the woods and of course it'll fill up with smartdevices. And each smartdevice has to have a person attached, right?" Morris has a finger wagging. "You should try getting burned by both parties, my boy. It can be quite liberating. Frees you to find the ridiculous in each." Morris shakes his head. "Don't have anything against Tom Jefferson personally, or even politically. Not really. But man, those henchmen of his play it so rough. Still smiting from that shit M'Kean pulled on me back in '00."

Rush remembers when Tom M'Kean first started riding around the state in early 1800. Most people thought he was on assignment for the Society of Cincinnati, but Rush knew right away what he was up to. M'Kean had started working for Jefferson. County by county he went, embarrassing the local Federalists by tying them to

Robert Morris. The old financier's real estate gambles had all gone bad. It was the last straw in a growing pile of financial disasters for the state's most visible symbol of Federalism. The deal had landed Morris in debtors' prison, which was all the example M'Kean and Jefferson needed. If the head of the state party can't keep his books in order, what does it say about the rest of the PA Federalists? Man, was M'Kean rubbing it in, and on Robert Morris of all people, locked away in debtors' prison where he couldn't say a thing back. M'Kean got the whole state legislature swung over to Jefferson, and all of Pennsylvania's electoral votes with it—Federalists never knew what hit them. Rush smirks in spite of himself. It was pretty sweet. But why they had to do it so mean, and to a Signer too. Rush remembers when Morris finally did get out of prison; the man was just plain emasculated. Balls never did grow back. One of the many events over the years which disassembled Robert Morris, piece by piece.

Morris says, "Wish I could go back in time. Bring that old Robert Morris here to be the one who's dying. Maybe he could do it with some dignity."

"It was nothing personal," Rush assures him. "Jefferson had that going on in every state. Burr in New York, M'Kean here in Pennsylvania. Chuck Pinckney down in South Carolina—last man to see Ed Rutledge alive. Bottom line, the Federalists had to be stopped. Adams, Hamilton, fuck, they had the Old Man out again."

Morris shakes his head. "It's true. Those high Federalists were on a rampage. And you're right—someone had to stop them. I don't hold nothing against anyone. But let us assume France *does* win this war in Europe. You think that's going to satisfy Napoleon Bonaparte? No. Whoever wins is coming over here next." He indicates the state of the room, its abject squalor. "I paid for the last war and look how I was treated." Morris leaves his gaze resting on the ramshackle furniture, the huge, swirling fists of dust that haunt the bare floor. Slowly a smile creeps onto his face, wistful and past-looking. "It was thirty years ago, Ben, that we signed that thing." In half a daydream, Morris pulls from his inner pocket a piece of paper.

"It's your letter," Rush says, laying a hand gently over his own breast pocket. He wants to ask Morris what it contains, but the doctor knows full well that no Signer is going to share the contents of his Jefferson letter.

Morris let the paper flop open so he can stare into the leaning script. "Jefferson is a puzzle that lies at the center of a maze. Just when you think you might know where you're going, the walls start moving around. The puzzle goes quantum, hides its angles in dimensions only Thomas Jefferson has visited. Strange physics apply in those places." Morris looks away from the page, at the echoes it leaves on his vision. "You get in Thomas Jefferson's way, you end up in the dirt like General Hamilton or Jim Callender. Or running around mad like Aaron Burr. On an Off-Worlder ship maybe. Or worse. Maybe end up like Robert Morris."

"*Colonel* Hamilton," Rush corrects.

"But there's one piece still left undone." Morris finishes a broad scan of his letter, folds it and slips it back into that threadbare coat. "If Jefferson is going to really win, complete the Revolution as you say, he's going to need to do something about George Washington."

W. H. looks just as confused as Rush. "George Washington is dead."

Morris indicates that smartpad, *The Life of George Washington*, a spine of hyperlinks leading any way you choose through the high, sweeping epic of the age that birthed the nation. "No matter how dead the General is, no matter how large the country gets, how high the population numbers soar, how low the taxes fall, someone's always going to point to George Washington and start talking about the good old days. And who's going to argue with that? At least in public anyway." Morris shakes his head. "Jefferson can have his minions hunt down every Federalist in the North, the South and the Cloud. He can annex Florida and Northern Mexico and Cuba and Canada, too. Hypnotize every Indian into loyal Enlightenment Americans. He can eliminate the judicial branch for good. Get elected over and over, and he probably will. He'll probably do all of it. And it'll probably be good for the country, too. He's already remade this whole place once, and I have a feeling he's just getting started. But taking George Washington down out of the Cloud, that's a program not even Thomas Jefferson can code."

Morris collects himself one last time. "Jefferson versus Washington, way up in the Cloud's cloud, in the dream of the Dream. Ain't two men worse to tangle with, alive or dead. If I were still a card-carrying Federalist, I'd run and hide while I still could. William," he says. "you're going to have to tell me someday how it all comes out."

Morris turns his face into the thick beam of sunlight. It comes through the window, all the way down from the broken-open Pennsylvania sky. Falls flat on him to chase away the shadows and a good chunk of years. A slightly younger Robert Morris goes still, then. His brief opportunity to affect the history of the universe has winked away.

No one can figure out what happened to George Wythe. Each of the three doctors brought in have theories that overlap only slightly. These are the best doctors in Richmond and thus (according to Richmonders) the best in all the South. But the only thing they seem good for is posting their half-baked theories to Newnet. Guys treat the Dream like their own personal sounding board, a place to store random ideas no matter how thin and unsubstantiated. When one posts a passing thought that maybe what's got Wythe is the first case of *The Death* in something like two decades, doesn't take but half a recycle for all the Dream to be atwitter with speculation and counter-speculation. People with only second- and third-hand information feel plenty informed to participate in the crowdsource. Non-doctors berate the "experts" and their tyrannical monopoly on the interpretation of data. Federalist screamers snap back from life support to sing the end of Jefferson, blaming the yet-unconfirmed outbreak on the liberalization of immigration policies and the reckless expansion and socialization of Newnet.

The only person no one is listening to is George Wythe. Every few hours he'll draw enough strength together to tell the doctors what really happened. "He came from the Dream," he keeps saying. But they chalk his fractured story up as just another symptom. Vomiting, diarrhea, light sensitivities, wild non-linear thoughts. Wythe lays there all but paralyzed; his tale never cracks the shell of the room. Never makes it to the Dream.

During Wythe's third full day of spiraling toward death, a fourth visitor joins the Richmond doctors. Comes into the sick room with a large canvas bag. Rests the bag on the floor and pulls a chair close to the bed. His head is covered with a hood. He wears thick, dark glasses, making his eyes all but invisible.

"Thomas?" Wythe inquires. "Thomas, is that you?"

"No," the man says. "The President is sorry he could not be here." The hood draws off. Glasses pulled to rest in his lap. If there were another twin left, there's no way they could be identical anymore. What chance could there be of two separate men being injured this same way, then healing the same way, all to end up with identical four-pronged scars like the one that wraps this face? Looks like the flaming hand of the devil has been laid on his cheek, left there until the searing reached bone.

"Thought you were dead," Wythe manages weekly.

"That was the conventional wisdom . . ." and realizing there's no one there to finish his sentence, ". . . was in a coma for six months." He holds up his right arm, revealing no arm south of the elbow.

Wythe's hand, moving for the first time in days, lays atop the last of what was once four identical hands. "I remember when Thomas first made you two. And now your brother is gone." Wythe eyes the grizzly face. "Still don't understand how M'Kean got out without a scratch."

"He's M'Kean," a smile pressed across the twisted flesh. "Mr. Wythe, I need you to tell me what happened."

"It came from the Dream." Wythe's tongue appears, to spread moisture across his lips. It dries and is gone. He offers nothing more.

"Mr. Wythe keeps saying he was attacked by a drone. But where would the *matter* come from?"

"Maybe it was John Marshall's boys," another doctors offers. "Trying to send the President a message. Take out his old mentor, the last Republican in Richmond. I'm going to post it."

The twin holds up a hand to silence the doctors.

Wythe coughs, clears his throat. "He brought me there. Into the Dream. He was a drone." Wythe stops, exhausted by the effort. "We came out again and I was *there* . . . really there . . ."

The doctors exchange confused looks.

"What did he show you, Mr. Wythe?"

Wythe takes a deep breath. "Through the Dream and New-net. Crossed through the old Internet, too. All these big frames . . . the uncompleted firmware of 3net. Way out, out to the west and there it was, right there below us. The Fissure." Wythe looks into the twin's eyes, sees them swimming with knowledge. "What is it? What does Thomas know?"

"Some rather credible intelligence of a pending attack, Mr. Wythe. An invasion, from the deepest sectors of the old Internet. Can you tell me who it was that came to you?"

If he could move enough, Wythe would shrug.

The twin shares a look with the doctors and one of them leaves. Probably to get the priest, though nothing is said. Wythe mumbles a few sounds more before the room goes quiet. In the silence, the twin turns from the bed, digs into the bag he's brought with him, lifts a contraption out to show Wythe, a crude leather helmet covered with wires and transistors. Wythe's interest piques a breath of energy. The old knight of the Enlightenment. "Is it . . . Thomas's design?"

"You know of Mr. Jefferson's collages. A bit from this, a bit from that."

"It's going to show you what I saw?"

"More or less . . . but it's quite a taxing procedure."

"You mean, I might not survive it."

"Everyone we've tried it on has. But they're all young men. Sleep for a day or two. A hangover of sorts."

"Haven't got long either way," and he indicates to put it on. "If this can help Thomas . . . then we'd better get . . . started."

The twin eases the cap over the front of Wythe's forehead, lets loose a light leather flap that folds over the old man's eyes. He presses a button, and invisible signals dart backward through the air, connecting to the smartpalm on that one remaining hand. Soundlessly, the machine begins to act. There in the palm of the twin's hand, Wythe's memories come to life. "My God."

Wythe, with his last breaths, "You've seen this before."

The twin nods. Inside his palm a section of cracked-open earth, huge jagged shelves of ancient rock framing a gorge of molten lava, flames lapping skyward to bend the air. "In Michigan territory," the twin says. "This is where Bartlett threw that first crystal. But . . . this is not what it looked like when we were there." The skin of his palm returns to its customized main menu, severed from the brain it was connected to. Well, not so much severed, as the feed is gone. The absence brings the twin back to the room, back from the edge of that Fissure, way out west.

The doctors are leaning over to see the finality. "Well," one says, "let's hope it's not contagious."

Twenty miles outside Eerie. Directly west. That's where James Smith has just moved all that's left of his existence, what little there is. For twenty years, he'd been off the grid, and not just off the Newnet grid—off the grid altogether. Hidden from society in all its forms, real and virtual. But then last week something happened that forced Smith out of the hole he'd dug in the surface of reality. His mansion—tucked between hills on the eastern edge of Bucks County—burned to the ground. A day later, winds came sweeping in from the west and blew it flat, a grayscale stain streaking the landscape. Not a thing left but the clothes on his back. Which is how James Smith likes it best. That old mansion was okay, but too much life dust had shaken off him there. Place was creating an echo a little too close to real.

About a week after moving out to his new home, James Smith can't believe it when he looks out his window one late afternoon. And strolling up the foot path to his front door is the former Vice President of the United States, Aaron Burr.

When James Smith opens the door, the colonel asks him, "Well, Jim, what do you think?"

Smith waits for Burr to duck his way through the door. And then the door's closed and everything's back to how it was a few minutes ago, except now there are two men in the cabin. "What do I think about what?" Smith asks.

"When you signed the Declaration of Independence, I asked you what you thought about it and you said ask me again in thirty years."

"Haven't thought about that stuff, since, oh, the Constitution, pretty much."

Burr smiles. "That's right, you've been off the grid. *Way off.*" Burr takes a few bold steps, letting his boot heels clack hard and sharp against the floor. The wall opposite bulges with heat, a small Franklin stove cooking the place right up. "Pittsburgh?" Burr asks. "All but off the map now, too."

"Map keeps getting bigger."

"No computer? An old textphone, maybe?"

"No Internet, new or old. No the Franklin's Dream."

"You can just say the Dream. Or Dream. And it's Patrick Henry's Dream America now, for whatever that's worth." Burr ponders it. "That fire of yours must have burned the bottom of the sky. Was the point so someone like me could track you down after all this time? Are you looking to get involved again, Jim?"

"You heard about the fire?"

"Heard about it? I've *seen* it. Everyone has. Went viral, all over the Cloud, for a couple of days anyway. 'Signer's home burns to the ground.'" Burr holds up a finger for James Smith to either see or count. "Your house burning down's not a moment anymore. It's forever in Newnet. I bet it's happening right now somewhere, for someone."

"And you guys wonder why I've been out so long."

"Jim, was your Jefferson letter in there?"

"How do you know about Jefferson's letters?"

Burr grins one of several grins he employs. "Thought maybe it was just a rumor, until now. Would love to get my hands on one of those letters. Maybe it's a way out of this one for me."

"Well, mine's burned up with everything else."

Burr appreciates it. "We're going to need a man who can live off the grid, Jim. These guys have the Cloud locked down, Newnet, the Dream, the whole fucking thing. Eliminating the opposition, in groups and one by one. They'll be coming for you soon, too."

"Which guys? Who's going to come for me?"

"Someone with the smell of Jefferson on him. The Governor probably."

"M'Kean? What's he care about whether I'm still alive? I haven't been a part of this fight since before the dissolve."

"M'Kean's been busting heads all across the state. Throwing Federalist screamers in jail, canceling Brainpage profiles, if you know what I mean. Oily snake even married his daughter to the Spanish minister. Like he's some feudal lord, assimilating fiefdoms. Who do you think set fire to your house?"

"I know exactly who set fire to my house, and it wasn't Tom M'Kean. It was me."

Burr is genuinely surprised, not an easy feat. "But why?"

Smith tosses a log into the fire. Leaves him with a chunk of bark in his hand. He puts a sliver in his mouth and chews. "Get rid of my data."

"Your data?"

"Don't give me that, Burr. You were there. We did some pretty dark shit back then. Back during the Revolution."

Burr waves his hand, but then his eyes settle, settle on that fire. "*The Death* was happening, remember? Washington had vanished. Seemed like it had all fallen apart. I was a kid, pretty much. Me, you, Read. M'Kean, too. He was a different man back then."

"We all were."

"You still got some of that old James Smith in you?"

Smith chews some more on that bark, says firmly, "We did what we did. But not anymore. Data's all gone. I die and the guilt dies with me. But you, you've been a busy man since leaving office, morally speaking."

Burr smiles wistfully. "It was the President's idea. Lure Hamilton into an affair of honor, let him flail and embarrass himself and back down in the end. Sounds easy enough. Of course, when the plan didn't go as planned, who's left holding the bag while Jefferson whistles out the other side?" Burr's smile looks the same but frozen. "They say I went mad, will be saying it all through the rest of history." But he does have to give it to Jefferson. I played a rough one too, he thinks. Really rough. "What about that letter, Jim?"

Smith shakes his head. "No more politics, Burr. Not for me. Not anymore. Stuff makes me sick. Always has." Smith steps to the window. Outside, the day has begun to break itself down. Amber replacing white dotted blue along the horizon. Shadows lost all constancy. "When Newnet came on, then the Dream, just seemed too noisy. Too temporary. Too much changing too often."

"Got to like that quiet deadliness of life when the Internet was illegal, when *The Death* stalked the land."

Smith turns back, spits the bark into the fire.

"We're going to take him down, Jim."

"Oh, yeah?"

"We're going to get us a tyrant. Connecticut River-style."

Smith smiles wider. "So what, you're going to sneak into the President's mansion and slice his throat? Because *that's* Connecticut River-style."

"And *that* is the old Jim Wilson. But no, killing Jefferson would never kill Jefferson. Slice that throat all you want. Put his head on a pike. Bones in the river. He'll be bee-bopping down the eway in the Dream the next day, most members in the history of group avatars." Burr leans back on the wall. "No, we've got to destroy Jefferson the old-fashioned way. And this bill of his, isolating the U.S. Cloud. This is our chance."

"Isolate it?"

"Section it off, huge firewall between us and the Old World. Not even a tickle gets through."

Smith turns to lean on the wall beside the stove. The heat up and down the front of his body is almost unbearable. "What's Jefferson's play? You were in there for a while."

"Not that far in." Burr shakes his head. "This *is* some shaky ground he's dancing out on, maybe the first mistake he's made. Even his lap dogs M'Kean and Madison are having second thoughts. Gallatin's taking a shit. A real shit. The fucking Swede." Burr shrugs, like it's so simple. "We've seen this before, restrictions on the Cloud. Some state declares its independence and Jefferson's going to tell them they don't have the right? The guy wrote the Declaration."

"So what? Dissolve again?"

"This time a fissure, Jim. Right down the middle."

"A fissure?"

"Connecticut, Massachusetts, those guys are itching for it." Burr smiles. "But we start it in the *West*."

"That's Jefferson's territory. He gave them the land, gave them free Newnet."

Burr smiles deviously. "Those crazy bastards out there. Suspicious as hell of Jefferson's virtual warfare, his experimental economic weaponry. Quasi-war, virtual war. What about a good old-fashioned war? And who's sitting right there asking for it in Florida? Those settlers have been itching to kick the Spanish out since they first moved down there and realized the Spanish were already there. Fill her, bust her."

"How are you talking about having a war, Burr? With what?"

"We got an Irishman out there putting up the money. Just like old times. We march down there and kick the Spanish out, prop up a government. Lookie, lookie and line on up. We trading free and clear with the Cloud down here. New England will fissure that second."

"A New England Federation, a Western Federation, a Florida Federation? How many Americas are we talking about?"

"The North and the West will be joined in no time. Big arc around the Mid-Atlantic. Maybe New York is its own thing for a while. Until the Clintons die, probably. Soon enough, though, it'll be Virginia and the Carolinas, maybe Georgia, all alone. Jefferson can be president of his little slavocracy, and *we* can finally get back to being real Americans. Maybe in a few years we come on in and take it over. Give Virginia to the slaves and see what happens."

Outside the house, just audible over the crackle of the fire, the unmistakable sound of a flock of birds breaking from a bush nest. Fast and violent fluttering fading as they disperse into higher air. Burr raises his hand to signal they should listen for whatever it was that disturbed those birds. Slowly, Burr draws back the curtains just enough to peek through. "You said you don't have a smartdevice here."

"I don't! No phone or computer either. No Cloud."

"Well, I guess the Cloud is here whether you've got a device linked to it or not." Burr shakes his head. "Damn, these guys are good. How the fuck did they find us?"

"*Us?* They followed you here. I should never have set that fire." Smith moves up beside Burr so he can see who's out there. "Who is that?"

Burr checks again. "Local Jeffersonians, probably. Society of Cincinnati?"

"Thought *you* were SOC."

"There are a few different branches now, if you know what I mean." Burr rushes over to the Franklin stove, pulling papers from his inner coat, actual papers. He starts shoving them through the open door, two at a time.

"I could deliver them for you, after they take you away."

"They're not here to *arrest* me, Jim."

Smith considers it a moment, rolls his eyes. "And me?"

Burr just looks back at him, gives him that Aaron Burr. All his documents in smoldering layers in the fireplace. "Sorry. This is where our paths diverge from destiny." Burr doesn't slow down. "What about that Jefferson letter, Jim? Already burned, right?"

"This is exactly what I didn't want," James Smith says. "Twenty years I managed to keep invisible. Then you show up. Well, give me a gun at least."

"Ain't gonna be no gun fight, Jim. These boys have some weird shit."

Smith lets the room operate around him a moment. "What's that tingling?"

Light Horse Harry Lee and Junior Heyward sit on opposite sides of a containment tube in Heyward's lab. It's the third-floor east wing of the mansion, where no servants are allowed to go. Not even the butler. Heyward's on the inside of the tube, which is where he's going to die at some random moment in the next couple of days.

"The plan was to set it loose during the inauguration," he's telling Light Horse Harry Lee. "Madison comes into office just as another outbreak is hitting. Republicans have been in charge eight years and so try blaming that one on John Adams. It would have been the end of them, Lee. The end of the Republicans: Madison, Jefferson, the Swede, the whole party."

"The inauguration is tomorrow," Lee says.

Heyward nods from the other side of the tube. "Madison's gonna stroll over to the Capitol, put his hand on the Bible and Jefferson'll be right there behind him. Rubbing their goddamned asses in John Marshall's face."

"Just a formality," Lee says. "Madison's been in charge for months. As soon as the election was over, Jefferson ported all his avatars and rode off for Monticello."

Heyward's not able to react. The idea fits into his schema of spite for all things Jefferson, but undermines his conspiracy theories about Jefferson's perpetual control of the American government.

"Look," Lee tells him. "I don't like these guys any more than you do, but another outbreak? Come on, June."

Inside the tube is where Heyward does all his most sensitive electrochemical work. It's in case something goes wrong. Which is exactly what happened a couple of days ago. While he was closing the last carbon octagon—the final touches on his latest creation: *Synthetic The Death*—something went wrong. Suddenly, the virus was active. The door to the containment tube slammed shut as all the lab's safeguards kicked in. The floorboards shimmied; it was the jammer signal beginning its transmission, a forcefield of modified sound waves that blocks out the Cloud. Can't let *Synthetic The Death* get out from his own lab. What's the point of an outbreak if it doesn't look like it was the Administration's fault? The only reason anyone knew to come to his rescue was a kill switch auto-text Heyward programmed to go out to the southern headquarters of the Society of Cincinnati: "code 76."

There was a time when that text would have gotten a door busted down a few seconds later. Some war veterans and a mid-level Federalist with a cigar. These days there's not much of an SOC left. Heyward was praying for some young upstart dickhead with a bloodlust for red meat. But who should show up and all by himself? Light Horse Harry Fucking Lee. Took that virtuous dickhead one look around the place to get an exact idea of what Heyward was up to. No way was Light Horse Harry going to open that containment tube. No way was he going to let *Synthetic The Death* get out.

Heyward had begged a little bit, for Lee to let him out or maybe even finish his plan for him. But Heyward knew that was all in vain. So he broke down and asked if Lee would just stay with him so he wouldn't have to die alone. They fist-bumped the opposite sides of the same piece of containment tube and so it was a promise. Now there they sit, on either side of the glass, swapping stories and

finding some ground on the middle-right where they can agree.
Whenever Heyward gets too worked up, Lee stands and pretends
he's going to leave. That always brings things back down to Earth,
and they can start to act civil again.

"Thought it was going to be more painful." Heyward lifts his
eyes from his stomach, gestures toward the desk on Lee's side of
the glass. "If you ever want it, Lee, I backed up the formula on that
old smartpad."

"The formula for *Synthesized The Death*?"

"*Synthetic. Synthetic The Death.*"

Lee shakes his head. "What was going to be your delivery system?"

"I was planning on embedding it in the Dream feed of the
swearing-in."

Lee shakes his head. "Christ, June, you've lost it."

"Remember when those feeds of the *Chesapeake* went viral?"
Heyward clicks. "British Sea captains hanging American citizens,
their bodies right there on the Dream for everyone to see. Storm
rains lashing them for days until their skin looked just awful. Never
had the Dream frothed so hard for war."

"I thought for sure it was coming. We all did."

"War with England's about the only thing could bring the
Federalists back. But of course, *fucking Jefferson*. Just massages it
right into his cute little narrative and what should have killed him
becomes his temporal swan song. Saves the country from war and
off to the presidential Dream." Heyward laments. "Had a million
feeds in the first hour. A *million*. And that was when the population
had just hit a million. That means that every person in America had
seen it in the first hour alone."

"Not sure about your math, June. Well, the math's fine, but the
equation is maybe off." They both laugh, legs all out straight on

the floor. If it weren't for the curved glass, they'd be back-to-back, leaning one on the other to keep both from falling. Really, it's the tube that holds them up.

"Madison'll fuck it up. You watch. Guy's had a boner about fighting England the whole time he's been at State. When that war comes, *that's* your chance. You find Gouverneur Morris. Burr, if he's still alive. You get some wedge issue in there real good, Lee, and you spread that fissure wide."

"No one in the SOC would ever clear that."

Junior Heyward scoffs. "The SOC has no leadership. No one gives orders. And no one takes them if they do. The SOC broke apart years ago. Just a collection of odd reactions ever since."

Lee thinks maybe Heyward is right. About the SOC, there can be no doubt. After Washington died, it kicked around for a while. Staggered about and limped and made a fool of itself. That shit Lachlan McIntosh pulled in Santo Domingo was pretty sweet. But now the SOC is just another piece of that old America Jefferson has pruned off. Lee wonders, though, if maybe Heyward is right about the country, too. A danger to itself the way it's headed now. "Look," he says. "If you think a war with England is going to revive the party, you're nuts. If that happens, it won't be safe to be a Federalist. Not in the Dream and certainly not in the real."

"Lee, you know the difference between us Federalists and the Jeffersonian-Republicans? The *real* difference?"

Lee has a feeling something crazy's about to get articulated.

But Heyward says instead, "We actually fought in the war. Actually saw it. How close it came. How important it was that we had an army, roads, guns and powder. Without the Federalist system behind it, the whole Revolution would have collapsed into a string of clever tweets. Republicans have been in charge for eight years now, and look at us. Look at the country. Ripe as a dangling dingleberry for any Old World power to come along, pluck us right off and have the biggest bite they want." Heyward pauses. "Lee," he says, "you at least have to take the crystal."

Lee looks over his shoulder, finds Heyward doing the same. Their eyes lock. "Dig it out of your stomach?"

"Find a Federalist, anyone who's left, Lee. You get them this crystal."

Lee cocks his head so it rests crooked on his side of the glass. His distaste with this idea is palpable. Heyward can feel it in the air, his grand plan unwinding into nothing in the end. He thinks through a spot of silence. Some dripping noise from inside a beaker, somewhere on Lee's side of the glass. "You think Madison can handle the Patrick Henry Group Avatar?"

Lee thinks. "He kicked Patrick Henry's ass in the real. Back when he was on our side, when he was a Federalist. Kicked Patrick Henry right in the ass and got that Constitution through. Saved the country, June. He was with the Old Man on that one."

Junior Heyward rocks his head a little in the concave of the tube. "Maybe when you die of *The Death*," he says, "you don't die fully, but go into the Dream. Maybe the Dream was always there and we've just now discovered it."

"Then where are all the people who died in the outbreaks?"

"Maybe the drones aren't drones but human souls displaced by *The Death*. Floated around for a while until they found some platform they could crawl into. Maybe the real purpose of *The Death* was to decide who could live forever in the Dream and who would have to stay out here, out here in the real."

From the streets, a shriek. Then another. Shouting rising up from several sources below them. Lee gets struck with a pang of fear. Maybe Heyward's *Synthesized The Death* has gotten out! He scrambles to his feet, rushes to the window. More shouts are flittering up. Images race through his head, sidewalks dotted with toppled-over Americans clutching their stomachs. But the visage evaporates when Lee sees what people are really shouting about. "You should see this." But when Lee glances back, Junior Heyward is slumped over against the inner curve of the tube.

Lee turns back to look out the window, a huge flying saucer floating over Charleston. He doesn't know it yet, but there are similar ships pulling into position above eleven other ports all over the world. Last day of the Thomas Jefferson presidency and the Off-Worlders have returned.

"Shit, June. Maybe I will take that crystal."

SAMUEL CHASE :: JUNE 11TH 1811

Associate Justice of the Supreme Court Sam Chase keeps a three-foot mirror in the chair opposite the chair he sits in most of the day. Really, there isn't anybody left to talk to. Federalists are an endangered species, especially in Baltimore. The ones left wouldn't dare be seen with Sam Chase the Bacon Face, certainly not going to return any of his tickles, texts or chats. They're all worried that copies of their correspondence will show up in the Dream some day, drag their reputations right down with his. "I'm just like my country," he says, "limping toward the sunset, half alive and shadows only."

He looks at his face in the mirror, cheeks like cooked beef, hair more like clouds around his head than something attached. Not hard to see why all the Jeffersonian-Republicans got to calling him Bacon Face. Sam Chase the Bacon Face. Some of his friends too, and with him right there in the room. He does have to admit it, though—his face really does look like bacon, like greasy slices of bacon laid atop a skull.

"The Royal Navy," he says to himself. "The most powerful sea force man has ever created. Against what?" A beeping begins to eke from a device attached to Sam Chase's wrist. But he doesn't seem to notice, just leans in, talking to that face that looks exactly like his but flipped. "This America Mr. Jefferson has built is about to get its ass kicked. Both cheeks." The beeping breaks from background noise to infest the consciousness of the room. "Oh, fuck you," Chase says. But this just makes the beeping louder, faster. "Fuck you," he says again, but softer. Softer still, "Piece a shit." He starts in on deep and measured breaths, lifts his arms high above his head, holds a breath and counts to five. As he does, the beeping slows, subsides. Chase relishes the silence. He looks tauntingly into the device, licks his lips and whispers, "That's right, motherfucker."

Chase settles back, props up his feet, looks past them at himself with feet propped. "War with England is inevitable now," he says. "No way to stop it." Not after what happened this morning. Baltimore dock worker practicing square knots looked over the pier edge, but instead of water, there was a human floating, an American sailor dead and drained of blood. By the time the dock worker came to grips with what he was seeing, he was seeing much more of it. The water between the two closest boats was filled with them, Dead Americans, bobbing there like driftwood.

Right after watching the first Dream feed about it, Sam Chase left to go see the bloodless sailors firsthand. His house is within a mile of the Baltimore Harbor, making this one of those rare modern moments when something happening in the Dream is actually within a crossable physical distance. Constant access to feeds from all over the country is okay. But nothing beats the buzz of actually seeing news happening in the real. Chase didn't get a block, though, before every Republican with a voice box was shouting him down and calling him Old Bacon Face.

"You're a rascal, Old Bacon Face."

"Hey, Old Bacon Face, why don't you get out of here?"

"Fuck you, Old Bacon Face! Go fuck yourself!"

And so Chase turned around and went straight home to look at the images on the Dream instead, just like everyone else. Fucking Baltimore, Paris of the East Coast. Right now, Chase is massaging his touchscreen, zooming and honing until a sailor's face fills the surface of the smartpad. Ghost-white and water-logged, eyes rolled back to focus on nothing, not on this plane. "The War Hawks aren't going to rest until America sees this same thing, in our mind's eye, everywhere we turn."

Chase knows it's impossible for the British to have done this. How could they have? Taken an entire ship's worth of American men, okay. But drained them all of blood? Ship set sail the day before and so they would have had to get it all done in twenty-four hours. Chase tries to imagine a little face-to-bacon-face with the War Hawks' new Speaker, Henry Clay. "So tell me, Mr. Clay, how exactly did the British accomplish this?" But Chase knows that plausibility's about to stop mattering at all, that explaining how the British are responsible for draining the blood of American merchants and sailors is exactly what Henry Clay is going to do, whether it makes sense or not. And Sam Chase knows another thing, too. The people are going to love it. So get out of the way. Hawks are finally going to get this war they've been champing at the bit about since they steamrolled the mid-term and came marching into town.

The beeping has begun again. Chase starts those relaxation techniques the hippie doctor taught him. Breathing, lifting his arms, holding a breath, letting it out slow. "Not sure I even trust this thing." He eyes the device. "Anytime someone's doing or thinking or saying something *the program* doesn't like, sends them a message, *calm down!* Humans don't run Newnet anymore. Newnet runs the humans."

On three separate occasions in his life, a severe heart attack has brought Justice Sam Chase to the very brink of death. Doctors say there'll be no fighting off a fourth. And so the device on his wrist is there to tell him when his blood pressure is putting his heart at risk, when he needs to relax unless he wants another attack. The first happened during the impeachment trial. Jefferson's foray into dismantling the Supreme Court. It was Samuel Chase who got up in front of the train. Survived impeachment, but the trial almost killed him. "Saved the Court," he tells the mirror. "And here I am, still alive. More than can be said for Hamilton."

For a while, Chase thought he could hold on until a Federalist got back in the President's mansion. Deprive Tom the First and his line of Jefferclones from filling his seat with some Jacobin democrat. But now Chase knows it's a fight he's not going to win. He could last another year, possibly. But the Federalists are running Dewitt Clinton. And Dewitt Clinton ain't got a chance in hell of taking Pennsylvania. And if he can't get Pennsylvania, he ain't got a chance in hell of beating Madison. Chase knows another five years is out of the question, and even if he could last that long, who's going to beat Monroe in '16? Not Rufus King, and not either of the Pinckneys, and certainly not Dewitt Clinton. *Dewitt Clinton?* The Federalists ain't got shit. The seat he fought so hard to save, some Republican is going to fill it with whatever slime they can scrape off some rock in the Deep South. A Jeffersonian, he thinks, sitting right there in Samuel Chase's Supreme Court seat. Fuck me.

Chase returns his attention to his smartpad, zooms out so he can see the whole image, all those dead sailors, hundreds of them. "Drained of blood," he says. He takes his eyes from it to lean back in his chair, looks into the face inside that mirror opposite. He watches himself say, "The Off-Worlders had something to do with this. Must have. Maybe they've made a pact with the British. But if so, why would they want to drain our sailors of blood?" Something doesn't add up, he thinks. "But less complete equations have been used to come up with war. And so war is what we're going to have. War with England."

Chase gets up. Leaving the mirror empty of himself and his face, however much or little real bacon there is to it. He goes to the window. From there, he can see the harbor in the distance. "All this time, Jefferson has been fighting a war with Britain inside the Cloud. And now it's here, crossed over into the real, and we don't have a real thing to fight it with." Beeping fills the room again. "I am calm!" he tells the device. He looks at the tiny words scrolling the screen. "How the fuck do kids even read these things?" He puts on some old-fashioned glasses and looks again in time to see: "DIE!!! . . . BLOOD PRESSURE ALERT!! IF YOU DO NOT CALM DOWN, YOU WILL DIE . . . BLOOD PRESS—"

"Oh, fuck you."

WILLIAM WILLIAMS :: AUGUST 2ND 1811

A daughter leans down over her paralyzed father and listens again for some form of communication. She's long given up on words, would be happy with a tongue click, an intentional pattern of breaths. After a few moments of nothing, she straightens herself from his bedside to face the mostly empty room. A few maids, a single doctor, a lawyer, her mother in the shadows. "Father says thank you all for your attentions." A look of disgusted suspicion from her mother, but the daughter seems to find strength in it, some reinforcement through defiance.

An hour later, William Williams's son-in-law comes bursting into the death chamber. "I hear he's talking."

Coldly from the shadowed corner comes a voice, "Yes, Mr. McClellan, that is what your wife would have us believe."

"Faith?"

Faith Williams McClellan nods to her husband. Loud enough for her mother not to miss, she says, "He *did*. He *did* talk to me."

Later in the evening, a pair of the town's young Federalists come knocking. "Word in the dinner halls is that Mr. Williams is talking again."

Faith lights up at the introduction of outside evidence to back up her claim. But when they're all hovering about the bed, William Williams just lays there as silent as a mummy. After a few awkward minutes, the daughter tells them, "His voice is very faint." And again she lowers her ear close to his spittle-crusted lips.

Boot heels come lifting off the floor as the two young Federalists lean in. McClellan steps in to rescue his wife, "Maybe your father is too . . ."

But she shushes him, rises and says, "My father says he's glad to see that the Federalist party of Lebanon, Connecticut, still cares about its Founders."

McClellan works back a sly grin, leans past his wife, toward those unmoving lips. Popping back erect, he tells the young men, "William Williams says you can help the party best by uniting behind Mr. Clinton for President."

"*DeWitt* Clinton?"

Little do both of them know that William Williams can hear everything they're saying that he's saying. He might not be able to speak or move at all, but the ears still work fine. And did those ears just hear *Dewitt Clinton*? For President? As a *Federalist*?

The next morning, Faith and John McClellan watch the maid hustle away from the breakfast room to answer the front door. "Ringing at this hour?"

When the maid returns, she's leading two lines of well-dressed Federalist office-holders. Just town-sized government is all, not any big-wigglers. By noon, the front rooms are bustling with them, these up-and-comers and just-made-it-theres. From every corner of Lebanon, Connecticut, they've come. A chance to hear the final wisdoms of an actual Signer. And Faith Williams McClellan is not going to let them down. She waits for a moment of calm, then leans over her father. The room falls silent. Rising, she coughs back some nerves. "My father says if Mr. Madison declares war on England," a glance at her nodding husband, "then the President declares war on *New* England, too."

Huzzahs and light clapping spatter the master bedroom. More trickle in from the long hall beyond. An hour later, they have to get the maid and stable hands to move William Williams into the parlor for better general access. And so now Mrs. Williams haunts the shadows of this room as she haunted the bedroom since the stroke.

From where his head rests, Williams can see the ever-growing crowd. Not a single one of them was alive for Yorktown, he thinks. Not one was ever a British subject. Young Federalists raised on Washington but come to manhood in the age of Jefferson. Only vague memories of the promise of a dying generation to go on. All they know about Off-the-Grid is what they've clicked on in *The Life of George Washington*.

William Williams notices, then, floating ineffectually about the room, his youngest and meekest offspring, William T., elbow-led by his cousin/wife, Sarah Trumbull Williams. Solomon, he thinks. Where is Solomon? But then he remembers that his eldest son died almost a year ago this week, suddenly and without warning in New York City. The cause very much still a mystery.

Rising up from bent over his father-in-law, young McClellan tells the room, "Mr. Williams declares his support for the northern states in their battle against the tyranny of the Virginia dynasty." He then launches into his own riff about the plunder of northern shipping, the Deep South, and western farmers and their land madness for Florida and Canada and Cuba and whatever else can be expanded into, the restrictions on Cloud commerce, the secret alliances with France and Russia both. "And now, gentlemen, I ask you to think about the potential aggregated power of a separate New England confederation. To the Fissure!"

For all their complaining about the dangers of the war, Williams gets the sense these young Federalists are rooting for it to start. Then they can root against the nation and then be there to say we told you so when the whole thing falls apart. War has become just another party issue, he thinks. Not a means for liberty or rights or property, but a means to prove the opposition wrong. Destroy

the country so you can be in a position to save it. Quite a formula
to follow as time goes by.

"Mr. Williams says the defenses of our very homeland have
been razed internally by neglect." Young McClellan has the attention of the room once again. "So diluted by the utopian fantasy of
a rational and peaceful world, Jefferson's party has turned us into
defenseless prey for any hungry nation or alien species."

From the shadows, Mrs. Williams just watches. She almost put
a stop to this whole thing when it first started. But then people
began showing up. In the age of the Dream, what more genuine
tribute to her dying life partner could there be than the actual gathering of people in a physical place?

"Excuse me," comes a voice, a young Federalist whom Williams doesn't recognize. He's standing there beside his bed, ready
to address the room. "Mr. Williams says this war is just the next
phase in a plot to create a global revolutionary government with
Napoleon at its head."

Faith Williams McClellan steps forward, anger flashing. But
she catches herself and melts again into her somber mourning. Her
husband takes her hand. One rule of politics is it never takes a fox
long to sniff out a fox. And so it was only a matter of time before
others would be in on the act, leaning their ears close and then
talking imaginary words out of William Williams' mouth.

"He's quoting Mr. Jefferson," another would-be listener tells
the room. "The tree of liberty must be fed from time to time with
the blood of patriots and tyrants . . . and all that stuff."

Some clapping.

"I hold these truths to be self-evident," and then a long list of
Connecticut grievances.

"If all men are created equal?" his daughter asks, retaking the
room. "Then why is northern industry being forced to prop up

southern agriculture?" And Williams has to admit, she does have a good point there. Might actually be something he did once say.

After a moment of pretending to listen, another young Federalist light steps to the center of the room and declares, "William Williams has told me that what we need is a *bold* act. To throw off the oppressions of this troll in the President's mansion."

"William Williams says that abandoning 3net has left our Cloud subject to the brute whims of Europe's old powers."

"William Williams says we should be making peace with the English, to defeat France and open up trade with the Off-Worlders on our own terms."

"William Williams says the rise of the common man will lead to either a tyrannical oligarchy or a tyrannical mob. Liberty itself will be extinguished by too much democracy."

If these are the ideas of this generation's Federalists, Williams thinks, I'd hate to hear what this generation's Republicans are coming up with. Never mind who's going to save the country from Jeffersonianism. Who's going to save the human race from Americanism?

Williams tries, then, to see some kind of American future. But all he can conjure is a constantly swinging pendulum where men without property vote for laws to destroy entrenched property and then men with property vote for laws to keep down those who seek to destroy their property and then those who can't get property vote for laws to destroy the men who vote to keep them from destroying entrenched property.

"William Williams says that free market ideas will welcome back the fiscal insanity of the 1780s."

Another tells how William Williams just warned him of the "fiscal irrationalities we thought could exist only under kings and popes."

"He's talking about currency irregularities that will make *gold* look stable."

Young McClellan takes command of the room and relates something William Williams supposedly said to him the night before in a long bedside session of father/son-in-law bonding. "My father warned me not to think of Jefferson and Madison as futurist creatures of the Dream. They seek only to turn the clock *backward*, to lock in an antiquated agrarian mode of life, forcing on the nation clothes it has long outgrown."

Jefferson, William Williams thinks, a conservative now. I've taken way too long to die. Then it's off into some other tunnel of thought. Some of these digressions can run pretty deep. He decides this is what death will be like when it finally does come, drift off into thought and never return.

"Mr. Williams," one young Federalist whispers to him, "can you tell me where your Jefferson letter is? Jefferson's letters to the Signers?"

Signers. The Signers, Williams thinks. When the war starts, the English will stomp right down the coast of this defenseless countryside. They'll hang all the Signers they can find. The ones still left anyway.

"To the Fissure!" he hears again.

That night, after all the Federalists have gone, his wife detaches from the room's thick curtains of darkness and comes close enough for Williams to catch a last brush with her scent. "I know you cannot hear me," she whispers.

But I can, he thinks.

"There are things, Will, things I must tell you. If not for you, Will, then for me."

William Williams remains still.

"During the Revolution, while riding west to avoid the British invasion, I was forced upon by the nephew of a Continental officer. I never told anyone, worried that someone would think me responsible. I'm sorry I thought this of you." She moves the slightest bit closer to him. "Years later, there was a man. I met him in a chatroom in the Dream. Not sure if it was love, but it was something close. We never met in the real. If that makes it any better, I don't know.

"I also stole pennies from you," she whispers. "Saved them away but never found anything worth spending them on. It was an exercise in independence, I suppose."

William Williams isn't aware of time having passed, but he's conscious next of the room around him empty. Completely. The candles all blown out and not even the lingering scent of their wicks and wax remains. Morning comes as he lays there awake. Another procession of young men and their wives filling up the room of the dying Founder. Connecticut's last Signer.

But then another sort of men begin to arrive. Older men. Men who *were* there at Yorktown, at Trenton, some of them actually there in person. The old Federalists of Connecticut. The Wolcotts and Goodriches, Huntingtons, Smiths and Swifts, and of course the Trumbulls. Full force. Governor Griswald and John Cotton Smith and his little trail of Puritan thugs. This development gives Williams the understanding that something more important and bigger than his death is happening here today. Even Federalists from other states begin dropping by. How long does it take these days, he wonders, to get from Northampton, Massachusetts, or the Port of New York all the way to Lebanon, Connecticut?

A young Federalist takes the opportunity to raise a toast. "To the men of the Revolution," he says. He sweeps his glass in an arc toward the older beings in the room. "To the men of Washington. The gods of Federalism. The saviors of our great nation of liberty."

"Gods," William Williams says then. Actually says it out loud for everyone in the room to hear. Most surprised of all are his daughter and son-in-law. Williams thinks, maybe we have reached the day I always knew would come, when men are made into gods who can say and do no wrong, their words as sacred as the scriptures. And anyone who challenges these will be banished.

"Our illustrious Founding Father," one shouts, "says that God is sending something to punish America for the way we have acted these last twelve years."

"He has sent Jefferson," someone remarks, breaking the room into polite laughter.

"To the Fissure!"

"To the Fissure!"

Williams now raises a hand. The look on his wife's face—first a word, now this—she clearly considers the possibility that he could rise right off that bed and be back to his old self. She wonders if she could live with him knowing what she told him. But it is not meant to be. This isn't a revival but an encore. "Bring me my son," Williams says. "Bring my son, Solomon."

"Solomon is dead."

"Oh," Williams says, remembering again the truth of it. "It was good, to spend a little time in this world, I guess."

PART 4 :: THE ATTACK OF THE VAMPIRE MILLIPUS

George Clymer always thought war rooms of the future would be big big big. Banks of paper-thin touchscreens and whole semi-transparent walls of holo-maps you could walk right through, zoom in on a flanking maneuver with a flick of your finger. But the future is here and it's not what this old man had expected. No maps at all and so how are you supposed to tell where the fighting's going on? No row of computer terminals, no hordes of scuttling aides. Both his son and grandson are neck-deep in western defense, but whatever they're doing, they're doing it all with smartlenses. The room is the same exact living room as before the war, fire going and tea in the kettle. Kind of cozy, actually.

Clymer can't help but wonder, if things didn't move so fast, if there weren't allchats and tickles, instant messages getting countered and redacted before they've even been read, reply-alls coming so fast, from so many different directions, then maybe things wouldn't get ratcheted up so quick. It's like a fever, the speed of communication these days. No chance for cooler heads. And so here we are, at war.

In order to see what either of the younger generations of Clymer men is up to, the old man can't just look over a shoulder. He has to have one of them redfang into his old smartpad and slave his display. "Why don't you just get a smartlens, Dad?"

"Yeah, Grandpa. They're cheap as hell now. You can get a G1."

"I don't like how small the display is. I want it *big*."

"Doesn't get any bigger than your entire field of vision."

George Clymer did try one of the smartlenses once but couldn't figure out how to stop seeing it when he was done with Newnet. "You just ignore it," they told him, "and it goes into ghost mode." *Ghost mode?* Yeah, no thanks. But even with his smartpad redfanged right in, he still can't get a handle on what they're doing. They move so fast they smear the Dream; all George Clymer sees are boxes and colors and text all mixed together.

"You look pretty old, Granddad, with that old smartpad."

Clymer looks up to see the teasing face of his grandson. "Well, you two look like a couple of haunts to me. Floating around the room like that, waving your hands at nothing, talking to no one." He finger flicks to his grandson's display. Curser's jumping from Brainpages through Dream feeds and chatrooms and allchats, right into what look like screen captures of a war simulation. Maybe they're right; maybe he does need a smartlens to understand all this. "What are you doing?" Clymer asks.

"Rebuilding the massacre."

"The massacre?"

"The River Raisin."

"Some Indians, Dad. Got drunk and chopped up a bunch of Kentucky militiamen *after* they'd surrendered." His son makes a motion like scalping himself with the edge of his hand.

"What were they doing surrendering?"

"Guess they were surrounded."

George Clymer watches the same cobbled video his grandson is watching.

"See, Grandpa. If this guy dies *here*, then *this* comes after *this* because in *this* he's alive."

George Clymer's face must reveal perfectly how baffled he is.

"You just link their face pattern to their Dream avatar. Use a little probabilities coding, you know, to fill in the gaps. The Dream does most of the work." Clymer watches the separated pieces of footage becoming more and more coherent. Gaps of time gone between captured instants, just like the kid says. "Once we're done, anyone in the Dream can step right in and *experience* it for themselves."

George Clymer whistles. "Sounds pretty intense."

"It's for the families, too. Now they can go in and see how their dad or brother or husband or whoever died. The surety is better." The kid taps his head. "Imagination can come up with atrocities that make reality just plain comforting."

"But who was capturing all this?"

"The footage came in on their smartlenses."

"No wonder we're losing the war. Messing with their smartlenses when they should be fighting."

"You can fight just fine with a smartlens on."

"And we are *winning* the war, Dad."

George Clymer thinks a moment. "Do you say *in* or *on*?"

"In or on what?"

"Do you say a smartlens is *in* or a smartlens is *on*?"

His grandson doesn't even stop to think about it. The kid's concentrating on some clip set to loop. Must be working some of that coding magic on it, breaking down the actions to ifs and thens, how this Indian went from killing this Kentucky soldier to killing the one who's running away a few clips before. Clymer watches a hatchet get slammed into a soldier's skull and the soldier goes so still he looks like an avatar on pause, his user gone for the great bathroom break. "Are you sure experiencing this is something Americans are going to want to do?"

"Don't worry, Grandpa, that soldier didn't really die."

"What?"

The kid laughs. "That soldier and that Indian. Looks like they're just some drones, snuck into the Dream feed after it went up."

"Snuck in? They weren't there during the fighting?"

His grandson laughs. "No, Grandpa. They're just drones playing around in the feed."

"I'm going to sit down." But George Clymer already is sitting down. No more down to go unless he wants to lie on the floor and really call it quits.

"Look at this one, Grandpa. This is a real one. No drones."

George Clymer watches what his grandson tells him is a *real* scalping, but he can't much tell the difference. He's not sure if it should affect him more or less. He unmirrors his display and watches the curtain billow for a few minutes. "Why the hell are you guys working on defending Michigan territory, anyway? What you should be worried about is defense right here in Pennsylvania."

"Got this guy out there, Dad, called The Prophet. Says he's going to summon the drones."

"You mean like the drones inside the Dream feed of the massacre? Summon them?"

George Clymer's son turns. He flicks his iris, shooting his smartlens display forward, to hover in the center of the room. A hologram of a clearing in the woods, a deep gorge of lava slicing lengthwise down the center of a long, sloping field. A strange red glow pulses from within.

"What the hell are you showing me?" Clymer demands.

"The Fissure."

His grandson pipes in, "The Prophet says he's going to summon the drones across the Fissure. Into the real. To join forces with the Indians and destroy America. Hand us right back to the British, or the French, or whichever old power will have us."

"W. H. Harrison is on his way," his grandson says. "And when his boys see what the Indians did to our soldiers . . . *Remember the Raisin*, it's the new big tickle."

Clymer sighs. "I got a feeling we're not going to have any choice but to remember it." The holographic fissure vanishes. "Remember the Raisin," Clymer mumbles. "Ben Harrison's boy, you say?" He turns things over in his brain, doesn't need any Dream feed to picture what it all could mean. "Those drones come streaming into Michigan territory, Pennsylvania's going to be next. Makes me wish M'Kean was still governor. He may be a back-stabbing SOB, but he knew how to kick a little ass. Would be kicking some British ass right now if he were still in charge."

"He tried last year, remember? Mustering that militia outside Philadelphia. The guy's *so* old, Dad."

"Just because he signed the DOI doesn't mean he's any good in a hyperwar."

"The *doy*?"

"Declaration of Independence, Dad. You signed it, too."

"Yeah, I guess so." Clymer lifts a finger. "You know, that SOB M'Kean one time, right in front of everybody, slapped me on the back and you know what he called me?"

Both son and grandson *do* know. They've heard this story at least once a year since the year it happened. And that was *years* ago.

"*George Social Clymer.*" Clymer laughs. He takes a moment of stillness. "Never would have won the Revolution if we'd had the Internet holding us back. Makes me wonder sometimes if *The Death* and the curse are connected somehow. Maybe it was *The Death* that started America and so it's fifty years from the appearance of *The Death* that the curse strikes."

"Oh, Grandpa, not the curse."

Clymer watches his son and grandson work a second. Maybe if they listened to the old folks a little bit, maybe they could get themselves out of this mess instead of further and further into it. He knows they think they're winning, that victory is some kind of inevitability, ordained by their nation's dedication to liberty. "When I was your age . . ." but Clymer stops. He was about to say, I was signing the Declaration of Independence. But then he realizes he was quite a bit older than his grandson is now. I was forty-two. Gosh, Clymer thinks, I should sit down. He looks at the chair he's already seated in.

"You can come, if you like, George."

Clymer snaps up because the voice is not the voice of his son or grandson. Hovering there before him is Francis Hopkinson, his outline anyway. Formed of a thin sheen of pixels, Hopkinson flitters and flashes, a cheap hologram of the man Clymer once knew so well. Clymer realizes he's standing now, and he turns and looks back and sees himself slumped over and still in that chair. Neither son nor grandson has noticed yet, they remain neck-deep in the Dream, rebuilding the past to steer the future through a war. "What is this, Hopkinson?"

Francis Hopkinson looks over his shoulder at a portal that shimmers and flits code. "Retake America, from the Dream side out."

"Retake it from whom?"

But Hopkinson only smiles. "You ready for one more adventure, George?"

J
ust another day for Benjamin Rush. He's had 24,000 of them or so over the years. But then Thomas M'Kean shows up and that changes everything. Not just another day anymore. Standing in the front hall of Rush's house, the two old Signers shake hands. "Mr. M'Kean. Actually here in the real."

"Hello, Ben."

Rush invites M'Kean into his study, where he has several feeds coursing in, separate live streams of the House and Senate, debating funding for naval construction and federal control of state militias, respectively. A small inferno burns in the fireplace beneath the screens, crackling and oozing heat. Rush clears his throat, points at the feeds. "What do you see, Tom?"

"John Randolph of Roanoke doing the John Randolph of Roanoke."

"No." Rush zooms the House display to highlight a single pixelated figure, half-there against the chamber's back wall. "Thought with Newnet we were getting rid of haunts and drones and all the awful things that used to pervade the old Internet. But now Newnet has all those things and worse. And it's more impossible to tell the difference between them and any real user."

M'Kean takes an offered seat. "We keep trying to eliminate the drones and the drones keep returning. Maybe they have nothing to do with man at all, were here before us and will be here after. The Dream's just opened up a place where our worlds can cross over."

Rush plops into the den's other chair. "The first hyperwar. We can watch it all from the comfort of our palms."

"A long way from wondering if Off-the-Grid is still alive. But you never did like the Old Man."

Rush smirks. "Like him fine now, compared with what these kids have to offer." Rush takes a long look at his guest. M'Kean has picked up a tremor, his age finally beginning to show; it shakes him a little while he sits there, but he's still as lean and angled and dangerous-looking as ever.

"I remember when the Dream was just a way to organize a press blitz." M'Kean waves a hand at it.

"Kids probably think it was like that from the dawn of man. Along came the old Internet and with it the Dream." They both laugh. "Physical locations are a fad. Soon, Congressmen and Senators will just stay at home in their subsidized mansions. I'm not sure who's the biggest threat: the English, the Off-Worlders, the Federalists or the Republicans."

"Coming apart, pulling together. Depends on how long a lens you take to it."

Rush shakes his head.

"It's just their way," M'Kean says. "These new Americans. We fought our fights pretty rough."

Rush holds fingers up like it's a list he's worked through a hundred times. "Standing army. Deficit spending. Permanent forts all over the country. Instead of fighting for independence, we're trying to take over Canada. They're even talking about 3net again. And that's the *Republicans!*"

M'Kean sits there a while, listening to Rush work himself through what sounds like his standard dinner party shtick. Boring as it is, it can be important, sometimes, to give people a chance to let their favorite noises hiss out.

"Baltimore's like a war zone," Rush says. "The Paris of the West. Poor Light Horse Harry. Killed by a mob in the street. An American mob. Here, in America! Brits show up, they won't know who to kill and who to welcome back to the Empire. I sure can't tell. Got their own private navy there in Baltimore. Running up and down the coast taking potshots at anything that floats the jack. How long before the tide tips and they can make more money doing the same thing for the King?"

"Yep, pretty wild."

"Andrew Jackson's down there running crazy in Florida like there never were any rules. You seen this guy John Coffee he's got? What laboratory was that monster grown in?" Rush shivers. "And we thought Jefferson's twins were creepy."

"It's good for the kids, this war. They need to work on making some heroes of their own. Not too many of us real ones around anymore." M'Kean shows off that palsy in his hand. "Soon there won't be any left. A perfect vacuum and some dickhead who's never done anything will get sucked in, be the next George Washington."

"The Dream sure makes the war look okay," Rush says. "But Admiral Cockburn and that attack dog, Lieutenant General George Ross, tearing up the entire Chesapeake Bay. They'll make a wasteland of the whole seaboard if someone doesn't stop them."

"You're going to hate me for saying this, Rush. But it'd be nice to have George Washington around. Someone's got to knock that prick Cockburn's block off. Do it myself if I were young enough. Try something like that now, and I'd just make a fool of myself."

Rush watches what's coming through on the feed, clearly thinking of something besides what's coming through on the feed.

M'Kean looks, too. "After all we've done, this is what we're reduced to, watching and complaining. Complaining and watching. Come on, Ben. Let's turn this thing off and just not worry about it."

Rush appreciates it, lets a breathy chuckle escape vague and unpointed. "I remember the day John Morton died. The day we uploaded the Articles." Rush ponders, his brain off on one of its meanders. "I always wondered if maybe those Articles had something else in them. Something maybe they got from John Morton, all that blood and phlegm splattered all over his laptop."

"Calling what we did back then the Immortal Congress," M'Kean says.

Rush sighs. "We lose this war, Tom, it's back to colonies, and everything we've done these last fifty years will be wiped out of the Cloud forever. Like it never happened."

"Why don't we just enjoy the afternoon, then? Us old guys, maybe we shouldn't be so worried about the war. How it might or might not come out."

Rush is measuring his words: "Because you think we won't live to see the end of it? You know something I don't? British on their way to Philly? Going to hang the two of us, finally, for signing the Declaration?"

"It's something in the Dream, Ben. Jefferson's calling it Central Programming."

"Central Programming?"

"Like scar tissue in the Cloud. Some of that coding that makes up the protocols of the Dream, of Newnet, sort of calcified at some point. Developed a nerve center."

"Are you saying the Cloud has grown a brain?"

M'Kean's eyes widen. "That's a scary way to put it, Ben, but yes, I suppose so."

The two sit thinking a few moments.

"Well," M'Kean continues, "we figured out how to tap into it. And one of the things we found . . . Central Programming, it can take your Brainpage, your Dream avatar, cross-reference it with all the other echoes you make in the Cloud—"

"It can determine the date of your death?"

M'Kean nods.

"And today's mine?"

"'Fraid so."

"How?"

M'Kean shrugs, lets silence be his answer.

"I feel okay."

M'Kean smiles. "You never were that good a doctor."

Rush laughs. "Awful big of you, then, to come and spend my last day with me."

"No patriot of your caliber should have to die alone."

Rush retains that smile. "Where's the cutoff line? What caliber of patriot do you need to be to be assured a visit by Thomas M'Kean the day Central Programming predicts you're going to die?" They look into the Dream feed. Rush takes a deep breath, lets it out slowly. He feels his body sinking away from the main courses of the world. "I watch this war now, it's like watching someone else's world." He stands, goes to the desk in the corner. "Are you sure about this Central Programming thing?" And it's the first time M'Kean has heard a bit of fear in the doctor's voice. "I really do feel fine."

"Sorry, Ben."

But even before M'Kean says it, Rush is waving it off. Comes away from the desk with a letter, twice folded. "You know what this is, right?"

M'Kean pats the breast of his coat. A few layers down, his own Jefferson letter. "Never leaves my side."

Rush is falling back into his chair. "I've wondered about these letters, Tom. What parts of something larger they all must be."

M'Kean lets the room slow down. "Knowing Jefferson, there's probably some code embedded in the layout of the characters. Corresponds to an address you can enter in the Dream and it takes you to a secret chatroom where all the Signers have been uploaded as they die.

A place where the great avatars go to hash out democratic philosophy on into eternity, ever toward greater and greater compromises that inch in half-steps toward perfection but never quite get there."

"I don't think Tom Jefferson's the kind of guy who's into private heavens. But yeah, I suppose they contain some riddle." Rush lets his letter fall open. He reads silently a moment.

"I could take yours," M'Kean says. "Maybe collect the others."

"Don't think that's going to be possible."

"Why not?"

But Rush just smiles, shakes his head a little. "I guess you'll see in a little while. Maybe . . ." The doctor works himself to his feet. "Gosh," he says.

"You okay?"

"Might be that I'm feeling something coming on." And he lays a hand flat across his chest. "Always thought I would die with the country at peace."

"What is it?"

Rush tries to take a step but can't. Goes down on one knee and there he is, wobbling like that. Central Programming was right, he thinks. M'Kean is up, spry for a man almost eighty. He helps his old friend to the floor. Rush lays there flat on his back, looking upward. "Anything I can do, Doctor?"

Rush grasps for M'Kean's hand. "Tell me I've measured up, Tom, even if it's a lie."

"You were right there the whole way, Ben. More than measured up. In some ways, you set the bar."

M'Kean watches Rush's face melt into a smile. The actual moment of death is clear, a stillness that settles in with unmistakable finality. M'Kean sets the hand, inanimate, across its owner's corpse, waits a moment out of respect, then looks to the table beside Rush's chair. But the Jefferson letter is gone, vanished. M'Kean smells smoke. *Is something burning?*

T he Paine girls have been thrown into a low-bubbling hysteria over videos that hit the Dream just a few hours before: a giant cephalopod thrashing small fishing towns up and down the coast of Nova Scotia. "Must have been that thing that sucked the blood out of those sailors," one says. Because reports are coming in about the bloodless bodies being dug out of the towns this thing has destroyed. And "destroyed" is the right word. Only a few leaning joists left standing. Footage of the thing is always bouncing two second clips, and then whoever's filming gets snatched up, too. Buildings falling into the blur of thrashing tentacles. Bodies flung left and right, all bloodless. Doesn't seem to be a human able to escape all those tentacles. Hundreds of them, maybe thousands.

The latest uploaded clip of the monster shows it swimming southward off the coast of Maine, then wasting a ship of the line with a few flicks of those tentacles. As the ship goes down, so does the monster, turns a big eye toward the shore and then dunks below the surface.

All of the Paine daughters are there. All four of them. Not one died in childbirth or rearing. None taken by *The Death*. Not one killed in a war, this one or the Revolution. Not one has fallen to disease or violence. When Robert Treat Paine has a daughter, that daughter grows up big and strong. Same can't be said for the boys. Of four, only one remains, serving on the *USS Frolic*, somewhere in the vast curves of the Gulf of Mexico.

"Maybe he'll return tomorrow. All the ships have been called in. The entire navy, so how long will that take?"

"I think we should tell Father," one whispers. "He has the right to know."

"Even if it kills him?"

Throat-clearing crackles from a bed in the corner of the room. "I may not be able to hear what you're saying, but that doesn't mean I don't already know." The girls look just in time to watch Robert Treat Paine take his last breath and go still. And so they call the doctor up from the downstairs parlor, where he's been camped in the liquor cabinet since he first arrived a few days before. The doctor comes in, turns a dial on a small transmitter beside the bed and just like that Robert Treat Paine comes back from the dead. "I've been to the future," he tells them. Which is the exact thing he tells them each time he's revived.

It was a few days back when the doctor injected some microscopic computer chips into Robert Treat Paine. The doctor told the Paine daughters that the computer chips were like little drones. He held up that dial for them all to see, turned it a few notches and back came their old dad. "It uses the parts of the Cloud that you're existing in at any one moment to vibrate your cells. Works pretty much the same as a smartlens, only in reverse, Cloud adjusts *you* a little." He smiles. "Smartlife."

Now every time the old man drifts off to the land beyond, the doctor will come from downstairs and turn the transmitter up a little higher. And Robert Treat Paine will flutter back from the grave and tell his daughters, "I've been to the future."

Deciding a hallucinating dad is better than no dad at all, one of his daughters settles in next to the bed. "Tell me about the future, Dad."

"The Fissure," Robert Treat Paine says. "It happens. The country splits. Rhode Island is destroyed in the fighting. Broken right off into the Atlantic. New England and New York become part of England again. Tariffs are less, actually, than under the Virginians. But none of that matters because no one can go in the water. Not the oceans, not the streams, not even the ponds. Turn on your faucet and it might come out and get you."

"What's going to get you?"

"The Vampire Millipus!"

The girls all look around. Who told him? But they're all shaking their heads and trading glances, and then looking back at their dad.

"It had babies," he tells them.

"Babies?"

"Planted inside some soldiers it ate on its way up the Mississippi."

"No, Dad, it's off the coast of Canada."

"Maybe *now* it is. Remember, this is the future I'm talking about."

They can't help but smile.

"The drones," he says. "They came across. All of them. Not tens, but *hundreds*. Hundreds of millions. It wasn't an invasion, they just filled the place right up. Filled up every city and country town and started making towns of their own. And if you think kids today are half in the Dream, these drones looked like what ghosts would look like if ghosts were real. Half there and translucent. You can see everything inside them with just a glance."

Robert Treat Paine takes a few long breaths. "The Cloud, the Dream, Newnet. None of it survived the war. All those drones came across and that was it. The Cloud couldn't take it, fell in on itself. Looked like a tornado, dust spinning, winds that spit eastward right to the coast. The whole thing collapsed. The air was buzzing for a week. And that's when the Off-Worlders attacked."

His daughters share a few concerned looks.

"Vaporized every army on earth. Not just here, but in Europe and Africa, too, Asia probably, but we didn't have any way to know.

No Newnet, no Cloud. People and drones alike, all watching the sky for what the Off-Worlders were going to do next. Avoiding any body of water bigger than a frog pond. Who wants to live in a world like that, where a sip of water could plant a Millipus larva inside you? Where there's no Cloud? Where the Dream is collapsed? And so humans started talking about a way to escape. And the only place they could think of was the old Internet."

"They went back through the Fissure?"

"Mary!"

"What? It's interesting."

"No. The Millipus had destroyed it. Swam right up the Mississippi and destroyed the Fissure. Knocked it back into the earth. All that was left was a field with some prints of its suction cups."

"But how did it get past New Orleans?"

"What's in New Orleans to stop it? It just bashed the place with its tentacles. Reared up like a horse and just fucking bashed the place."

"You sure were gone awhile, Dad."

"What about the President?"

"What president? President of what?"

"The President of the United States."

"States? There were some left in New England. The rest were all dissolved. Dissolved and fissured until there was nothing. Just drones guarding shacks with old muskets. Small bands of humans scavenging for clean water. The Capitol was burned to the ground and left there in ashes forever."

"And the Off-Worlders, I suppose, turned the whole world into a farm to make more of those crystals."

"Probably would have," he agrees. "But we found a way. Americans found it. New Englanders," he says. "It was the last place where humans were still human. The last place with a connection to the real. Everyone sacrificing, everyone contributing. They reorganized the entire society around finding a way to reopen the Fissure. Some way across. A way to escape and save the human race. And then, there it was. They found it and in they went. Back into the old Internet to live on. And not just the humans but all the drones and the AIs, too. And the old haunts. And then it was the real world that was the wasteland. Carcasses of starving Millipi putrefying in the skeletons of destroyed port cities. For centuries that seemed like minutes in the old Internet."

"None of that's going to happen, Dad. We're going to win this war."

"I believe him," one daughter says.

"If you've really been forward in time, Dad, then when do you die?" The other daughters all look at their sister, eyes like the eye of the monster for even thinking such a thing, much less asking it. But then they all glance dadward to see what he's going to say.

"Funny you should ask . . ." but his words trail off. Dead again.

"Get the doctor!" the eldest daughter commands. And when he's rushed into the room, she tells him, "Turn it up, Doc."

"Okay, but that's as high as it goes. Can't go any higher."

Robert Treat Paine's eyes flutter open. He points them in the general direction of all the faces looking down at him. "Don't you people know how to let a Founder die?"

The doctor laughs. "End of the line for me, ladies." He makes for the door. "I'll be in the liquor cabinet if you need me."

The room back to just Paines, daughters circling their father for a last look. "I'm sure Henry will make it home," one says.

Robert Treat Paine smiles. "Remember, girls, I've been to the future. So I already know."

"Well?" one asks. "What happens to him?"

"Does Henry make it?"

"Will we see him again, father?"

"Has he been eaten by the Millipus?"

Robert Treat Paine just pats the closest hand and goes still yet again.

"Judge Paine!" someone yells. And the girls all realize it's the doctor. "The Off-Worlders!" he's shouting.

The daughters all rush to the window, throw open the shutters to look out at Boston harbor. The Off-Worlder ship that's been hovering since back before the war has left its position and is headed southward.

"The Off-Worlders," one of the daughters says.

"They're moving." And they look back at the bed where their father lies, too dead now for any smartlife to wiggle him out of this moment in time.

"**M**ister Vice President!"

Gerry opens his eyes to watch a young aide stumble into the room. The kid's boots are covered in soot from a scramble through the burnt-out Capitol. Gerry had, just a few minutes before, sunk back in a soft chair and was almost in nap. Now he's perking himself up, shakes off what little sleep he's gathered and asks the kid, "You find the Senate Pro Tem?"

The aide is taking big breaths, hands gripping pants fabric into bunches on his knees. Swallowing, shaking his head, "John Coffee, sir, is on feed from outside New Orleans."

A smile from the Vice President. "The Cloud is still up, then. And Jackson is still out there."

"For now, sir. But . . ."

"What is it?"

"The Off-Worlders, Mr. Vice President. That's what Coffee's calling about."

Gerry tries to patch into the feed on his smartlens, but there isn't any signal. He moves to a few different spots, his lucky place by the window that sometimes gives him a bar or two. Head shaking, he turns to the kid.

"I've got two horses out front, Mr. Vice President. We've got to get you to a terminal."

Gerry cracks a smile. "Cloud on the flicker, troops marching the coast, Redcoats lurking around every bend. Just like the Revolution."

In the saddle, the Vice President and his aide cross over from Georgetown, then pick their way down trash-strewn Pennsylvania Avenue. Slaves and poor whites scurry from their path, arms loaded with whatever loot the British have left unlooted. Gerry takes it all in. "Looks like the war has finally reached America."

"It's pretty bad, sir." The kid nods to the wreckage of the President's mansion, just a blackened shell.

Gerry disengages from the conversation. He's looking into the roasted skeleton of the President's mansion but not really seeing it. "If this isn't the curse, then I don't want to be around for what is."

The kid's thinking of something else. "The Millipus," he says. "They say it's not even fully in the real, sir. That it's been seen in the Dream now, too. How do we kill it if it can slip back and forth at will?"

Gerry shakes his head. "If we're to survive long-term, we're going to have to get used to these kinds of multi-platform threats." He straightens himself in his saddle, forcefully clicks his horse into a trot, nods at where the Capitol building once stood. All that's left is the foundation. The rest has been burned and sucked into the earth. It makes the destroyed President's mansion look like a mansion. Gerry rolls up a sleeve. Old Sons of Liberty tattoo has faded some, but it's still there. "Don't worry," the Vice President says. "We'll rebuild it."

They descend into the guts of the archives, the only building left standing among the punched-out teeth of the National Mall. In the screen of the one working terminal, Gerry can see the choppy form of Captain John Coffee, Andrew Jackson's right-hand man. The image cuts backward and forward, showing code through the pixels; it's about the best you can get out of the Dream these days.

"How's the general?" Gerry wants to know. "Worried you guys were wiped out. You can hear me alright, Captain?"

"Pretty okay, Mr. Vice President." Coffee's big head fills the screen, flickering, starting, stopping. His words come out disconnected from the image. Looks like a bunch of still photos talking.

"Got some strange reports up here," Gerry tells Captain Coffee. "That the general's been executing our own soldiers. You know, there are some Indians down there, Spanish, too, if you just *gotta* kill somebody."

"We need a way of keeping the militia from going off to the races every time they see a line of Redcoats."

"Yes," Gerry says. He nods and nods. "It's a good thing you young men have a handle on this thing. Us older guys don't seem to have a clue." He glances upward, a gesture toward the burned-down Capitol teetering all around them. "Now, what's this I hear about Off-Worlders?"

"Their ships. They've converged over New Orleans."

"They're attacking?"

"No," Coffee says. "Just watching, it looks like."

"How many?"

"Twelve ships. No sort of formation, just a little cluster pocking the sky. General Jackson doesn't like it one bit."

"Can't imagine he would."

"Where's the President?"

Gerry shakes his head. "You should see this place, Captain. Government's scattered. President's in the hills somewhere. We hear he's sick, maybe on his death bed, maybe shot. Secretary of War, well, there's isn't one. Not really. Monroe rode through a couple of times, seems like he was starting to put things together. But now we've got word he's captured or killed." Gerry tries to brighten it with a little of his working-class charm. "Some people say they can get on the Dream. We're picking it up a little here. But for whole parts of the country, there's no signal at all. Brits aren't any better off, at least. Their cloud's infected, too. Cross-infected. Barely holding together." Gerry stops himself from continuing, asks the Captain, "What's General Jackson's plan?"

"We're going to have our hands full with Wellington's troops when they land. We'll be here to meet them, but that's all the plan we have." Coffee cuts in and out. He's there and gone and then frozen and then moving forward in halts. "If the Off-Worlders jump in on us while we're fighting the Brits . . . we'll have to see what they've got and improvise." Coffee tries to patch in a feed of the Port of New Orleans, but it's frozen and filled with grain—not a single hard edge. "Hickory says the plan is to kill anything that gets in front of our guns—Redcoat, drone, Indian or Off-Worlder."

Then Coffee's voice is gone. On the screen, the vague outlines of the Off-Worlder ships hovering over New Orleans dissolve into static only. "Talk to me, Coffee." But that's it. Communication with Jackson's ragtag army is severed. It reminds Gerry of those days before the Constitution when the Internet was first reopened and there wasn't a single rule or regulation. Everything was just piles of unchecked links, impossible to find or use.

Some shouting and gunfire bring Gerry back to the real. He turns to see that aide of his laying face up at the foot of the stairwell. Some British soldiers have entered the room. They stand there on pause, their rifles pointed at him. Into the doorway behind them steps Admiral Cockburn himself, the terror of the Mid-Atlantic. Uniform looks just pressed, pressed and polished under that huge cockade. This is the man who gave the orders to launch the invasion that destroyed D.C., sent the American government scurrying.

"Admiral Cock Burn," Gerry says. "You Brits have finally caught up with me. After all these years."

"It's '*Coh-burn,*' Mister Gerry. *Sir* Coh-burn. But what kind of King's English can we expect from the son of a reverend from . . . *Mhalbilled Mass?*"

"Nothing quite like a proper English dandy, fresh off the tit of the King, putting on a Boston accent. Gives me a boner every time."

Admiral Cockburn examines something under the tips of his fingernails. "They say the Cloud is coming to pieces because of this fissure out near Detroit."

"You imperialist pigs are the ones who diddled with the Cloud so long. Impressing other countries' signals. Partitioning all of Europe and South Asia. What did you expect was going to happen?"

Cockburn frowns. "One hundred million drones, they estimate. About to enter the great Northwest. And Francis Hopkinson is leading them. Funny, no? One of your Founding Fathers—a Signer no less—back from the grave to ring in the destruction of the country. Be here in a few weeks, I imagine."

"You believe everything you read in the Dream, *Cock Burn?*"

Admiral Cockburn looks around the room, largely untouched by the royal troops who burned the city. He takes a few steps, clearly hoping Gerry will join him in a leisurely stroll, but the Vice President stays right where he is. "Shame about General Ross," Gerry says. "Headed back to that King of yours in a keg of rum. That's what you get, I guess, when you fuck with the American Capitol."

Cockburn's face reddens. "Not only have you sunk to assassinating officers, but you're proud of it, too?"

"Officer is the same as any other soldier in my book. And any soldier can get shot. If you're in the war in this country, then you're in the war in this country, whether you're a reverend's son or the son of some duke or lord who gave up on England long ago."

Cockburn draws his saber and cuts a shape into the air. Just misses Gerry three different ways. And Gerry felt it, too, felt the tip of that blade flick his cheek. Cockburn rests the point of the sword on that faded Sons of Liberty tattoo, the segmented snake, JOIN OR DIE. "Terrorists," Cockburn sneers. "You Americans are terrorists." The Admiral stays still a moment, only his lip moving, a slight quiver that breaks into an evil grin. "The Royal Navy is in control of Maine, Mr. Gerry. Most of the eastern Great Lakes. This little armpit you colonists call the mid-Atlantic doesn't look much better than your burnt-out Capitol. Seems I've pretty well gelded the men of this continent."

"Forgot your lunch, though, at Fort McHenry, when you got taken to school."

Cockburn presses a smile. "There's something cute about a self-diluted subject, cracking wise at the tip of a sword, in the pit of a burned-down provincial city." Cockburn steps away to circle again the edge of the room, the cockade changing the shape its shadow makes on the wall. "I wonder, though, Mr. Gerry, if His Majesty's Empire is what you should be worried about at all. Captain," and one of the royal soldiers steps forward, "show the Vice President what's happening right now in Connecticut."

"Yes, sir," and the captain flicks forward his smartlens display. A hologram in the center of the room shows a crackling feed of a parade ground, two armies marching in threatening review formations with the gap between them shrinking.

"New London, Connecticut," Cockburn says. "That's your state militia squared off against your federal army." Cockburn chuckles. "You colonists, always imagining you have some role in the unfolding of your destiny. Really, your revolts have been little skirmishes on the edges of a world war. Well, that war is over now. France is defeated. Your side has lost. The American Revolution will be a few links in the database, not much more."

Cockburn snaps and the captain flicks his iris. The projected display dissolves into an ocean. A few seconds of a looped feed shows the shadowy shape of the Millipus, its tentacles lashing through the waves at its sides. "Sent to us by one of the Spanish governors in Florida. Looks like our little friend is headed into the Gulf. Maybe New Orleans? Don't look so surprised, Mr. Gerry. If the monster doesn't want ships in the ocean, it makes sense to destroy the biggest port in the hemisphere." On cue, the British captain switches the display to a map of the entire North American theater. "Your own armies are fighting themselves on one side, drones coming in on the other. When this squid thing reaches New Orleans, this little country of yours is going to be taking it three ways. Three ways hard."

"It's a Millipus," Gerry informs him.

"Ah, yes, *Vampire Millipus*. And what of the Off-Worlders, Mr. Gerry? What side are they on, I wonder . . ." Cockburn puts out a hand. An officer steps up and slaps a revolver into his palm.

"What's that for?" Gerry wants to know.

"My daddy," Cockburn says. "Always wanted to kill a Signer. 'A Signer and a President,' he always said. Said if I ever got the chance, I shouldn't pass it up."

"Kill me? I'm eighty. Wait around a few weeks."

"Afraid that would be a little slow for my tastes. Plus—" The projection cuts out, stopping Cockburn mid-sentence. The room feels suddenly empty.

"No signal, Admiral."

Cockburn shrugs. "War could be over any minute now," he says. "They're just trying to figure out some fishing rights. But who's going fishing with that . . . *Millipus* out there? Probably we'll come out of this thing on the same side, Mr. Gerry. Humans versus the Off-Worlders and their monster." Cockburn lifts the pistol, points it at Gerry's chest. "Guess a Signer and a *Vice* President will have to do."

"**L**ast day on Earth for Thomas M'Kean." He struggles up from his chair to stand tall and all himself. He's alone there in his office, tucked back in the corner of his mansion. "Was hoping for some sun," he says. But it was cloudy, all day long, every time he checked the sky.

M'Kean takes his cane from a groove that's been rubbed in the mahogany siding. He pushes through the thin office door and into the hall. The tilting warble of his guests reaches him now. As he cuts his shape into the ballroom's far doorway, M'Kean looks down at the skeleton of a crowd. Most of the city is home nursing the hangover of a presidential visit. A solid week of constant parades and open-air festivities, dinner parties with toasts already fading the crest of a 3net viral. All throughout the city people poured to see the man who'll make the country whole again. Really, Philadelphia was just a tune up. President has a week of parties planned in New York and then its time for the real test: Can James Monroe get the Federalists of New England back on board, make them forget about the dissolve and the Fissure forever?

M'Kean made it to one of the ceremonies. Just a drop-by, a drink and then on home. It was strange, all these heavies from both parties there in the same place. All doing their best to pretend the last two decades didn't happen. Right from Washington to Monroe and we're all one big happy family again. *The Era of Feeling Good.*

M'Kean laughs at it. He had to fight that horse-faced dolt like hell to get the Constitution ratified. He still remembers the kid over with Patrick Henry—the real Patrick Henry—predicting doom and the end of man if the Constitution became law. Luther Martin so drunk he was passing out on his feet. And now that anti-Federalist jackass James Monroe is President.

M'Kean takes a drink from the first tray that passes. Leans on his cane, sipping. Some kind of watered-down white wine. A man approaches with his free hand held up high for M'Kean to see. Lowers the hand and M'Kean gives it a shake. "It's me," the guys says. "Your new Senator."

"I know who you are." But really M'Kean has no idea.

"Thank God you guys had 3net ready."

"Was the Federalists who had 3net ready."

"You were a Federalist, M'Kean."

"Not then I wasn't." M'Kean pats the guy on his suit shoulder, looks past him, sees the current Governor has just made his entrance. Simon Snyder. This is a man he recognizes. Took over when M'Kean stepped down, almost got the Vice under Monroe. But, of course, it went to a New York man instead. Just like that, the bubble burst on Snyder. M'Kean wonders if the guy even knows it yet. He starts to pick his way through, keeping one eye on Snyder opposite, doing the same. The two governors, past and present, circle each other like old crows. Short glances up from breezy conversations as they close in. Then they're beside each other once again, each stirring a drink by wiggling it in his free hand.

"Maybe this new President is the curse."

M'Kean's eyes bound around the room a little. "Why you want to be talking about the curse, Simon?"

"Off-Worlders gone, Millipus dead, 3net is up and running, running smooth . . . what else is there?"

"Suspect there's plenty left around to worry about if we just look a little."

The current governor tilts his glass toward the north edge of town, where Monroe and his entourage rode out as the sun was rising. "Four years this guy has and then he's out."

"You really did want that Vice."

Governor Snyder smirks. "Wasn't Monroe that made the country whole at all. It was Jackson."

M'Kean rolls his eyes. "Lachlan McIntosh all over again."

"Well, better than another of these Virginians."

"What's wrong with Virginia that's not wrong with Andrew Jackson?"

They laugh. "But this kid, Monroe," Snyder has to admit. "Live 3netcast of the Fourth of July from Boston Harbor?" Snyder shakes his head, a touch of genuine admiration. "Could have done it from the White House, opened a 3net feed and patched it in. But he's going there. To actually be there. Right there in the port. No need to worry about that sea monster anymore, or the British or Off-Worlders either." Snyder smiles. "I tell you, he's got the Old Man act down pretty well."

A handshake, a pat on the arm and they roll, then, away from one another. M'Kean strolls a bit, finds a chair for his old body. A few minutes of nodding to people as they pass, then it's up again to mingle.

"Can't figure it out," one of his guests scratches. "Today's date. June the twenty-fourth?"

The guy's wife bobs there in one of those huge dresses. "Well, it's not your birthday."

M'Kean sipping.

"Is it some holiday we don't know about? A day you're trying to make a holiday? You trying to let us know some event occurred today worth celebrating? You announcing something, Tom? Coming out of retirement? Tell me, why the party?"

"Hannibal," M'Kean says. "Defeats the Romans at Trasimene." M'Kean smiles, nods at the thin crowd, changing shape only slightly around him. "Thought it was about time for a party is all."

M'Kean moves from room to room for a while, on whomever's arm is available. Still just as tall but thin-looking now in the door-ways he passes through. Greeting and moving on, muscle memory of a time when the strictness of such procedures made them all but brain-less. Now you have to work a crowd like you're not working it. Some things are just tiring to democratize. M'Kean can stand a few minutes at any one time, then he's looking around for the closest chair to sink into, down one layer under the festivities. Politicos of the B level and wigglers of industry bend as they pass. Their torsos all look the same. Their wives move the same way. Skin all the same shade of orange.

When M'Kean stands again, he recognizes the face of Caesar Rodney's nephew, Caesar A. Rodney. "I remember when your uncle rode that horse through the storm . . ." but M'Kean lets it trail off. "Heard that one enough by now, I'm guessing."

Rodney pats him on the back, sweeps the room with a tiny wave of his fingers. "So when does General Jackson make *his* tour?"

The two fall in line, walking slowly along the edge of the ball-room.

"Surely he's next," Rodney says. "This man of the people. Shut down the Dream and slayed the Vampire Millipus." He swirls his martini a little. "Scared off the Off-Worlders, too."

M'Kean smirks. "That's what they're saying?"

"Tell me, M'Kean, a little too convenient? That there's not one single second of feed?"

"Can't get a feed of something, Rodney, if there's no Cloud to upload it to. Jackson didn't just shut down the Dream; he shut down the whole thing. Dream, Newnet, the old Internet."

Rodney, as if seeing the nonexistent feed across his smartlens right then, Jackson's horse rearing up under the tentacles of the

Millipus, sword drawn. "Wonder who gave him the idea. Lure the Millipus into the Dream and then shut it down. You think that maniac came up with it on his own? Hanging deserters, chasing Indians and Redcoats through the swamp is more his speed. The occasional duel. Fistfights is what he's good for. And where did he even get that crystal he supposedly used."

"Lighthorse Harry Lee gave it to him, just before he got beat to death by that mob, the poor SOB."

M'Kean watches Rodney sorting through it all. "Madison?" Rodney posits. "He's never been in love with the Dream, not really. Patrick Henry Group Avatar, goes down with the ship? Jefferson maybe, from some terminal he's got set up at Monticello?" Rodney sighs at the ridiculousness of it all.

"George Washington," M'Kean offers. "Maybe he was in there, watching over us from inside the Dream. Got his hands on Hopkinson at the last second. Pow! No more drone invasion. Then reached out and grabbed that Millipus. Just fucking wrassled it. Killed the thing and saved the country again. Probably died in the fight, too, this time for real. Washington dead forever and gone." M'Kean looks at Rodney's face. "Underestimation is the best favor you can do a man like Andrew Jackson."

They separate. M'Kean weaves his way through the edges of a few different circles which loosen and bulge as he approaches. It was nice to be around a shadow of the old Caesar Rodney, even with all its inexactness. Might be the closest thing to a Signer that shows up at this party. Unless Jefferson does decide to attend. Suddenly, some young buck is pumping M'Kean's hand a little too forcefully. "Just want to let you know, General, that the Federalists might be gone, but the Society of Cincinnati is in good hands and as strong as ever."

M'Kean looks at the kid and his little phalanx of young officers, all medaled up from the war just passed. Probably believe they won the thing. And there they go, off through the party like it's not happening around them, right out the door, business done. "Don't these guys stay for a drink anymore?"

"What's that?"

M'Kean turns to look at . . . who is this? He pats the guy on the shoulder. "Need a break from all this bustle," M'Kean says. "You mind helping me back to my office?"

Back down that same thin hall, M'Kean hanging on the guy's arm, leaning on the cane on the other side. A loose summary of state-wide issues trickling odorless in the air, the smallest kind of talk. They pass through three separate doorways and into the study. "If I'd known I was going to live this long," M'Kean tells the guy, "I would have made the house smaller." Which is funny because M'Kean did know he was going to live this long. Knew exactly when he was going to die.

Helping him down into a chair, the guy asks, "You alright, Governor?"

M'Kean chases him off with assurances. Loud sharp click of the door closing behind him. The party now barely reaches him. Could be a recording of a party, any one of the hundreds he's heard muffled through these house walls as he sat back here. Back in the office with some big wigglers, taking care of the *real* business of the get-together. Now it's just M'Kean. All alone.

There's a knock on the door, then, and in comes the last of the twins. Same age as always, but now with that mangled cheek of his, whole side of his face split open like hamburger let dry. He takes a chair, looks like it hasn't been sat in for a while, lets that remaining hand curl around the arm. The one person Central Programming couldn't give an end date on. And so M'Kean knows that at least one of three things must be true: Central Programming is wrong, this twin outlives Central Programming, or the twin and Central Programming both live forever.

"Mr. Jefferson's not coming," M'Kean says.

The twin nods. "Too far for him to travel, but he thanks you for the invitation."

"He knows what day it is."

The twin lets a gleam break his eye. "So today is your day? Your last day?"

"Tomorrow, technically. A few minutes after midnight. A little scared, I guess." M'Kean brings himself back to the room. "I've always wondered if Jefferson told you guys about Central Programming."

"He told us about it, what you two found, that time you were digging in there, way down deep in the Dream: a database of future dates, the day and time that every human dies."

M'Kean smiles. "Jefferson never looked, did he?" M'Kean seems more amused than surprised.

"He looked at his own date, and that's it." The twin gets that smile that people get when they really know Thomas Jefferson. "He always says, 'There are far too many interesting things in Central Programming to worry about the days that humans expire.'"

"But he couldn't resist seeing his own?"

"No one's perfect."

Now M'Kean lets a full smile creep. "And so you know, too, that Thomas Jefferson is to die exactly fifty years after the birth of the country, the day the curse comes . . . the end of America. Central Programming hasn't been wrong once. I've done a fair share of cross-checking."

"To believe that, you'd have to believe in the curse. What do you think, M'Kean? Can America survive Thomas Jefferson's death?"

It's a question not meant to be answered but only pondered further. M'Kean wonders how much of this back and forth was scripted ahead of time, instructions from Jefferson. Still don't feel too bad, he thinks. "We *were* friends once, Tom Jefferson and I."

M'Kean settles his eyes on the twin. "But really it's *you* I wanted to see. I want to apologize. About your brother."

"Because you knew?"

"I knew he would die that day and that you and I would not."

The twin forces a smile, head shaking in spite of Thomas M'Kean. "Of all the stuff we did, *that's* what you regret most? Enough to get me all the way out here so you can get it off your chest?"

"I guess I'm not the kind of guy who has lots of friends." M'Kean starts digging in his breast pocket. "I'm going to do you a favor."

"Is that your letter from Jefferson? From when he was elected?"

"Watch what happens to it." M'Kean barks a quick laugh. "Seen it once before. When Rush died. Damnedest thing if I know how Jefferson did it, that old kook." M'Kean looks at the paper, flopped open on his desk. When the last Signer dies, he thinks, there won't be anything left of the letters. They'll be gone forever. No back-ups, no cache ghosts of them floating in the Cloud, whatever cloud there is then. M'Kean wonders for the last time if it *is* going to be true, after all these years of knowing, the exact time of his death. He chases off the wonder, smiles, really smiles. He works himself to his feet, takes the cane. "Well, if you'll excuse me."

"You're headed back out?"

M'Kean pauses a moment before continuing. "I'm thinking one more swing through the people, however few are left out there." They shake firmly. "Now, you watch that letter." Then M'Kean ventures out, down that same long hall. As he crests the main room, he feels some tightening in his chest but presses on. Breaths are starting to come hard. M'Kean has to force them out and suck them in. He looks down at his smartpalm: ten of midnight. He wanders between some conversation circles until he gets to the big glass doors that let out onto the back veranda. Someone's saying something to him. M'Kean nods, then limps his way into the cool evening air. Overcast still lingering. So there'll be no more stars, not in his lifetime.

In the new quiet, M'Kean can hear his own wheezing, can hear the slow thumping of his heart. He crosses to a bench that was carved into the railing when the mansion was first built. Cool and damp from some condensation already forming. Not a soul out here with him. He can see their vague colors splashed on the glass. "So it's alone," he says to himself. "And this here, this here's the spot."

He turns his head to look out at his fields one last time. They shine a little with the dim diffusion of the sky laid over their dewy blades. In the distance, those awkward, crooked trees. The clock starts striking midnight. The official start of his last day. He's not going to make it much into it. M'Kean looks up at the clouded-over sky. "Would have liked one last clear night."

The doctor bursts in to find William Ellery by the window as always. "You're dead!" the doctor says. He points to his eyeball. "Came into my smartlens a few minutes ago."

Ellery looks at himself, his body half in that crooked parallelogram of light, comes from the sun, way far away from the Earth, to make this same shape every day.

The doctor steps into the room with a few big steps, starts glancing around. "Says you have no pulse, that your heart isn't beating, that you're not breathing."

Ellery stops all things for one moment. Perfectly still . . . listening. "I think I'm alive. But if the smartlife says I'm not, then I guess it must be true."

"You should have had the thing implanted, Ellery, like I said. I could up your meds from the office and save all these trips. I mean, why get a smartlife if you're not going to have it implanted? Lots of old folks are doing it." The doctor takes a chair that's sitting against the wall farthest from the window, lets his long jacket flop over either side. He sighs. "At this rate, Ellery, you might outlast the country."

"The country? Why, what's wrong with it?"

"You've seen what's going on out there." The doctor pulls out some kind of smartdevice. The thing is huge, the size of an old smartphone but sleek and devious-looking. When he talks now, the doctor is half talking; he's half in the room and half scraped off, into that thing he's got. "Commerce is all but frozen on 3net. People are talking about bringing back precious metals."

"Someone's always talking about bringing back precious metals."

"But now they're *really* talking about it, Ellery. These electronic transfers ain't worth the pulse they're sent on if no one believes in them. Talking about actually requiring face-to-face business transactions. Actually handing money over for things, *in person*."

Ellery turns to look down at the town center, gridded out below. Newport, Rhode Island. Ellery was made its collector the day after the Constitution was signed—George Washington's very first appointment—and has had one eye on this port ever since. "I've seen plenty of things in my years," Ellery says, "and this *panic* of yours. It ain't shit."

Only enough of the doctor peeking out of 3net to scoff. "The complete collapse of the financial system? *Ain't shit?*"

"The eighties, now that was a financial crisis."

"I was only a boy then, Ellery."

"The next time people talk about 'the eighties,' it's going to be the 1880s they're talking about." Ellery looks over at the doctor, looking into that smartdevice. "What is that thing? Don't think I've seen one of them before."

"Yes, you have. It's a smartlife."

Ellery looks at his old wrist model with its numbers all zeroed out. "Sure doesn't look like mine."

The doctor tells him, "This is the G5. But they should call it the H. Links right in with your smartlens. I'm following the market, watching the President's speech, reading some feed, trying to get this damned 3net app to accept the changes I made in its coding." The doctor holds his device up proudly. "Pretty soon the smartlens will be the smartlife and you won't have to have both."

Ellery rolls his eyes. He settles deeper into his chair, puts his forehead into that grease spot on the window where he leans his head sometimes. Can watch the outside world without having to hold anything up. The golden age of Newport, he thinks, long gone. "Once we competed with New York," Ellery says. "From all up and down the seaboard they came here, right here. From up and down seaboards the whole world over. Persecuted in Massachusetts, chased out of Russia and the Orient. Pilgrims from the land of pilgrims. Jews from Portugal, fleeing the Inquisition. Adventurers from countries it was the first I heard of when they told me where they were born. All that energy bottled up in their family trees since the beginning of time. Just waiting for a little freedom to shake it out. Newport. A new port. An island on the edge of a new world." He sighs. "Now the state capital's been moved to Providence. We're just an outpost for smugglers and pirates and damned slave traders. A hangout for old kooks and social rejects who somehow got their hands on way too much money."

The doctor creeps back and forth through the tides of 3net, all wavy and mixed in like it is these days. "Why don't you retire?" he says. "Enjoy your last few years of undead."

"Retire? Retire from what? 3net has automated everything." Ellery fixes his eyes on a far-off ship, floating just on the edge of vision. Kind of ship waits until night's dark to unload. "Don't need collectors of the port anymore. Captains can just scan their cargo, and the tariffs are calculated and deducted from their account. No inspection needed. These shippers now, so long as they're flying the Stars and Stripes, they're free to do whatever they want. That's why we fought the war, right? To free the Cloud for commerce."

"Isn't *the Cloud* anymore, Ellery."

"I know. 3net. It's the latest big tickle. Really, not much different, though, if you ask me. Same old things. Brainpage, Franklin's

Dream, but now with new names. Not long before drones start showing up. Then haunts. You wait."

"A drone on 3net?" The doctor laughs into his smartlife. "What I'm worried about is this damned panic."

Ellery wonders if there's a strategy to this type of listening. If the doctor tunes in at certain times or just waits until there's some quiet, recalls enough words to fashion a response that seems at least tangentially related. Or maybe these new humans have mastered it for real. Maybe living in two planes at once is just regular living to them. "Fifty years from the launch of 3net," he says. "Maybe that's when the curse strikes."

There's the long grinding pause of the doctor, pulling himself together from scattered bits. "The curse?"

Ellery smiles. "I remember when a Founder was dying every day it seemed. Not enough of us left for that now." He looks at his body, and he has to admit, it does look dead. "I signed the Declaration, you know. The Declaration of Independence. I stood right there, right behind the secretary and watched each man's face. Each face as he signed his name."

"You've told me this story."

"We really did think the Brits would end up capturing at least a few of us. That they'd string us up and we'd be martyrs for the cause. Revolution started *here*, you know. In Newport. In 1769, when we hacked into the logs of *HMS Liberty*, let those worms loose in the British mainframes. Things scrambled the links to all their shipping protocols." Ellery laughs. "Should have seen those captains with their big cockades, pacing their decks, all of a sudden had no idea which side of the Cloud was up." He watches on the street below, a little pack of merchants walking into a tavern, oblivious of everything. "*The Death* showed up, you know, not long after. I always did wonder."

"Wonder what, Ellery?"

But Ellery has moved on. He taps the window glass. "If I'm dead and still alive, does that mean that I can't die? Or that I'm really not here? How long have I got, Doc? Give it to me straight, I can take it."

The doctor crests his edges through 3net just a sec. "I suspect any moment. The fact that you're not turning cold right now, Ellery, is not short of a miracle."

"Well, I guess I'm going to sit here and watch the port like always, then, and see what happens."

"You want me to stay?"

Ellery looks at the doctor, but the door is already closed. He slipped out so gently that Ellery didn't even hear the knob click, or maybe he sunk into that device, portaled himself just as easy as sending an old tickle. Ellery turns his focus back on the tiny town square, a half-block set in from the water and the ocean it lets into. Just going to watch this port, he thinks. Just going to sit here and watch this port.

"**G**reat-grandpa."

"Great-grandpa."

"Great-grandpa, look at my smartlife."

Floyd looks down at the little twins, each with a forward projection floating in front of their face. Links aren't links anymore, but little looping snippets of realtime, all portaling off into the vast layered stretches of 3net. "Life don't look so smart to me."

"Smartlife, Grandpa," his granddaughter tells him. "It's kinda like an old smartphone, except—" but the old man is winking at her and so she blushes and turns away. Still a little of that little girl in her. "Put your smartlifes back in your lenses," she tells her kids. They flick their irises and the projections vanish.

"Don't need a smartlife or a set of dentures," Floyd is telling his granddaughter. "Don't need a cane or a feeder. I *own* a smartlens." And he taps his eye. "Know how to use it, too." Floyd reaches down to heft one of the seven-year-olds into a chair along the long table.

"Careful, Dad. Take it easy."

"I don't need to take it easy." But he does, then, need to sit down and take a rest. He watches the kid jump out of the chair and go scurrying off. Then what was the point of lifting him into it? Floyd looks over at his son, the only other person seated. It's a flashback to how the family table looked right after the second outbreak. All the other Floyd fathers and grandfathers and mothers and grandmothers, wives and sisters and brothers, too. All killed by *The Death*. It was just William Floyd and his son and the little granddaughter, still in her crib then, and they had no idea if there would be a country for her to grow up in.

Now that son is sixty-two years old, that little girl has a husband and twins of her own, and the Floyd family table is becoming its old self again. It recalls to Floyd the Saturday dinners of his youth, with long strings of healthy Floyds and their gracious old-money wives.

His granddaughter's husband comes over and sits. "You seen these new clubs, Granddad-in-Law?"

Floyd turns to the guy.

"In order to find out where the meetings are, you have to actually go down to the corner of 112th and Broadway and pick up a piece of paper from a box they put out every morning. And then you actually have to go to the place where the meeting is, too. It's hilarious. The meeting's *not* on 3net."

Floyd's son tells him, "New numbers this afternoon, Dad. Show that the panic is officially over. We are *in recovery*."

"It's goodbye panic and back to the Era of Feeling Good."

Floyd's granddaughter and the twins take their seats around the table as the help emerges from the kitchen to put down hot plates of food. Floyd looks from one twin to the other. They're the same but for hair length. "World's filling up, again," he says. "Funny, we used to worry so much about population."

"You used to worry about population, Granddad? Do I remember that? What, like that there were too *few* people?"

Floyd's grandson-in-law says, "I remember when I was a kid, my dad checking it on Newnet. And then saying how Thomas Jefferson was a slave-driving Socialist pig," and he laughs, with his mouth wide open.

"We're slaying them now, though, Dad, with all this immigration. People everywhere want to get a piece of what we've got here. To think, population numbers used to decide elections."

"Is that true, Great-grandpa?"

Floyd shrugs. "There was *The Death*. Not that hard to understand."

"*The Death*," his granddaughter repeats.

Floyd watches the twins. At the table but not even looking at their food. Must be into those smartlenses. Was easier when you could slap an actual device out of someone's hand. Now what, poke an eye out every time someone's drifting off to 3net? Might knock them the rest of the way in. He tells his granddaughter, "Shouldn't let these kids spend so much time in 3net."

"You all spent plenty of time in the Dream."

"You know perfectly well we didn't have Franklin's Dream when I was a kid. We had the old Internet and that was plenty."

"They're just slipping into other people's lives, Grandpa-in-Law. No harm in that."

"It's good for them, Grandpa, to use their smartlens to experience a bit of how other people live."

"There is no smartlens anymore, Mom. It's smart*life*."

"Then what are you accessing 3net with, William?"

The kid looks equally disgusted with his mom's advanced age as he is with his grandfather's and his great-grandfather's, too. "3net *is* your smartlife."

Floyd has looked horrified through all this. "Slip into other people's lives?"

"Anyone with a smartlife, Dad."

"Or a smartlens," his great-grandson tells him. "But then you can only *see* it."

"Someone on 3net could be linked into my smartlens right now?"

"You never set up your privacy settings, Dad?"

"Privacy settings?"

One of the kids gets up and slaves William Floyd's smartlens. "There you go, Great-grandpa. Now you have to grant access if anyone wants to experience your life."

Floyd rolls his eyes, "And it's Jefferson who's the Socialist pig."

William Floyd's great-grandson says, "I'm experiencing someone starting up a startup."

"I want to go inside 3net and come out in the West."

"What?"

"How far west, Willy?"

"As far as there is."

"Wait," William Floyd is demanding, "you can do that now?"

"No Grandpa, he's only kidding."

"No one's allowed to tell me I'm too young to start a startup."

Floyd sits as far back in his chair as possible. "Never thought I'd hear myself say this, but *the way kids talk today*."

Floyd's granddaughter is scooping more mashed potatoes onto her children's plates even though they haven't touched the first scoop. Her husband watches, says, "Now that the panic is over, maybe our generation can finally get down to the business of making this country."

A bit aghast, Floyd says, "Business is done. We took care of it."

There's some light chuckling from various spots around the table. "A lot harder to build something new, Granddad, than to knock down something old."

Floyd spits some unswallowed food into his napkin. "Knock down something old? Is that what you think we did?" Hard, sharp sounds of an old man clearing his throat. "You should have seen this place during the Revolution. Americans with their stomachs all dug out and their eyes, too, from carrion birds. Dead Americans putrefying along the roadsides, in piles at the edge of every town."

"They weren't Americans then, Grandpa."

"What does that have to do with it?"

"It *does* make a difference, Dad. She's right."

But Floyd can't figure out how. How that could be right, or how his son could think so, too.

"No more panics," his granddaughter says. "No more dissolves. No more crashes. We've finished with all the apocalyptic talk. We've got a new America now. Real independence. Not weighed down by all those *old* problems."

"Wasn't just talk," Floyd says. "The world really was ending. Look at them in the streets. People hungry for a little of the old Dream, if you ask me."

"What's the Dream, Great-grandpa?"

"This panic's going to show people," Floyd says. "How much money can be made on an economy they've invented just by voting for it. Soon they'll be imagining something that's going to make 3net look like an old email editor. And then they'll be voting for that, too. It'll be like the Cloud all over. Bigger and bigger and bigger and bigger. And when *that* Dream collapses, watch out. The gravity of it's going to suck the whole world in." He has a sip of wine, swallows some food he didn't realize was still in his mouth. "And no amount of Andrew Jacksons or George Washingtons or Thomas Jeffersons are going to be able to stop it."

"But Grandpa. Multiple American realities *are* possible. Simultaneously, too. Not only possible but beneficial."

"That's the *real* point of 3net, Granddad-in-Law."

Floyd shakes his head. "Everyone keeps telling me what the real point of 3net is, and every time they say it, it always sounds different."

"Don't know how you old bucks keep talking about different when everyone's on 3net and so how different can we be?"

"All I'll say," William Floyd says, "is that when the pot boils, the scum rises to the top. You guys already crashed 3net once. But instead of maybe slowing things down, instead of maybe changing your behavior, you just insist there are safer ways to keep on ramping it up. Now there's your curse."

But no one is paying attention to him anymore. Eyes all down into their plates, or off in their smartlenses, tunneled into some other dinner table with some other family where the old man of the house is gone and so no one has to be bothered by the crappy old revolutionary generation. "Well," he says, "someone better start worrying about the curse. You've only got five years left."

"Is Great-grandpa having one of his spells?"

Floyd turns to his great-grandson. He wants to ask the kid who told him that. That he has spells. He wants to ask the room, *Do I have spells and no one tells me about them?* But he can't make words. He tries to figure out if he's choking. He hears voices, faintly, looks up to see the same family faces he recognizes but now bleary, sucking their colors off from the lines of their bodies. He tries to say one last thing, but it's no use. Some kind of last words, he thinks, ranting about *the curse.*

Part 5 :: 50 Years Later
. . . The Lighthouse
in the Sky

There was a mountaintop in this spot once. But then a human came along and knocked it right off. Built a home that folds its octagons symmetrically aside, then raises its last in a high dome to bask all eight sides in views of the valley. Spreads its wings and dips them underground to never be seen. Octagons and octagons, lined out in every dimension, the floor plan hinting spatial riddles all throughout its topography.

Hung from the mansion's northeast pillars, a drooping footpath ensnares the lawn, its edges laced with flowers last spored half a world away. Rows of experimental vegetables slice sideways into the hillside, like the veranda of some ancient temple. Each carrot and snow pea, each marigold—like the octagons and the doorways, the widths of the footpaths and stairwells, the alloy content of the transistors being pressed out by the slaves along the row—all facets of an ecosystem plotted out in databases that cross-link through decades of meticulously kept spreadsheets.

In the mansion's rear corner study, light pools through windows and glass double doors, capturing what seem to be multiple versions of a risen sun. Set out from this octagon's center, at an angle one degree short of two o'clock, Thomas Jefferson sits back thinly in a chair that popped into his brain one morning while riding the plantation. Humming softly and still but for his dancing eyes, the third President is typing up one final Brainpage status update: *th@ all r cre8d =; th@ they r endowd by their cre8or with certn inalienable rights; th@ among these r life, librty and the purst of happines.*

He reads it over a few times to himself—as if the phrase were not already a constant echo through his mind. "There it is, Sally. The most important 140 characters in the history of man. The DNA of our Revolution. The core tweet of the American character." Jefferson goes back to humming. Bach toccatas in the same octave the house groans while settling. Today is the first day Jefferson has been out of bed in almost a month. Teetering on the edge of death for weeks as that twin stalked the place, telling the doctor how important it is that the ex-President survive until the Fourth of July.

Sally keeps busy, tidying the cluttered shelves that stack strange objects toward the high trim. "How you all going to still have the Cloud I'll never understand."

Jefferson has slipped into 3net. His avatar lounges in a digital model of this same octagonal room. The digital room sits in a digital model of this same building. Not hampered by the restraints of temporal geometry, the floor pattern can be broken from the wall and folded into a perfectly truncated cuboctahedron. Back and forth between this and the other Monticello so often over the years, Jefferson has forgotten which came first, the visualization or the actual building.

"All these Thomas Jeffersons," he mumbles. "Mustn't leave any behind, Sally. Some Calvinist hacker gets inside and uses me to tyrannize the minds of good Virginians."

The old sage has spent his last few months programming the architecture of what's about to happen, this joint finale. And grand it shall be. A simultaneous end for all the online Jeffersons. All around him, portals poke and web through the farthest quantum tunnels of 3net. Others reach back farther, into the ghosted caches he's meticulously archived, the echoes he's preserved of older internets man has left behind. Each portal ends at one of his Jeffersons. Looking in, he can see what domestic and intellectual world each has made in its own curling universe of code. All the drones he's reformatted and reprogrammed, the haunts he's brought back to life, given purpose to again, the group avatars from the Dream, step back profiles he's replicated from other masked accounts. "I wonder, Sally. What it will seem like for them. Like death? Or perhaps a liberation, their bits freed to not be collections of my protocols any longer."

"Death for a computer program?" Sally shakes her head. "How is it, Tom, you go so simple from having no god to believing some strange things, and like you were a crazy person, too?"

"Doesn't have to be a god to be worth believing like crazy in, Sally." He raises his hands. Lets them hover above all those Jeffersons, like bringing some vast orchestra to noise. Each of their faces, at that moment, turns up to see his palms. With mirrored, arcing swoops, he slices the air and every one of them goes to sleep. Pixel by pixel, they fade to just the outlines of their shapes. Then nothing.

Of course, this mass death is just an aesthetically pleasing manifestation of these accounts all being terminated permanently. Wiped from the Cloud for good. Jefferson thought their ends deserved a little beauty, a touch of dramatic flare. Not that he would ever need to again, but if he were to recode this same protocol, he could brainstorm a few places for improvement. Oh, well . . .

When he stands now, Jefferson really does stand. Not in 3net but in that corner study, in that mansion on that mountaintop he flattened. He checks off a task from a list he has open in his smartlife. "I am officially out of the Cloud." The humming begins again. Whenever Jefferson is not talking, he's humming. When he's not humming, it's because he's talking. As soon as the words are fully out of him, the toccatas start back up, right where they were paused.

He offers Sally a smile as he slides past, into the adjoining room, to the bolted stacks of harddrives. From floor to ceiling, they line the walls, set two-deep and packed with data that arcs back to the days when the Cloud was actually connected. Inside these harddrives, all his collected caches of the old Internet, Newnet, the Dream, every generation and incarnation of Brainpage. All of it saved right here for later historians to sift through, discover whatever continuities they need to enlighten their age. This is the greatest collection of information the world has ever known. If 3net were to crash for good, if all human knowledge were lost, here is where man would begin to rebuild.

In the center of the room, a stone pillar rises to waist level. On the circular platform, a single harddrive spinning speeds which suck in its own noises. Modified with Off-Worlder crystal technologies, this harddrive backs up the data of all the other drives combined. And that only begins to scratch the surface of its storage capacity. Jefferson rests a palm on the black shell, feels its low, pulsing coolness. "When the Dream was shut down and the Cloud collapsed, we piped it all right through here and it held things up just long enough."

Sally's voice comes clear from the adjacent room. "Well, congratulations."

Jefferson flips a switch on the back of the harddrive and its lights go dark. He picks up the device, holds it gently in his hands. "Storage enough for all the brains of every human who ever lived or died."

"You the one going to die today," Sally tells him. "That's what you always said, Tom."

Jefferson steps back into the study, places the harddrive on a small end table.

"It was a computer told you and so it must be true?"

"Actually, it was Central Programming that told me. It's not really a computer." Jefferson rests a hand on the desk, as if holding up his arm would be a needless waste of energy. His fingers touch a twig he found on his final walk around the plantation, broken into bits to make the shape of the Big Dipper—the walk and the twig. His last morning walk.

"You might have been an awful mess these last weeks," Sally says. "But you look fine now." She shivers. "Keeping you alive with that thing? Unnatural. I think if it's going to happen, let it happen. If it's not, then let it don't." She turns away, dusting a shelf of antique smartdevices, humming her own song now, something deeper, improvised, as beautiful as any Bach.

Jefferson watches her, listens, watches. "I remember the first time I saw you," he says. "A woman had dropped a crystal glass. I could tell it was crystal, Sally, because I could hear it keep on breaking, breaking smaller and smaller into sharp spears of dust. I looked up and you walked in and the room really gasped at it. It was strange, too. Like music that was just then invented. First time ever heard. My life had been over since the day your sister died, and then there she was, walking right back in."

Sally shakes her head. "Wish I knew, sometimes, Tom, if it was me you've loved all this time, or her."

Jefferson has slipped back again into his Bach. He lets a couple notes drag into the room, forgotten-sounding and dull. He checks that list only he can see. Then he's glancing at that harddrive, there on the end table. "It will have to be destroyed, Sally. As will all my artifacts from the Off-Worlders. Crimes against humanity if history finds out," and he rolls his eyes. "To talk with another species about something more substantial than who is urinating on whom else's feces. Why is it the stupidest dogs always bark the loudest?"

"Them dogs ain't like you," she tells him. "Digging through those old harddrives all hours of the night. ABC," she says, "you *always be consuming.* Them dogs got mixed up in consuming as much information as you, wouldn't be dogs no more, just be normal humans, I suppose."

"That would be nice, but still they're dogs. And so this will have to go into the brick oven. Burned up and gone."

She takes the harddrive out with her and so it's Jefferson, all alone. He checks another item off that list, then sits down and flicks his iris. A hologram takes shape from the bank of soft displays stretched above his desk, the amorphous torso with hundreds of curving tentacles. "The so-called Millipus." He lowers his eye to the eyepiece of a microscope. In the slide, tissue samples taken from the saving of New Orleans. Wires untangle from the microscope's base, snaking back to smartpads he's modified into bio-monitors. Using this data, Jefferson has constructed what he likes to think is a pretty exact 3D rendering of the monster.

"Working on that Millipus guts," Sally says, coming back into the room. She closes the door behind her. "Your last day on Earth, maybe you want to relax a bit."

He compares data-imaging models with scans that hover over the smartpad screens. "Seven hundred nineteen tentacles," he says. "Far short of a thousand." He hyper-slides down some tunnel lined with animal classification vocabulary. "Cetni-septa-nana-septapus." He thinks. "Centiceptipus." He winks at Sally. "This *is* relaxing."

"You know more about that Millipus's guts than you know about anything else these days."

He looks at her. "I can think of some other tissues samples I know just as well."

"If that's a dirty thought, Tom, then that's a *dirty* thought." Sally comes to the hologram of the monster. She places a hand on the skin. Her fingers crackle as they pass through. "They been saying what happened was *The Death* came across."

"Have you been sneaking onto 3net again?"

"But they been talking about it in the house, too. And all along the row. That those Off-Worlders didn't cure nothing. Just brought *The Death* across and let it loose in the ocean. Maybe thinking it would never bother no one again. And that's where it's been this whole time."

Jefferson smiles at her. Then back into the microscope.

"Some of them slaves thought maybe that Millipus was going to come and set them free."

"I doubt it had much in the way of intent, Sally, virtuous or not. Poor thing, really. Brain the size of a lima bean."

The hologram tentacles writhe in slow motion. Sally rakes her fingers through them.

Jefferson brings himself up from the eyepiece. "So much that can't be got in the wrong hands. This will have to go into the brick oven, too." But when she moves to take it, Jefferson's hand wraps itself ever so gently around her wrist. "Do it later, Sal."

She sinks back into the room, lets her hand find rest on his shoulder. "You think you're the only one got a piece of that monster? That it can't find some other way to get loose than escaping from Thomas Jefferson's library?" She pats him, then moves to the window.

Jefferson watches the sun tick her edges for a moment or two. "People seem to want to forget," he says. "If it wasn't for the Off-Worlders, the whole human race would have died in that third outbreak."

"Why they going to wait, then, until 80 percent of the world was already dead?"

Jefferson stands, joins her at the window. "Maybe saw it in a telescope from their planet, way on the other side of the galaxy. It was a race to get here in time, and the only way back was the oil we gave them. Most successful humanitarian intervention in the history of the Milky Way."

"Or maybe they were behind the moon the whole time," Sally says. "Just waiting so they could knock us down easier."

"I suspect if the Off-Worlders were going take over the Earth, they would have done so by now."

"Maybe they already have, Tom. Millipus, *The Death*, the Cloud all falling in. Maybe those are its weapons and we down here just too stupid to see they giving us whipping after whipping."

Jefferson is pulled back into the Revolution, just for a moment. It all plays before him like a feed in fast forward. Even the parts where there was no feed, when the Internet was illegal and *The Death* seemed like it was going to suck the whole continent into the Earth. He comes out dizzy the other side, wobbles, catches himself on the back of a chair. Turns in to her, right into her grabbing arms. "Sally," he says.

"Tom!"

Slowly he begins to take back his weight. Then he's himself again, standing all on his own with Sally a step away. Jefferson gazes at her, but she's looking down, at something she's holding in her hand. He looks there and her hands are empty. "Don't be scared, Sally. People die. It's what happens."

"I can't help but think of someday in the future when no one's going to remember any of these things you spent so much time on."

"But you'll remember."

"I'll remember how much time you spent on them. Time you could have spent otherwise."

He looks long at her. "Me too, Sally."

"You too, what?"

"I wish, too. That I knew. If it's been her I've loved, or you."

Sally just waits there for him, not moving, getting herself ready for what his touch always does. He seems to have recovered from his spell. But she doesn't know what to think, not with this smartlife thing involved.

"If we could pick a spot," he says, "anywhere in the world. Locate that one singular position in the schematics of the 3net code. Then why can't we make that spot corpuscular? 3net, the Cloud, it can't be made of nothing. There must be particles of some kind. If we made the Cloud of matter, can't we change the type of matter that makes the Cloud?"

"Sounds like you talked yourself into another circle there, Tom."

He smiles. "Yeah, that one needs a little work." He takes her by the shoulders. Breathes once. Thinks, *Well, more or less I've already told her*. Then scolds himself for the half-lie. Starts to speak but stops or can't go on.

She keeps his eyes. "That smartlife thing, it's starting to wear down?" And when he doesn't answer, she reaches out and holds his face firm, forces his eyes into hers. "What are you thinking in there, Tom? Don't like it when you're all stepped back in one of your places."

Finally Jefferson manages, "I think it's time we gathered up the family."

Sally looks disappointed or indifferent maybe. Jefferson watches her fade and then slip out, leaving dim the shapes of the study.

Jefferson had always meant to get down in that same old chair for his last minutes. His favorite place in the real to sit. But before he realizes it, he's tucked himself into the alcove of the bed. So enclosed a place to die, he thinks, but he knows he won't be getting up again and so decides to make the best of it. By the time the Monticello circle all comes filing in, he's faded noticeably.

His daughter Martha is there, looking more like her mother than ever. Nick Trist and young Jefferson Randolph, the few grandchildren Martha has pried away for a summer at Monticello, that one twin with his burgered face. They all go still in silent anticipation. These are the people in the world who really know this man. And to really know Thomas Jefferson is to expect something you can't imagine until it happens. Why would death be any different?

Sally is the one who breaks the silence. "You going to slip over there, Master, into that cloud? Then maybe we'll see you again someday, you become corpuscular, like you said."

There are a few odd looks, coming out of context as it does for all but her and her Tom. But then the focus returns to the bed and the sage passing there. Jefferson's eyes are the only parts of him still moving, slowly searching the fading room for faces, a last comparison to the shapes and patterns he's burned into his brain as they've changed and developed alongside time's passing. Finds the last set of eyes and stays there, those lips parting one last time. "Sally—"

"Thomas Jefferson is dead."

John Adams looks up from his smartpad at his niece Louisa, seated behind the desk he never uses anymore.

"Just came through on the 3net feed, Uncle."

A bit of a tremor in the old President's hand is the only movement. His breathing has slowed to all but inaudible. "Central Programming," he whispers. From where his easy chair has been placed, he can see out upon farmland that doesn't stretch quite so far as it used to. They're in the upstairs study on the east side of Peacefield, just a little country house in a field. Ever since March of 1801, home of Farmer John. This is how their lives have been organized these last years. Louisa runs the farm while John Adams sits propped in that easy chair or downstairs by the fire. He spends most of his time with his face buried in an old smartpad, reading through the classics for a third or fourth time, bouncing off to troll 3net, sending out emails and terrorizing messageboards, trying to wedge a place for himself in the epic of his lifespan. Louisa here, John Quincy off in Washington being President, but the rest of the family is gone, picked off over the years by various workings of the organic world.

"Thomas Jefferson dies on the Fourth of July." Adams snaps up from his wander, leans forward, reaching for Louisa. "Give me your smartlife," he says.

She rolls her eyes, stands, begins a long loop around the desk. "Use your own."

"Mine's in the bathroom." Arms straight with fingers grabbing until she has her smartlife out and into his palm. Adams calms, bends his face toward it. Head coming back, blinking. "There," he says. "There we go."

"Thought you don't like to use smartlife."

"Well, I'd read a *webpage* if someone would put the news in one. How does it god damned!" He stops to poke a finger in his eye. "How do you work this goddamned thing? Wait. There. Okay." His pupil dances. "Thomas Jefferson," he reads, "passed away this afternoon at his mountaintop home." He looks past the smartlife to where his niece stands above him with her arms looking frozen. "He was my oldest friend, you know, young Mr. Jefferson."

"You haven't spoken to him since the turn of the century."

"We talk all the time."

"On *email.*"

"How do I check if Charles Carroll of Carrollton is still alive? Wait. There it is." He sighs. "Nope. I'm not the last Signer left, not yet."

"Uncle!"

"Goddamned thing!" John Adams is rubbing his closed eye. "Never, never work the way they're supposed to . . ."

"Well, don't use it, then, if you hate it so much."

"Today is the day the curse is to come, you know, the day America is to be destroyed. If you believe the things witches and computer programs tell you."

"Oh, Uncle, not the curse." Louisa lowers herself onto the couch opposite, under the portrait of her Aunt Abigail.

"He told me this would happen, you know, that he would die today."

She looks at him.

"Thomas had grown a little soft up here." He presses his temple with one of those sausagey fingers. "He imagined he was communicating with some all-knowing computer system." Adams wobbles a little, back and forth between the room and 3net, never fully in either. All throughout the virtual corners of America's newest incarnation of the Cloud, majorities have gathered to revel in the Age of Jefferson. Black bars line the frames of every feed. A contest to see which source can be in gravest visible mourning.

Adams digs though it all, scanning, moving on, scanning. He may play the part of the lost old man, swallowed by the present, but he can slide across 3net with the best of them. "The fifty-year anniversary of the birth of the country, and Thomas Jefferson has hijacked another one. Bipartisan love fest for our nation's third President, party chieftain, Signer and *supposed* author of the Declaration. Add it to all the lies they've been stacking on top of this Revolution since the day I started the whole thing." Adams reads, scoffs. Reads some more. "They'll have you believe Jefferson just wiggled his fingers and the Dream came out. Began in the morning, had it done by dinner. Really, the whole thing started when I uploaded my *Thoughts*."

"Your thoughts? You *uploaded* them?"

"My *Thoughts on Government*, an annotated database of foundational documents. Uploaded it to the old Internet and it went viral. Seeded every constitution this country's produced since." Adams shakes his head. "No one ever talks about that, though. How can you sell an operating system with *this* face on it?" Adams indicates his own owl-like visage. "*John Adams's Dream America*. Ha!"

Louisa says tiredly, "Everyone knows you're the hero of independence."

"Oh, just of independence? My presidency wasn't monumental enough for you? Saved the country is all."

"Saved the country from what?"

"From the Federalists."

She rests the back of her skull on the cushioned back of the couch. "Uncle, you *were* a Federalist."

"Don't give me that confused-old-man tone. I was never a Federalist." Adams returns a good portion of his attention to 3net, talking as the feed streams by. "The last independent American is what I was, what I still am. What I'll always be is for the future to decide, wisely one would hope. Hamilton, Pickering, *Waaaallll-*cot. The Society of Cincinnati. Now those guys were Federalists. The standing army. 3net. But not *this* 3net. The elimination of the Dream, the establishment of a hereditary soldier class. A state where finance and the military are supreme. All it takes is a war every thirty years to keep that going." Adams wiggles down deeper into his chair. "Wasn't Thomas Jefferson who stopped it or the Dream or Newnet. It wasn't the Patrick Henry Group Avatar. It was John Adams." He touches his own chest with a few fingers curled back. "In 1798. I'd lured Jefferson right in. I'd sprung my trap. Toppled the man. He was dead in the water. War fever took. I was never more popular than when I had that sword strapped on, marching around like some little general. The country was ours to do with whatever we please. But they'd gone mad, Walcott, Hamilton. The whole rest of them." Adams shivers at the image. "I did what Washington and Jefferson would not. I threw it all away, sacrificed myself and brought the whole Federalist plot down with me." He smiles, grim. "You know how to tell who the *real* hero is, of course."

"How, Uncle?"

"The real hero is one who is most unpopular."

"Well, you've got them there."

Adams breaks into a full belly laugh, or what passes for one from him these days, more like a reedy cackle.

Louisa is tapping her lips silently with the tip of a finger. "Is all that stuff that true, Uncle? The Society of Cincinnati, the High Federalist plot?"

Adams smiles coyly. His face changes a bit as he moves through different channels of thought. Which Adams you get depends on which Adams is looking at which Adams—the vast linear parallaxes of the true Founding Father.

He leans as far back as the chair can go, his eyes toward something higher, a plane above the things which gravity has dictated placement in this room. "Just lucky to have been alive for it. We got to remake the world, to define the age."

Louisa sighs. "These men today, though, Uncle, jealous young Americans. Trying to remake an age that doesn't need remaking."

Adams shrugs, nods feebly. "We certainly did unleash a kind of spirit in this world." The sun comes out then, takes the rectangular window and makes of it a perfect square of light. Lays it on the floor, just missing Adams's chair. But then it's gone. Storm clouds now raking in their first edges. Adams eyes the darkening sky. "Maybe this is it. Maybe this is the curse."

"No one believes in the curse, Uncle. Not anymore."

Adams smiles, laced with something clandestine. "That's where you're wrong. No one ever did." He holds up a fist that looks more like a tiny throw pillow. "The simple gathering of diverse minds, the natural and wonderful conflicts that result, a potential energy that can fuel a society for years. But not forever. More *The Deaths* will come, more Off-Worlders and trade wars. There'll be another Millipus of some kind. And we'll beat it. And get stronger and stronger. Again and again. Right up until the last one. The last struggle that finally breaks us and brings us down. And it won't be because the calamity is too big for America but because America will be too small for the calamity."

Adams thinks back over this day so far. The Fourth of July. Spent a good chunk of it not here but wiggling through the past instead. He removes the smartlife, lets it rest in his palm. "Take this thing," he says.

Louisa gets up to make diagonal across the room. "You sure you don't want to experience some more of the Age of Jefferson?"

"I think once was . . ."

"What is it, Uncle?"

Adams has taken hold of his head. He screams, forces open his eyes, looking wildly. "Is this happening to everyone? Is this the curse?"

She looks at her hands. "Just you, I think."

By the time the doctor arrives, the pain has subsided. Adams lies in that same chair, mostly gone still. One look and it's clear that here is the spot from which this one-term President is going to leave the Earth.

They patch a feed into John Quincy right away. His face sits in the frame of a soft display. He doesn't really look like an earlier version of his father, but that's the idea in the old man's head. *There I am,* he thinks, *President John Adams.*

"We've got a clean feed, Dad. Some scramble coding of my own design. Not going to have anyone breaking in and posting any of this to 3net, so don't you worry."

The elder Adams looks into the faces around him. Then into the empty spaces between. Wish we had group avatars of all the Adamses, he thinks. So they could all be here. All of them, from all throughout time. And Abigail, too.

"Dad, how do you feel?"

"He's been talking about the curse," Louisa informs the room.

John Adams cracks open his droll mouth. "Don't need no curse. Same for people as it is for countries as it is for clouds as it is for solar systems and universes, too. Some miracle, some struggle, some coming together, a burst of energy, then the slow burnout."

"Mr. Adams," the doctor tells him. "You've had a major stoke."

Adams nods, pats his niece's arm. Reaches out for John Quincy but only bends fingers on the screen. "Dad."

His hand hangs there forgotten. Louisa tucks it gently to his side. "He looks sort of cute, doesn't he, John Quincy?"

The old President lies there with eyes barely open, the little slivers wet and welling water along their edges. Like brain or soul leaking out of him. A small noise. The two present lean in to hear, John Quincy turning up the volume with a flick of his iris. More lip licking, light and wet. "Today, John Adams dies . . . but Thomas Jefferson lives forever."

epilogue

The Carrolls of Carrollton have gathered finally for the end. The death of the last Signer of the Declaration of Independence. Hot November at the tail end of a hot Maryland summer. Off-prime year for the cicadas and so only an occasional whirring reaches them through the manor walls. Good to have some of those old sounds mixed in, however faint, to bring a little organic chaos to the harmonies of Realnet.

"Great-grandpa!" A child comes flittering, loads herself onto the quilt bulging crookedly over Carroll's skeletal frame. "Tell me again what things were like before Realnet."

Other voices ebb and swell in the ether, ordered in protocols to fit each silence perfectly. Odds and ends of sentences hung together in the counter-pattern of code. Sounds toned down or up to meld perfect keys with other sounds filtering through. In Realnet, everything is like music: Andrew Jackson has just been reelected, and America is swimming along.

"Imagine," he tells the girl, "if you were the last one who understood. The last one left alive. Come closer, my darling."

And she phases toward, whole sections sliced and stacked upwards of themselves in the big poster bed. Charles Carroll of Carrollton works a sinewy arm out from quilts all warm with body air. At the arm's very end, a hand holding a paper, a single twice-folded sheet. Giggling as she takes it. "Great-grandpa, it's blank!"

The old man giggles, too—not but a dozen teeth between the two of them. "Damnedest thing," he wheezes. "Only *I* can see it. Must be linked to the coding of my DNA." He reaches for the letter but the little girl holds it away, and so he lets her have it. "Thomas Jefferson sent me that letter. The day he was elected President."

"What's a letter?"

"And some day they're going to wonder how humans ever survived without whatever comes after Realnet." He pats her chubby, little hand. "I want you to put this paper in the back pocket of your father's pants." Both of them back to giggling as she smears her colors over the surface of the room. Collected all up behind her dad, that Whig prick, still blabbering about Henry fucking Clay. Little girl with her finger pressed to her lips as she slips the paper in. Be a nice surprise for our young Whig. One last burn from the Sage of Monticello.

Little girl the shape of quilt lumps comes back full of his attentions. Right there Indian-style denting the spread. Kid's a wiz on Realnet. Probably this whole new crop of Americans, Carroll thinks. And we thought Doctor Benjamin Franklin's Dream America was just the wildest thing. "Tell me, my sweet, why do you want to know what life was like before Realnet?"

She spins a finger into the dark hole of a nostril. "I do, Great-grandpa!"

The others have all dissolved from their places in the room, left conversation feeds forgotten to take up shapes around the bed. One is seated at its foot, another weighing the mattress down with the little girl, the rest all standing. All the Carrolls of Carrollton. No excuse not to be here when you can Realnet your way on over.

"Tell her one of your stories about George Washington, Grandpa."

"We had smartdevices," Charles Carroll of Carrollton tells them. "And they were connected to us. Right here to your fingers.

Then your eyes. Then your brain. The Internet and the real world were different things. And separate, too."

"That's scary."

"Don't scare her please, Dad."

"Grandpa, she'll be up all night."

"Tell me, Great-grandpa!"

"We had webpages. And information could move faster than a human being."

"She *has* a horse, Grandpa."

"Ah, a horse is a toy now. She has a toy, you mean."

"Grandpa, why don't you tell us what's the greatest thing you ever saw."

"The launch of Realnet."

"Before that. Something else."

"Do you want me to tell you or not?"

"Is it true that Thomas Jefferson invented Realnet?"

And his father, that Clay-loving SOB, gives the kid a bop on the side of his head. "Some fucking teachers they got these days."

"I said no politics."

"What was it, Grandpa?"

"What was what?"

"What was the best thing you ever saw? The Constitution? The Dream? 3net?"

"Don't know about the best, but the coolest thing I ever saw was when Jackson killed the Millipus."

"You didn't see that. No one did. There's wasn't any feed."

But everybody else besides that Clay-lover is listening. "Jackson had it right there, caught between the real and the Dream, and he shut the whole thing down. Not off the grid. No fucking grid. The monster, it was sliced clean in half. Half collapsing in the crash of the Dream and the other half falling dead at Old Hickory's feet.

He killed the Millipus and *The Death*, too, because that's what that thing was. It was *The Death* come across."

"Wish there was some feed of it so we could experience what it was really like."

And here comes that Clay-loving grandson-in-law. "Right, but no one *can* because there's no record it happened at all. A little convenient, don't you think?"

"Convenient you're not hanging in some Off-Worlder crystal farm."

"How many elections does Andrew Jackson have to win before you'll shut up about it?"

Charles Carroll of Carrollton silences them by lifting one emaciated arm. The sleeve of his pajama shirt falls to reveal skin and bones and not much else left. Little strings of muscle that hang up there. "Whether it was *The Death* or not *The Death*, a sea monster climbed out of the ocean to swallow America. And a guy rode out there and killed it. On a horse. Now, if that guy wants to be President, maybe you better shut up and let him."

*the author would like to thank those whose
support made this book possible*

Louis Armand

David Vichnar

Equus Press

Yishai Seidman

Joshua Mensch

Donna Jaffee

Scott O'Connor

Jim Ruland

Jerry Lee Atwater

Marx Cafe

Amherst Cinema

Steve Ober

Ellen Herlihy

Katherine Singer

Damien Lincoln Ober is a novelist and screenwriter. His work has appeared in *The Rumpus*, *NOON*, *B O D Y Literature*, the *Baltimore City Paper*, *VLAK*, and *port.man.teau*. He was nominated for a 2012 Pushcart Prize, and his screenplay, *Randle Is Benign*, was selected for the 2013 Black List.